Till the Wind Blows Silent

By Bernice Bohnet

Print ISBNs
BWL Print 978-0-2286-0207-1

BWL Publishing Inc.

Books we love to write ...
Authors around the world.

http://bwlpublishing.ca

To: Betty

I hope you enjoy
this book.

Bernice

Dedication

For Doreen, the kindest and most loving mother imaginable. Your unconditional love has made me the luckiest person on the planet.

I would also like further acknowledgements besides that of Service Alberta: I would like to thank Judith (Jude) Pittman, Publisher, for seeing potential in this novel and patiently and capably guiding me through the publication process. You are a true professional.

I would also like to thank Nancy Bell, Editor, for all you contributed to this work. You are not only brilliant with language but also considerate and efficient.

I appreciate the fact both Jude and Nancy worked with me despite my technical shortcomings. BWL is an excellent publisher.

Most especially, I would like to thank my husband, Bruce, for his support and encouragement. You read over completed chapters, offered suggestions, and encouraged me when I grew disappointed. I could never have completed this book without your help.

Thanks also to my sister, Gerry, and, of course, Doreen. You two are terrific.

Thank you as well to the many friends and family who are eager to buy my book and even help with promotion. I am fortunate to have so many wonderful people in my life. Your enthusiasm is contagious.

Acknowledgments

BWL Publishing Inc. wishes to thank the Government of Alberta for their support.

Alberta
Government

PART 1
LONDON ENGLAND
1944-1945

Chapter 1

Anna's sensible shoes thudded on the pavement of London's deserted streets. Fear hastened her steps.

She'd caught a glimpse of the man several blocks back. He looked about her age, from what she ascertained in that brief moment, that and the U.S. Army uniform of khaki with russet shoes.

There was no sign of life in the buildings crowding the street this early in the morning. Without pausing she pushed a loose strand of hair behind her ear and wiped the trickle of sweat from her temple.

Why hadn't she decided to have a lie in herself? What a silly idea it was to visit the park on a quiet morning. She shifted the easel and large paint box into a better position and tucked her purse more firmly under her arm. Burdened down like this, there would be little chance to fight off an attacker.

Fighting to control the situation and her growing panic she picked up her pace. A peek over her shoulder showed the bloke remained a few feet behind. Switching tactics, she slowed down. The soldier matched her pace and stayed the same distance behind her. Perhaps he was harmless and not a threat as she perceived.

She crossed the street and so did he. The shops were closed on Sunday so there was no escape by ducking into one. Maybe this was God's punishment for her sins. She really should have gone to church with Mom and Dad this morning, not hurrying through the deserted street lugging easel and paint box.

Her heart pounded and fresh sweat broke out on her brow. Could he be some sort of pervert? He looked respectable enough but so could a rapist and murderer. The entrance to a tube station was just ahead, but if she dared to descend into the murky depths of the tunnel he might grab her before she could board a train.

The persistent ache in her side decided her.

Anna entered the station, hoping to lose the soldier among the other commuters. The chill sent shivers over her as she left the warmth of the sunshine outside. She ran down the stairs and tripped on the last one, banging her left knee sharply. There'd be a bruise tomorrow. More penance for skipping church, she supposed.

In her haste, she failed to excuse herself to any of the people she bumped into. Reaching the metal turnstile, she almost dropped her purse as she inserted the ticket.

She sent a prayer of thanks to God when a train almost immediately pulled up. She felt more blessed when she found a seat by the window. No one sat beside her; an unusual occurrence because often when she rode the tube she felt like a tinned oyster.

When the door closed, she radiated joy, certain she'd lost the soldier. Her hands ceased to shake and her breathing eased.

Anna managed to smile. She could still go to the park and paint the beautiful trees just as she'd planned. She settled the paint box and easel against her knees. Her day off wouldn't be wasted.

Soon the car moved and Anna swayed to its movement. Goodness, how silly the whole escapade seemed now. She'd probably just imagined that man had been following her.

Anna leaned back and closed her eyes. The earlier tension melted like butter on toast, and she allowed herself a cat nap. A presence beside her brought her instantly awake. Opening her eyes and turning her head she smothered a gasp. The soldier occupied the seat beside her. How did he get on the train without her seeing him?

Anna opened her mouth to scream but no sound came out. Oh Lord, it was just like one of her nightmares. She looked about frantically for a bobby, but could see none.

The American soldier didn't grab her or even seem to notice her. His attention seemed captured by a large, foldout map of London. It must just be coincidence he showed up beside her.

Several minutes passed without the man acknowledging her existence and curiosity began to replace her terror. Anna peeked at the man beside her through lowered lashes.

He was more than a little attractive, she decided. Not tall, but certainly in good shape, and those large, expressive brown eyes made her wonder if they lit up when he smiled. The smattering of freckles on his nose was endearing.

Anna straightened her spine and assumed a pleasant demeanor. She almost forgot that only a few minutes earlier she'd been too scared to scream. Now she hoped to get to know him.

She clasped her hands together and she searched for some way to start a conversation, but came up with nothing.

Anna shifted in her seat and cleared her throat. The soldier never looked up from the map. She went from being frightened to disappointed, in a very short time.

Nonetheless, it pleased her that she looked much better than she did on workdays when she rode the Underground with her hair pulled back into a bun and dressed in baggy, shapeless trousers.

Today was Anna's twenty-fifth birthday and in honour of the occasion she wore a special dress, a rare treat. She had traded a pair of gray work trousers for the dress, clothes being rationed, and she was grateful for her cousin, Miriam's, practicality.

The blue flowered dress nipped-in at the waist and the large, white, lace collar suited her. It made her feel

8

attractive and she'd danced to an imaginary Strauss waltz around and around her bedroom when she'd put it on earlier this morning.

When she least expected it, the bloke turned and seemed to notice her for the first time. Anna put her hand over her heart, it beat so fast. The handsome man smiled and indicated the map he held, and said, "I wonder, Miss, if you know your way around London? I wanted to go to Charing Cross station. Am I on the right train?

"No, Charing Cross is in Westminster right by Trafalgar Square. You'll have to take the northern line. You're on the southern. I'm sorry. Your journey may take a while."

"That's alright. Thanks for the information. I appreciate the help. Londoners are a friendly people."

She liked his accent.

"Besides, it's fun riding the Tube on a peaceful Sunday morning with a most helpful British lady."

Anna blushed.

The soldier held out his right hand, smiled enough to leave crinkles around his eyes, "I'm Harold Dexter. It's great to meet you."

The subway carriage rounded a curve and the momentum pressed Harold against her. Her nose twitched with the spicy scent he used combined with an under note of soap. The thigh pressed alongside hers was solid and strong. Glancing up, she noticed the hint of stubble on his cheeks and chin.

When the car straightened again, Anna reluctantly moved away. She extended her hand, "I'm Anna Marshall. It is nice to make your acquaintance." She hoped she didn't sound like an ancient grammar teacher. The hand that gripped hers was warm and dry.

Harold didn't seem put off by her formal manner. "Anna, what a beautiful name. I love it. It's a very romantic name." He smiled and she noticed how white and even his teeth were.

Anna nodded her head. She wished her own teeth were whiter; all the Yanks seemed to have brilliant smiles. Anna

9

refrained from commenting on his name. In her opinion Harold was a horrid name and she couldn't tolerate false flattery.

Harold deftly continued the conversation. "I see that you're an artist. That is wonderful. I'd love for you to show me your work."

It pleased Anna that he seemed to want to see her again.

"Yes, I paint but I wish I had more talent. The last time I went to an art gallery I saw one of Monet's water lily paintings, the most beautiful thing I've ever seen. Sometimes I wish I possessed genius like Monet rather than a mere, small ability."

Anna blushed. Why did she go on so with a complete stranger?

If Harold noticed colour staining her cheeks, he didn't comment on it. "Maybe someday you'll do a painting for me. Do you think my wish might be granted?" He spoke tentatively.

Anna forgot any embarrassment in her enthusiasm. "Yes, perhaps. What subjects do you like? Landscape, portraits, still life? Oh, or abstract versus the more traditional styles?

If he liked landscapes, she might give him something she'd already painted, like that one of the cliffs of Dover. She'd even painted a bluebird on it, just like in the song.

"Whatever you choose is fine with me. I'm sure I'll like it." He waved a hand dismissively.

Anna drew back a little and hid a frown. A small suspicion entered her head. Perhaps this Yank wasn't an art lover; he probably didn't even know who Claude Monet was. Nonetheless, he did appear to be trying hard to get to know her.

She wished their carriage would lurch again. The thought of physical contact was exciting.

Harold's gaze roamed over her and squashed the tiny thrill that ran through her. It was as if he saw right through her dress down to the safety pins holding her underwear together.

Several awkward minutes passed with only the rattle of the Underground breaking the silence. Harold straightened up as if he'd made a decision of some kind.

"Here, I have a small gift for you."

From his pocket he produced the finest pair of silk stockings Anna had ever seen; in London, in 1944, they were a highly-coveted luxury.

He pulled the sheer items from the Harrods packaging. Expensive items, especially with rationing, her heart skipped with delight. Harold held them up so they shimmered in the dim light.

Anna reached out and ran the luxurious stockings through her fingers, careful not to snag the delicate material. Their soft, classic shade of light brown; and very straight seams sorely tempted her. Wouldn't they look marvelous with her new dress?

Caution overcame temptation. "No, I couldn't possibly accept these. This is much too fine a gift for someone you just met. Thank you, though, for offering."

Harold shook his head vigorously so it looked like his hat might topple. "No, I know a way to make it all right. I have rented a hotel room. It's just at the next stop. Please say 'yes.'"

Harold put a hand on her arm and she looked up, lost in his deep brown eyes.

The pressure on her arm sounded alarm bells as Anna realized exactly what he was offering. All the rubbish about painting and wanting to see her work was just that, rubbish. He thought she was a floozy who could be bought for a pair of silk stockings. That certainly wasn't her idea of love.

Anna shoved the stockings back at Harold, no longer concerned about snagging them, "How dare you suggest such a thing? Please remove yourself.

Harold's beautiful eyes pleaded with her. "Please, Blanche, please. I'll be careful. I've got a condom. I think I'm in love with you."

The soldier's voice sounded far too loud, even with the rattle of the carriage. A few heads turned in their direction and Anna was suffused with anger and embarrassment.

"You are not in love with me." She enunciated each word carefully. "My name is Anna, not Blanche. If you don't remove yourself, I'll scream and accuse you of molesting me."

Wordlessly, the Yank shoved the stockings into his pocket and stood up.

He kept his hands in his pockets even though he swayed as he walked toward the exit doors. He had the audacity to smile and tip his hat to a woman holding a baby as he passed. Anna was appalled at the cavalier attitude and gritted her teeth in anger when he leaned against the post and whistled that ridiculous ditty, *Yankee Doodle Dandy."*

The soldier got off at the next stop, and Anna sent a silent prayer of thanks to God.

Tears pricked at her eyes so she reached into her pocket and pulled out a hankie her mother had embroidered with daisies. Why had she been so silly as to think any man would be interested in an old maid like her? Everyone said if a woman hadn't caught herself a husband by the time she was twenty-one, and here she was twenty-five. Twenty-five, for heaven's sake!

She'd dabbed her eyes, picked up her purse, and dug until she found the ancient compact, complete with cracked mirror, she always carried.

At that moment she hated her mirror. True, it revealed her best feature, freshly washed, blonde, shoulder-length hair; but it also revealed a thin, pale face composed of a long nose, thin lips and gray eyes, presently slightly damp; altogether not an encouraging sight.

She sighed; her figure had its problems as well; a long, angular body with small breasts and protruding pelvic bones, the result, at least partly, of food shortages. If only she had curves like her sister, Patsy.

The train shuddered to a stop at the next station and almost immediately, a pretty, sexy, blonde woman in a short, clinging red dress; came to sit beside her. Anna smoothed her dress and straightened her posture.

The girl reminded her of Patsy. Just like Patsy, the girl tried to catch the attention of a handsome young man in uniform standing nearby.

Anna resisted the urge to say that she knew a well-paid American soldier with rare, elegant silk stockings that came at a price she wasn't prepared to pay. Anna believed this girl would take the stockings, and so would Patsy.

Thoughts of Patsy caused Anna to take a deep breath and conjure up the scent of the inexpensive toilet water her sister favoured.

Anna missed her sister almost as much as her nephew Robert, Patsy's so-called love child. Patsy worked on a farm seven days a week, her contribution to the war effort; and Robert had been evacuated to green, leafy Wales, one of the safest places in the United Kingdom.

Some of the neighbours called Robert a bastard. Anna hated the word and all its connotations.

The disembodied voice announcing the next stop shook Anna from her thoughts. It was her stop, only a block away. However, she felt too overwrought to paint.

She decided to stay on the train until the end of the line and then ride back to the station near home.

When Anna returned home she somehow expected Margaret to know all about the incident with the Yank. Her mother always seemed to have a second sense when it came to her children.

However, Margaret's face only broke into a smile of pure devotion. Anna reveled in the love and acceptance and found herself forgetting about Harold.

"Did you enjoy painting?" Margaret said brightly.

Anna freed herself from the easel and paint box and dropped them on the floor. "No, I guess I just wasn't in the mood." She avoided meeting her mother's gaze.

She was too ashamed to tell her mother what happened, while at the same time she craved her mother's support and comfort.

Margaret gave her daughter a sharp glance and turned back to the bread dough she was working on. As she expertly kneaded the loaves she hummed a Brahms lullaby, a sound that always soothed Anna. The dull green dress strained across her mother's shoulders, plump in spite of rationing. She pushed a strand of graying hair from her pretty face with the back of her hand. Anna wished she'd inherited her mother's looks, but Patsy seemed to have gotten the lion's share of those genes.

Margaret wiped her hands on a tea towel, clapped small, fleshy hands together and started a new song, "Happy birthday." She sang boisterously.

Because it was Anna's twenty-fifth birthday, a party was planned in her honour. Her mother insisted such a red letter day shouldn't go unnoticed.

War rationing aside, family and friends had pooled their resources for a feast. Uncle Sidney would bring a whole bottle of excellent gin, enough to give all adults a small drink.

Anna's mouth watered when she remembered there would be roasted lamb, (not mutton) a terrific change from the usual diet of Spam, and a one-egg cake. Sugar rationing made any sweet a wonderful, heavenly extravagance.

Margaret finished the last chorus of the birthday song and turned to regard her daughter. "My, you look pretty in that dress." After a brief hesitation, Margaret continued, "I'll put the kettle on. Thanks for queuing up so we can have a cuppa. Imagine, Earl Grey. You're a fine daughter."

Margaret reached for the old kettle and Anna inhaled the delightful aroma of roast lamb permeating the air.

She knew better than to ask if her mother needed any help. Margaret liked to work alone in her kitchen so instead Anna took a seat at the large, metal Morrison table that dominated the room.

The Morrison table made her uneasy now. It had always been the centre of family meals but now it evoked thoughts of sheltering under it when the air raid siren sounded and they didn't have time to take refuge in the Underground. *When would this wretched war end? Apparently, D-Day had been a success yet still the war went on.*

14

Anna looked out the window, the heavy blackout curtains drawn back exposing the lush sunny beauty of the day.

Sunlight reflected off the bright red kettle on the stove and highlighted the gold rug glowing warmly against the brown linoleum. Myriad African violets and a huge shamrock that came all the way from Ireland filled the corners of the homey, comfortable room. Here, with her mother, she could forget the war and arrogant Yanks.

"There's a bit of sadness to mar the day. I heard on the wireless east London had bombs dropped on them again last night. They still don't have a death count." Margaret's voice was grave.

Anna nodded. "I hate the war. I hate the noise. I hate the smells. I hate the pounding of my heart during the air raids. The siren gives me the willies."

Anna clamped down on her rising panic. "I'm sorry. Let's be happy. It's my birthday and I appreciate the party more than you imagine."

The kettle whistled shrilly and Margaret abandoned the lunch preparations to make the tea. She wrapped the pot in a tea cozy and set it on the table. "I know exactly how long this brew should be steeped. We Wellington women make excellent housewives and an excellent housewife makes incredible tea."

"I have your Wellington blood and I like to think I'd make a good wife and mother, but it doesn't look like it's going to happen. I guess it's just not meant to be." Anna sighed wistfully and silently damned Harold for raising her hopes.

"You're wrong." Michael Marshall's strong deep voice filled the kitchen.

She turned to greet her father. The affection on his face warmed her heart. Michael Marshall, aged fifty-one, was tall and well-built with blond hair touched with gray, a longish nose, gray-blue eyes and high cheekbones, good looking in a hawkish, powerful way.

He limped, his only physical flaw, because one leg had developed several inches shorter than the other, something

15

Anna only rarely noticed. Today he wore his best blue dress trousers, a white shirt and blue suspenders.

"Your twenty-fifth birthday is going to be even more memorable than we imagined. Only the end of the war would be better than this." He grinned in happy expectation.

"I see you're wondering so I'll come right out with it. Charles Harding has just asked me for your hand in marriage. Of course, I said yes. He wants to propose to you right now."

Michael reached out his arms and a confused, frightened Anna walked into them. Her father smelt of pipe smoke and shaving cream, comforting scents from her childhood. Anna trembled.

Michael released her and held her at arm's length, a huge smile creasing his face. "Go to your fiancé, daughter. He's a good man." He pointed to the door and then waved her through it.

Anna clutched her hand to her heart. Her first marriage proposal, why oh why did it have to be Charles Harding? She could never love him even though her father adored the son of his business partner.

Michael's words at dinner last night played through her mind. "Our business at Marshall and Harding Limited is flourishing since Charles joined us. He has such capital ideas for displaying merchandise and understands hardware as well as his father. We'll have to offer him a partnership soon."

Anna's emotions beat inside her like moths battering against a glass jar. She allowed her father to push her out the door. Charles stood beside one of her mother's rose bushes. She couldn't bring herself to look at him and kept her head down.

Anna's stomach turned at the thought of kissing that mouth with its crooked teeth stained pink from his bleeding gums, and stench of his breath reached her even from two feet apart. The possibility of the more intimate acts of marriage made her want to bolt.

Drawing near, his polished shoes came into her line of sight. She raised her head and was surprised to see him dressed in an unfamiliar grey suit. *Did he buy it just for this occasion?*

A pang of guilt sliced through her. Was she putting too much emphasis on his appearance? The idea rankled as it was one of her pet peeves in others.

Charles took her hands in his clammy ones. "My dear, it is time for both of us to be married. I'm ready to settle down, and so I imagine are you, pet. Not to mention our union will please our parents. I am well able to take care of you. I expect to be offered a partnership in the near future, so you have no worries in that area.

Anna couldn't have imagined a less romantic proposal. He seemed to take it for granted she'd say yes and fall into his arms. She studied their clasped hands and searched for something suitable to say.

A tiny gasp escaped her when Charles pulled her into his arms and pressed his chapped lips to her cheek. She nearly gagged as his fetid breath seemed to steal the breath from her lungs. In spite of her best efforts she cringed away from him.

Charles must have misunderstood her reluctance. "I hope you don't consider me a coward. I didn't enlist because the army rejected me. I have a heart arrhythmia."

"Of course, I don't believe you're a coward." Anna regretted the words almost before they passed her lips. Perhaps Charles might have changed his mind if he found her to be overly critical of him.

She disengaged herself from him and breathed more freely. Dear Lord, how was she supposed to get out of this ridiculous arrangement? She regarded him with a dubious expression.

Charles seemed set on reassuring her the marriage would be a success. "I have it on good authority, dolly mops mostly and they should know; that I am an excellent lover.

The words stunned her and left her speechless.

A salacious smile twisted his face. "I assure you I can satisfy you. Of course, I like a woman with more than a handful in the bosom department. However, you'll do nicely, and at least you're a virgin. Not like your slut of a sister."

Anna almost screamed. Dear God, had he slept with Patsy? She wouldn't put it past either of them. He had the gall to brag about his liaisons with prostitutes and only wanted to marry her because she was a virgin.

She finally found her tongue. "I don't want to marry someone who prizes my virginity over me."

Charles' face darkened with anger and superiority. "What's gotten into you, girl? You've always seemed so biddable. Where is all this nonsense coming from? He stiffened his spine and looked down his hooked nose at her.

"Men and women are different and different rules apply. Of course you'll marry me. You will be a suitable wife and I will be a suitable husband."

"Do you love me?" Her voice shook and she forced herself to look into his face.

"If its love you want, of course I love you. You'll make a good wife."

Anna backed away and folded her arms across her chest. She couldn't stand the thought of being near him. Those prostitutes really had to work to earn their money. "Why do you love me?"

Charles' voice filled with exasperation. "You're Michael Marshall's daughter and he's my father's partner. It pleases them both. You're an obedient daughter. You'll make an obedient wife." As he spoke, Charles smiled and lit another cigarette.

Anna uncrossed her arms and clenched her fists. "Charles, the man I marry has to want me for who I am. I can't just be a convenience. You don't know me, and even if we were married for eighty years, you never would."

Charles regarded her as if she had suddenly grown two heads. "You will marry me and you will be happy and you'll have my children. There's no sense fighting this, you know. You don't want to be an old maid forever, do you?"

Anna chewed her lip and considered his words. If she looked at it coldly and without emotion, there was much to be said for marrying Charles.

She would have the status of being a married woman and she could have the family she always wanted. Perhaps, best of all, she could quit her job at the factory. Maybe Patsy was right and love wasn't so important. Real love, not the physical kind.

Even as she considered it, she couldn't bring herself to agree. The man talked like she was a brood mare he'd negotiated to purchase at the horse fair.

Anna looked down at her beautiful dress, the pleasure it brought earlier fled. Life with Charles would be cold and colourless and hateful.

Life as a spinster wouldn't be that bad. She could join the suffragettes and be her own woman. With no man in her life she could paint to her heart's content and she'd already proved she could earn her own money. Nursing or teaching would be viable options, she supposed.

She pleated a fold of skirt in her fingers and met Charles gaze. I won't marry you and no one can make me. You just march inside and tell my father I said no.

Her courage faltered for a moment. Her father would be furious with her, but it couldn't be helped. She would not marry that repulsive man for all the tea in China.

Chapter 2

Anna cringed before her father's rage. "How could you reject one of the best men in London? And don't give me some silly twaddle about how he doesn't understand you. What's to understand? You're not complicated."

Michael swayed; the result not only of his limp. "I'll be ashamed to see Ronald, the best partner a man could ask for. We've always been proud of you. Now you're acting like Patsy."

Anna lifted her head and stamped her foot. "You can't dominate me like you do Mom. I have your genes and they tell me I need a spine. *I will never marry Charles.*"

Margaret rushed to give Anna a hug. "You're right. Your father dominates me and sometimes I resent it, yet I wanted a strong man so I must be happy."

Margaret's pretty features twisted into a smile, a futile effort to hide unshed tears. Anna suppressed a pang of sympathy regretting the pain she'd caused her mother. However, she was too angry to take the words back and tried to ignore Michael's retreating back. She winced at the slamming of the door.

* * *

Anna managed to revel in the company of family and friends at the party. Charles and Ronald Harding were conspicuous in their absence. The partiers played the phonograph, danced and laughed, the war many world's away.

At the height of the merriment, Michael abandoned his chair beside Margaret and ignoring his limp, danced with Anna.

He whispered in her ear, "I love you daughter, no matter what."

Tears of gratitude filled her eyes.

* * *

Anna paused on the steps of the factory to inhale the pure, fresh air. She felt like an escaped prisoner leaving the noisy boring job behind her. The only good thing about the factory was the music they played to relieve some of the monotony. Anna thrilled to Mozart and Mantovani's Orchestra. She also savoured the independence the two pounds a week gave her.

Anna clutched three oranges. She'd stood in a long queue to retrieve them. They should placate her parents. Her mouth moistened in anticipation of the juicy taste.

Anna rubbed her forehead where a headache plagued her and used the now soiled handkerchief to dab at her sore eyes. The shift at the factory always left her covered in dirt and grime and longing for a warm, sudsy, fragrant tub. With any luck today she wouldn't have to settle for a sponge bath.

Anna glanced around and sighed with pleasure. Thank God. There was no sign of Charles. He wouldn't be attempting to "walk her home" in his usual fashion.

The man was incorrigible, insisting on taking her hand in his large, sweaty paw and trying to kiss her despite the lack of privacy on the busy street. Anna always pulled out of his embrace but Charles insisted he would never give up until she consented to marry him.

Michael radiated happiness whenever he saw Anna and Charles together. Her father couldn't seem to give up the idea of their union. He already hinted for a grandson.

Anna decided to enjoy her newfound freedom by taking the long way home, something she never did in Charles' company.

The day was perfect for walking, with sun-filled skies and everything lush and green. She thrilled to the singing of birds.

Her euphoria withered when she paused to watch five children playing within the rubble of a building. Their tattered clothes hung on their dirty, poorly nourished, and pale bodies. She shook her head at the memory of the rosy cheeked children of pre-war London. *Thank God we sent Robert to Wales.*

Nonetheless, the youngsters exuded happiness. Anna allowed herself a bittersweet smile. Children had the capacity to live in the moment, something she appreciated more and more in these war-torn times.

Tears darkened Anna's gritty eyes. Such a shame for innocents to have to play in an environment filled with such desolation. Anna rubbed her arms to dispel the sensation of ugliness and filth.

The realization her feelings were derived from more than her surroundings was a small revelation. She hated the brown, loose-fitting trousers and olive green jumper that did nothing for her complexion. Her long hair was pulled into a snood, a bag made out of fishnet and elastic that prevented her hair from becoming entangled in the machines. For some reason her hair style was a final insult.

Shaking her head, she pushed the feelings aside and continued on her way. She managed to enjoy the rest of her walk. The route took her past a movie theatre showing *Gone With the Wind.* If she and her parents ate spam for the next week, she could probably treat her mother to the movie while her father visited the local pub.

* * *

Anna clutched her heart. Air raid sirens wailed. Would she have time to get to the tube? A loud, terrifying buzz filled the air. Dear Lord, it must be one of the vicious

22

German V1 bombs that were as frightening as they were deadly.

She opened her mouth to scream, but the sound stuck in her throat. Anna scurried futilely in circles. Where to run? The tube was too far away. Finally, she stood still and prayed while she counted what she thought to be five seconds, the way to discern the bomb's location.

The five seconds stretched like five hours. Five, Four, Three…she could still hear buzzing, Two, One…Nothing. *No sound meant the bomb hovered directly overhead.*

Anna dropped to the pavement on her stomach and clamped her hands over her ears. There was no time to get to the tube. She prayed silently for an eternity that was only a millisecond. *"God, let me live. Please let me live."*

The bomb impacted with a torrent of crumbled stone. Shards of glass rained down around her, one just missing her wrist by inches. The precious oranges rolled from the suddenly nerveless fingers of his left hand.

Anna's heart pounded in her ears. The odd taste of fear filled her mouth. She could barely move. She coughed in vain attempting to dislodge the soot, ashes and dust filling her mouth. Heat suffused her body; it felt like she was on fire. Dear God, was everything on fire around her?

Surprisingly, she could see a little bit. Bodies and bits of bodies littered the street where blood flowed like water. Anna tried to call for help, but it turned into a cough.

She struggled to move her arms and legs and realized with certainty her left arm must be broken, the pain sent spots dancing across her vision. Her right arm and legs didn't particularly hurt, but she could move them only a little. Where were the fire fighters and rescue crews? If they couldn't find her, she'd die in this stifling, confining pile of rubble.

Time passed and she must have lost consciousness for a time. A certain sensation of resignation stole over her, somehow calming the terror gibbering in the back of her thoughts.

In a curious detached way Anna wondered if she would gaze upon the gates of heaven or the infernos of hell.

It was hot enough for hell. Did she even believe in heaven and hell?

She closed her eyes and swallowed. At least, she was still alive, but for how long? The pain made her dizzy and she was parched for water. Every part of her body ached.

* * *

After what seemed like an eternity, hope arrived in a flurry of sirens and commotion with the arrival of fire engines, ambulances and sniffer dogs.

Anna was reminded of their family dog, Brandy, when the two black Labrador Retrievers scrambled and sniffed in the rubble. Anna had loved Brandy and cried for a day when she died. In wartime, food was scarce for people, non-existent for pets.

Anna gathered her strength, determined to scream loud enough to be heard. She strived hard to draw attention and each time ended up coughing. She refused to give up. Finally, success. She dislodged enough obstruction in her throat to make an audible sound.

"Help."

Buoyed by her triumph, she tried again and joyously detected another voice. It was male and weak but she could make out his words. "Help, is someone there?"

Thank God. She wasn't alone. "Yes, I'm here, not too far from you as well as I can tell."

The voice grew louder. "Good, good. Let's yell for help. Maybe someone will hear our two voices. I know they can't see me because I can't see a thing."

"*I can see out*. It's a terrible sight but I like your idea. They'll be more likely to hear two voices."

Anna and this Godsend yelled and yelled and finally Anna heard a rescuer. "I hear voices but can't see you. Keep yelling and we'll find you."

Anna continued to call, fighting the pain that threatened to overcome her. She longed to rub her sore eyes but the only body part she could easily move was her head.

The rescuers continued to collect the dead bodies. It reminded Anna of sweeping the house clean. She shivered although she felt satanically hot.

With relief, she discerned a savior's voice. "Finally, I see you. We'll get you out as soon as we can. We just have to wait for more equipment. Can you hold on?"

Anna could just make out the rescuer, covered in dirt with a tattered plaid shirt and overalls, more apparition than man.

"Yes." She had no choice. At least it wouldn't be dark for hours. She strained her voice, "There's a man trapped nearby."

"Don't worry. We can't see him but we can hear him. We'll get him out. Keep talking to each other. It will pass the time."

Anna bit her lip hard enough to draw blood when the emergency workers moved away.

* * *

The evening dragged on and Anna's terror reduced the pain to a dull presence. She continued to converse with the trapped man. She learned his name was Daniel. He had the pleasant accent of one of the brave and perennially polite Canadians.

"Even if I'd had time to put my gas mask on, it wouldn't have helped with all this soot and dust. I feel like I'm going to suffocate. At least we're not covered in glass. It can do terrible damage."

Anna cried out. "A shard just missed my left arm, which hurts like crazy. It's probably broken."

"I'm sorry. I didn't mean to frighten you. With me, it's my shoulder. It's filled with shrapnel but that happened before…on D-Day. I'm 'getting a Blighty one.'"

Anna knew the term. While Daniel may not have life-threatening injuries, he had been hurt badly enough not to

25

be sent back to the front line. "War is hell. Do you think poorly of me?"

She'd heard similar words from Charles. Men all wanted to be considered brave, but fear was a human condition.

"Of course not, you're just being honest. I'd feel the same. Anna started to cough and found she couldn't stop.

When her coughing finally subsided, Daniel continued as if there'd been no interruption. "Now I'm damned miserable and craving a cigarette so bad I fear I might die."

His voice sounded raspy, the result of either cigarettes or the rubble? She suspected it was a combination of both.

"And *I'd* like a cup of tea. Thank God that's one pleasure Hitler hasn't been able to take away from us. We would lose the war for sure without tea."

Daniel's voice revealed he was only a foot or two away and she found this proximity made for a special intimacy. "Tell me about yourself, Anna."

She excluded little. She talked of her love of art, her work at the factory, and her family. In spite of the conditions Anna found she enjoyed talking to the man. He seemed to be genuinely interested in what she had to say.

Daniel reciprocated by describing his life in Canada. He lived in a vast country on a vast piece of property. If she escaped this rubble she vowed to find a book about Canada.

He rambled on about army life. "I hate all the rules. Yet, somehow we need them. I commanded a tank and have the rank to go with it."

Did she detect pride in his voice? No, she didn't think so. Instead she sensed the heavy mantle of responsibility.

Daniel groaned. "I can't wait to get back to the farm. It's my life. Funny, I don't share my private thoughts with most people. You're a special lady, Miss Anna."

Anna's eyes watered. She didn't know if it was from the debris or because no man had ever felt worthy of her confidences before.

Daniel's voice grew faint. Anna strained to catch the words. She silently prayed, *Dear God, don't let him die. Not like this.*

Fortunately, his next words were stronger. "My parents are extremely religious and established a church. It's almost cult-like. Mom and Dad are pacifists. Yet, despite the hell I've gone through, I think I did right by enlisting. Hitler is probably the most evil man ever born and there have been some bad ones."

"I agree. For one thing he's attempting to annihilate the entire Jewish nation." Anna moaned at the sight of three very small bodies pulled from the rubble. The war they'd just agreed needed to be fought was more terrible than words could convey.

Daniel began to cough violently.

Anna held her breath, waiting for the fit to subside. *He couldn't die. He just couldn't.*

As if reading her thoughts, he continued, "I survived D-Day in a destroyed tank and now I'm trapped in rubble. I lost all my company. Why can't I die?"

"Daniel, you said I'm special. *You're the special one.* I can tell you're a kind man."

* * *

Their rescue worker from earlier finally returned. Anna recognized his torn red shirt. The news wasn't good. It would be at least another thirty minutes before they could free Anna and Daniel.

Anna was comforted by Daniel's voice. "You sound young and pretty. What do you look like? You English girls all have such beautiful skin."

Anna softly sighed. Everyone wanted a pretty girl. "I'm not pretty. My nose is too long and my face is too thin. Actually, I'm too thin everywhere. My sister got the looks. I'm an old maid but a fussy old maid." Anna explained about Charles, his lack of love, his selfishness. Trauma must begat honesty, she decided.

Daniel's situation was similar. His parents wanted him to marry Nancy, a woman devoted to religion. "I don't love her. I don't even *like* her. She's a hypocrite. She's

27

constantly spouting love and compassion, but I saw her kick a cat for no reason. Besides that, she's plain as mud. Who wants a woman who is neither pretty nor kind?"

Anna gasped as more dead bodies were pulled from the rubble. She'd never before been so close to death. Perhaps she and Daniel were speaking too intimately. Who might be listening? She pushed the thought away; she had to keep speaking with him. It was the only thing keeping her from hysterics.

Daniel's desire to continue their conversation appeared equally strong. "I don't believe in my parents' fire and brimstone religion but I do like the idea of purity. You, Anna, are pure, and I don't just mean because you've told me you're a virgin. You have a purity of spirit, so different from me because I have seen such atrocities of war."

Anna struggled to smile. Could she be falling in love? With a voice, was it possible?

* * *

Just before dark, the necessary equipment arrived and worked its magic. Anna and Daniel were released from the rubble.

They freed Anna first. She held her left arm steady while they helped her climb out of the rubble. Free at last, she took a deep breath and found the untainted, crisp air the sweetest thing in the world. Her stiff limbs moved slowly and awkwardly at first, then they gained strength and she could move freely. *Thank God. I made it. I'm alive.*

She was just telling the rescuers about a trapped Canadian soldier when a man who must be Daniel appeared from the debris. He clutched his shoulder. She knew he was a young man, yet at the moment he looked at least eighty. Ash covered him and his eyes were red orbs.

She caught glimpses of a tall, strong, athletic body through the ripped and torn uniform. Somehow, even in that condition Anna found him attractive.

Daniel walked stiff-legged to where Anna stood and grinned.

"We're to go to the hospital with the other wounded."

She followed the direction of Daniel's gaze and looked down. Her jumper and trousers were torn and gaping open. She clutched the jumper closed and Daniel averted his gaze. She found it had been easier responding to a disembodied voice.

Daniel did not seem to suffer from the same condition. He gathered Anna close with his good arm, careful of her injury. She leaned into him, he felt wonderful, all strength and muscle.

"We made it! I know this isn't exactly the right time or place but will you see me again? I'd like to take you dancing."

Chapter 3

The ringing of the phone sent a spike of excitement through Anna. "I'll get it. It's probably Daniel." She almost collided with Margaret as she rushed to answer the strident summons. Anna ignored Margaret's, "Be careful. Or you'll break the other arm."

"Hello." She'd caught it on the second ring. She beamed. *It was Daniel.*

It took four days before the air raids let up enough to allow Daniel and Anna to go dancing. Even while she chaffed at the delay, Anna cherished those days. Daniel phoned every evening. Thank God. He'd committed her number to memory despite the fact he had no pencil or paper. She connected with Daniel in a totally different way than anyone else, including her parents.

Margaret hovered in the background, supposedly dusting or cooking, but shamelessly eavesdropping.

* * *

On a warm, sunny Friday evening, Anna anticipated spending time with Daniel when they would be able to do more than talk. She pressed her hand against her heart where it throbbed with excitement against her fingers. Margaret aided Anna as she dressed, which was a big help because of Anna's broken arm. However, the fracture came with a benefit. Anna could avoid the factory until her arm healed.

Margaret zipped Anna into her almost new outfit. "This dress suits you. I'm reminded of a daisy, all bright and fresh. Thank God, you're safe. We almost died of fright the day you didn't come home."

Margaret hurriedly changed the subject. "Are you sure there's no future with Charles? I've always liked him."

"No. He's already taking me for granted. I can't understand why he's still hanging around. I don't encourage him."

"It's simple. He's in love." Margaret sounded like she was just about to devour a chocolate, all happy with anticipation.

"He's not in love with anyone but himself. I'd rather die a lonely old woman than marry Charles."

Margaret blushed. "But you're dating a Canadian. Canada is a barren wilderness. It's very cold and primitive and they have mountains of snow. I'm sure you wouldn't be happy there. And remember, you'd never see England again."

Anna winced because Margaret hit a nerve. She cherished fresh, green, quaint, charming England. If she moved to Canada, she *would* miss her home.

Yet, how silly. After today, she'd probably never see Daniel again. She could only guess what he looked like. She remembered he was tall and well-built, but his features and colouring were a mystery. And since she was no looker, he might take one glimpse and scatter.

Anna thoughts were interrupted by a loud bang on the door. Was Daniel here already? She'd finished dressing so she rushed to answer it.

To her dismay, the open door revealed Charles. He blew smoke through his nose. "Aren't you going to let me in?"

"Yes, of course." Before Anna had time to adjust to Charles' presence, he lunged at her. She managed to duck behind the door and chastised herself for not slapping his face.

"You don't have to act like a frightened rabbit. I heard about the rubble and just wanted to see if you are okay. I see, except for a broken arm, you are."

Anna broke into a toothy smirk. "I've a date with a Canadian soldier. I really like him." She hoped the news would send Charles scurrying.

Charles looked aghast. "Canada is a wasteland and Canadians are all hick farmers. I'd be a soldier in a fancy uniform, if it weren't for this heart problem."

Anna saw her mother standing, mouth agape, arms crossed over her chest. She shook her head back and forth.

"It's not the uniform I'm attracted to. Daniel understands me." Anna spoke in thundering tones.

You're talking nonsense. I'm the man for you." Charles took a couple of steps towards her. Anna cringed away before she could stop herself.

She silently prayed for courage and found it. She raised her head. "Leave now. And don't ever come back." She fixed him with what she hoped was a steely stare and pointed at the door. To her relief, Charles turned on his heel and left, slamming the door behind him.

* * *

Charles had only been gone a few moments when there was a tap, tentative and undemanding, on the door. With shaking hands, she answered it. The gorgeous man with beautiful hazel eyes looked down at her. Anna's breath caught in her throat, the strong masculine features were capped with thick dark wavy hair. How could someone who looked so darned good be interested in her?

However, the handsome face appeared anguished. She'd encountered the look many times in the expressions of returning soldiers.

"You're right. You're not pretty." His voice was playful. Anna sighed. Of course, she wasn't attractive enough for the magnificent Daniel. Daniel smiled. "You're beautiful, very beautiful, in a fresh, clean, wholesome way. You have the best kind of beauty."

Daniel fumbled in his pocket and extracted a package wrapped in gold paper and tied with a white bow. "I got you something." He held it out to her.

Anna's hands shook as she extracted the gift. She hadn't had a wrapped present in years. It was a small, perfect bottle of Chanel No. 5 perfume. Surprise and happiness at the unexpected gift flooded through her. Impulsively, she reached out and clasped his right hand. Big, strong and warm, she doubted she'd ever want to let it go. "Thank you. Thank you. I will cherish your gift forever."

* * *

The evening was perfect. By the time they left the house and walked the three blocks to the underground, the sun began to set.

Daniel said, "I've never seen a more beautiful sunset."

Anna pranced like a race horse. This handsome, empathic man thought her beautiful *and* noticed sunsets. Anna had a picture of a sunset she'd painted and decided she would give it to Daniel.

They both hastened their pace when they passed the rubble of the movie house; a mass of boulders and ashes and old traces of blood. She shivered although the night was warm.

Anna said, "I never heard how many people died. There were so many bodies. It makes me scared all over again. But we both survived. It's like we were meant to meet."

Daniel didn't speak but reached for Anna's hand and gently squeezed it. He moved cautiously and his eyes picked up every movement. Was it because of the rubble, or his experiences in the war? She suspected the latter.

* * *

At the underground station they left the beauty of the evening for the hot, stuffy tube. The training was bursting, so they had to sit close together. Daniel's broad shoulder touched her own. Excitement thrilled through her. How could she find Charles repulsive and yet think Daniel heavenly?

They didn't speak but sat in comfortable silence. Many of the passengers were dressed elegantly so perhaps they were also going to the dance. The scent of Chanel No. 5 infused the air.

Anna inhaled Daniel's sensuous, uniquely masculine scent. On him, even the smell of stale cigarettes was attractive.

Outside again, Daniel spoke softly as if he didn't want to alert the Germans to their presence. "It's another few blocks. I hope you don't mind the walk. We'll have to move slowly. It's getting dark."

"Actually, I love walking. It calms me." She appreciated the sliver of moonlight shining the dark sky.

"I like walking too, but in Canada we go everywhere by car. There are a lot of things about England I'll miss."

Anna flipped a strand of hair off her face. "Tell me about Canada."

"Well, the prairies where I'm from, are as different from England as white is to black. We rarely get drenched and in winter we sometimes get walloped with snow. The wind blows loud and ferocious.

"I miss Canada, but on the farm we don't have indoor plumbing or electricity or a telephone. But, we've got plenty to eat and the prairies are spacious and beautiful. I'm trying to be accurate."

"I think I'm starting to get the picture. I'm waiting to receive a copy of a book on Canada from the library."

"I'd like to read it too, if that's alright?"

Anna heaved a sigh of joy, revelling in the pleasure of having a man friend. In the past, Anna had mostly just gone out with groups of friends. She'd only rarely paired off with anyone.

* * *

Daniel led Anna into the crowded, smoky, dimly lit hall. They soaked up the energizing atmosphere. She'd

34

never been to a dance hall before. She gaped at the 8-piece band, all attired in black suits with gleaming white shirts and black ties.

A singer wearing a clingy, white dress crooned a slow, sultry blues number in a breathy sexy voice. Except for breasts, she was built like a man and epitomized 1940's fashion. Anna frowned in distaste. She didn't like the singer, or the blues. She preferred happy songs.

The singer left the stage and the band played "In the Mood." Myriad dancers crowded the floor. There was much changing of partners and some women boogied with each other. Anna smiled. Everyone looked happy. Despite the war, people still needed pleasure in their lives.

Daniel took Anna's hand and steered her past empty tables until he came to one occupied by another couple. Several women ogled Daniel. He held out a chair for Anna. *Such manners.*

The music halted while the band took a break. Daniel introduced Reg and Julie. Reg looked handsome in his Canadian uniform. Anna warmed to his wide grin and offered her hand in greeting. "It's a pleasure to meet you. Were you in the tank with Daniel?"

Reg stared at Daniel and started to choke. Anna was aghast at her *faux pas* and stared at Daniel. His face had lost its colour. *What did she say wrong?*

"No. He has a desk job." Daniel's reply was curt.

The tension ended when Reg told a silly joke. It was his grin as much as the punch line that left everyone more comfortable.

Julie's accent and black, elegant dress reeked wealth. However, Julie greeted Anna with warmth. There was no trace of stodginess or condescension. Was the class system eroding? If so, something good had come out of the war.

Reg said, "It's about time Daniel got himself a girlfriend. And a fine girl you are." Anna had to lean in close to hear his words. The dance hall was crammed with noisy patrons.

"Now, don't be getting ideas. You've got a beauty yourself. Julie is almost as beautiful as Anna." Anna saw the pain leave Daniel's eyes.

Daniel offered to bring everyone a drink. There was some debate, but finally it was decided they'd all have a scotch and water.

Reg lit a cigarette. "Our Canadian rye whiskey is just as good, maybe even better than scotch. If Julie ever consents to marry me, she'll be able to try it."

"I didn't know you were asking." Julie's wide smile revealed teeth as white as Daniel's.

Daniel launched into a description of how he and Anna met. Reg and Julie both listened, wide eyed, leaving their drinks untouched.

"My goodness that was certainly a close call, how lucky both of you escaped unharmed." Julie gestured at Anna's arm.

Reg grinned and changed the subject. With twinkling eyes he bragged to Anna he came from a gopher ranch. "We have about five hundred head."

Anna nodded. She hoped she looked knowledgeable. She didn't know a gopher from a cow, but figured Reg must be a product of Canada's elite. It might explain how he had attracted Julie.

Daniel started to laugh. It was an honest, hearty laugh. "Reg, you bum. Gophers, or Richardson Ground Squirrels, *are* kind of cute, but they're also a nuisance because they dig holes. There's a bounty on them. We have at least five hundred head at our place too.

Reg chuckled. "You're spoiling all the fun."

The music started up again and Anna and Daniel danced to the "Tennessee Waltz." It wasn't easy with their collective injuries, but Daniel held her as close as her cast would allow. She placed her head on his good shoulder. He oozed strength and power and smelled heavenly.

The band played a couple of jitterbugs and Anna found Daniel had natural rhythm. All of the exercise made her legs weak and she wasn't up to a third lively dance.

They seated themselves and Daniel put his arm around her shoulder. She blushed, but enjoyed feeling protected and desired.

* * *

Back on the tube Daniel and Anna sat close together. Daniel enclosed her hand with his large one, and Anna glowed. Touch must be the most intimate of all senses, she mused.

"I hope you enjoyed yourself?" Daniel's smile was brief. The vulnerability in his expression touched her heart.

"I did. It was fantastic. Thank you."

"So you'll come out with me again?"

The carriage lurched and Anna found herself squashed against Daniel. Anna turned her face to Daniel. Their lips were only inches apart. "Nothing would delight me more."

"You and Julie, you Brits, you're all kind and fun." Even in the dim light Daniel's eyes sparkled.

"I'm glad you think so.. I believe we've become more relaxed with the hardships brought on by the war. That British reserve seems to have melted away a bit. Sometimes good comes out of bad. Personally, I like you Canadians with your wit and good manners."

Daniel hesitated for a moment before he spoke. "I wish your mother felt the same. She treated me like a wet mongrel."

"My Dad's worse. None of it's your fault. They both adore Charles. I can't see why." Anna hung her head and spoke to her lap. "If you have some extra money, it might help if you gave Mom and Dad simple gifts. The rationing is hard on them. I hope I don't sound overly materialistic and I'm embarrassed to even suggest such a thing.

"No, not at all. I realize how bad things are. I'll see what I can do.

* * *

Two days later, Daniel suggested they go to the movies. Anna had originally nixed the idea. She would never forget how frightened she'd been when trapped within the rubble of a movie theatre. What if another bomb hit while they were inside? However, desire for some fun overcame her fear. They would even be seeing *Gone With The Wind*."

Daniel arrived at Anna's door step carrying a box of chocolates and five apples. He offered them to Margaret when she answered the door in her new house dress.

"These are for you."

"Thank you. Thank you. My goodness, you must have queued up for hours. You're very generous. Please come in."

Daniel's shoulders relaxed a little, some of the tension drained out of him. In a flash, her demeanor shifted, taut lines etched her face and her eyes shone cold and hard as marble. "You seem a nice man, but my daughter is engaged to be married. I think you should know this," her voice was equally as cold as her expression. A white-faced Anna rushed into the room and grabbed her mother by the shoulders.

"Charles and I are *not* engaged, and you know it. Admit it. You saw how belligerent he can be. How can you say such a thing?"

Margaret wrung her hands. "Well, Charles wants to marry Anna, and we, my husband and I, are in favor. We don't want our daughter going to dangerous, primitive Canada and never coming home again."

Daniel hid a laugh behind his hand. "It's much safer in Canada now than in England. I want to keep seeing Anna,,, and I would like your blessing."

"Anna is an adult. She can do as she pleases," snipped Margaret. She lowered her head and spoke in muffled tones. "I won't stand in the way of her desires. I just wish she'd listen to reason."

At that moment, Michael entered the room. Poor Daniel, thought Anna, as she introduced the two men.

Michael looked fierce. "I don't want you getting any ideas. My Anna is a good girl."

Daniel's handsome face radiated sincerity and respect. "I would never hurt Anna. I like her a lot. I would certainly like to go on seeing her. I hope you can understand."

Michael sighed, but said nothing. He limped from the foyer into his bedroom. Margaret busied herself in the kitchen.

Anna and Daniel quietly exited the house.

* * *

Anna groaned when she spotted Charles on the way to the underground. *Could the day get any worse?* For years, she rarely encountered the man. Now he sniffed her out like a blood hound.

Charles' lip curled into a snarl. "Is this your Canadian, and what are you doing with him? You should be with me."

She expected him to pound his chest.

Anna drew herself up and prepared for battle. The situation needed to be dealt with once and for all. "Stay away from me. I've told you many times I will *not* marry you. So leave me alone." Her voice was shrill.

Charles loomed closer and Anna took a step back.

She had almost forgotten Daniel and exhaled in relief when he intervened. The Canadian towered over Charles who retreated rapidly. .A tiny thrill ran through her at the thought of two men fighting over her. *Thank God. Daniel is the obvious victor.*

Daniel grabbed Charles by the collar of his shirt. The Canadian's shoulder didn't seem to be a bother. A button popped and hit Charles' pallid cheek.

"Anna is my friend. She's told you she's not interested. You need to listen to the lady. Do you understand?" Daniel jerked on Charles' shirt so his head wobbled on his scrawny neck.

Charles' teeth chattered and he bowed his head. "I understand." His face was white with fear. He slowly shuffled away when Daniel released him. Daniel

39

unclenched his fist. "Imagine. The nerve of that guy! If he bothers you again, just let me know and I'll take care of it."

He took Anna's hand and they continued towards the underground. "If I were the smaller man, I would have taken the beating. Physical hurts heal. I'm not so sure about the others."

"Daniel, thanks for protecting me and getting Charles to let me be."

Daniel chuckled. "Nonsense, my pleasure." He turned to her and stared intently into her eyes. "I fell for you as soon as I heard your sweet voice in the rubble. At first I thought I'd bought it and you were an angel. You're everything I want in a woman. And I'm going to try to get a desk job so we can spend time together."

Anna swooned when they embraced.

* * *

Anna loved the movie. Even though she hit her head when they ducked at the same time during an intense scene in the movie. The onscreen gun fire brought their own war far too close once again. All too soon for Anna, Clark Gable uttered Rhett Butler's famous last line. The lights brightened and Anna and Daniel squinted in the sudden illumination. They exited the theatre and rejoined the drama of wartime England. The passing cars drove slowly, with shuttered head lamps. The danger from the Huns was always near.

They walked companionably, hand in hand.

"Anna, I want to be honest with you. I have nightmares and difficulty concentrating. I don't know when, or if, that will change. They don't know much about shell shock and the doctors are more likely to think a guy is just trying to get out of going back to the front. If we continue this relationship are you willing to put up with that? Daniel squeezed her hand tight.

"The more I'm with you, the more I come to like you. Shell shock or no shell shock."

Daniel tripped a little in the darkness and Anna clutched him tight. A maternal instinct rearing its head in her chest. If only she could protect him from the war. The closeness led to a tender kiss. Daniel's arms were strong, yet gentle; his breath fresh and clean. He was the complete opposite of Charles, and embodied everything she wanted in a man.

* * *

Anna mostly avoided their neighbourhood pub, *The Wolf and Hare,* because she felt like a ninny going with her parents. It looked like she couldn't find a date, true; but still embarrassing.

It was a thrill to introduce Daniel to the quaintly decorated tavern. She loved the heavy, dark table and chairs; chips as a snack; and delicious dark beer. Even if Daniel complained about its warmth.

A game of darts brought out Anna's competitive side. She always took the white darts and Daniel the black. Anna won a game and leapt up and down, squealing "I beat you. I did."

Every patron turned in her direction. *Oh God. How mortifying.* "I hope you don't mind." Her voice dropped to a whisper.

Daniel tossed back his head and laughed. "I like everything about you. Absolutely everything. I don't mind if you win every game."

Daniel gazed at his surroundings and a smile lit up his eyes. "British pubs are great. They're much better than our beer parlours in Canada where all a guy can do is sit and drink. Women are only allowed in some of them if they are with a man."

* * *

Since both of them enjoyed the outdoors, a day of fishing was appealing. Anna brought her paints and toiled at a close up of a sunflower. Her face screwed into a frown as she struggled to get the colours perfect, paying particular attention to the light.

Daniel stood on the banks of a picturesque stream. He whistled softly as he cast his line in the clear, swift-running water. Here, he could almost forget the war.

No fish took the bait, nor did Anna create a masterpiece, but neither cared. The voice of the water sliding over the rocks and the chorus of bird song sounded almost magical. Bright sun caressed their faces while they laid an old plaid blanket on the grassy bank and sat companionably close.

"How's it going with your job, Daniel?

True to his word, he'd snagged a coveted office job.

Daniel jerked the fishing rod and frowned. "It's a hell of a lot better than being fired at in a tank. But I can't type fast enough and my spelling's not so hot. I don't know how long they'll keep me here."

Daniel took a sip of tea still warm from the thermos. "Farming is my life. I love the way the land stretches for miles and miles. I work with my Dad and he lets me do as I please. As soon as I get home, I'm going to buy my own quarter section."

A bee buzzed just above their heads. Anna inhaled the scent of wildflowers. The beauty of the day was marred by Daniel's words. Why did he have to mention going back to Canada?

Anna brushed a strand of hair out of her eyes and looked at the man beside her. Even though she felt comfortable with him, what did she really know about Daniel? Taking a deep breath she ignored her innate reserve and asked what was to her an invasive question. "You say your parents are very religious. Do you believe in God?"

"Yes, I do, but I don't think he wants us to constantly worship him. I think people should just to try to live fair minded, forgiving, responsible lives." He took another sip of tea.

Anna softly clapped her hands. "That's exactly how I feel. I'm so happy you're not bound by rigid religious rules."

Daniel blushed with pleasure.

Anna decided to abandon her painting for the rest of the day. Chatting with Daniel was more pleasant. She found her cleaning solvent and the small plastic pail she carried and carefully cleaned her brush.

Daniel ignored his fishing rod and gazed affectionately at Anna. "You're my favourite artist."

Anna gently kissed him on the cheek. He made her art worthwhile. Charles hadn't even realized she painted.

Anna licked her lips. Thoughts of Charles prompted her to ask Daniel another revealing question. He'd be leaving soon. She wanted to know everything about him *now*. "Do you believe men and women are equal? My father bosses Mum around. That worm Charles only wants me because I'm a virgin. I don't mind being a virgin, but it shouldn't be the sole reason a man wants to marry me. Am I crazy?"

Daniel snapped his fingers. "No, you're not crazy. I believe in equality as well. In my parent's case, Mom's the boss, He paused and a blush coloured his face. I'm a virgin too. Maybe we can learn together?"

* * *

On their fifteenth date, a Saturday, Daniel startled Anna by asking her to lunch at a "charming café". Anna blushed with enthusiasm. Dining out was expensive. God bless Daniel's soldier's pay.

She mouthed a silent prayer that Daniel would never return to Canada. The attraction wasn't just the excitement of getting to know someone new. Anna found herself wanting to share with him the joy she found in the minutiae of everyday life.

Rain failed to mar their enjoyment of each other. Anna and Daniel huddled under Anna's umbrella. Daniel's had been stolen. They found moving difficult and both were left damp. Her feet squished in her sensible oxford shoes.

Anna laughed in mock protest. "You need your own umbrella. We'll look a horror by the time we arrive at the café." She leapt aside when a car splashed water as it passed. Fellow strollers jostled her.

Anna sighed with pleasure. "My, but this rain smells good. I guess I'm a total English woman, because I like it. How about you? Doesn't this weather grow on you?"

Daniel grinned in astonishment. "Actually no, I'm not a big fan of rain. Where I'm from, sunshine's abundant. It rarely rains. It's beautiful."

* * *

Anna hugged Daniel when the café came in sight. It had once been a large, vine-covered house. Laughing, they went up the path and through the entrance.

They stashed their umbrella in the stand by the door. There was little room for another sodden parasol. Water pooled beneath the stand. Anna glanced around the cozy room where a fire crackled in the grate.

Daniel led Anna to a table near the fireplace where a candle glowed. They removed their soggy coats and seated themselves. Anna combed her hair with her fingers. She could feel the warmth from the fire drying it.

Almost immediately, a slim, petite, dark-haired waitress appeared. She sounded more French than English. She smiled and took their order of tea and ham and cheese sandwiches.

Anna leaned closer to voice her approval of the cafe over the sounds of dishes being gathered and patrons' chatter. The table was near a large, square radio and they caught snippets of the BBC news broadcast. Anna exhaled when she realized nothing extraordinary had come out of the speaker, a blessing in these times.

Their tea arrived and Daniel wrapped his hands around his cup. "I wrote to Mom and Dad. I told them I'd met a special girl. I hope they got my letter. I haven't gotten a reply." His eyes shone in dim light.

Anna flushed. "Thank you. It's fantastic to be considered special." She took a sip of tea.

A beautiful little blonde girl about five years old came up to Anna and held out both hands. "Don't my nails look pretty? Mum put polish on them. I'm so pretty."

Anna reached out and grasped the small hands, soft as butter. "Yes, you are beautiful." Anna's eyes moistened. "You remind me of my nephew who's away from London because of the bombs."

A slender woman, beautiful as the girl, grabbed the child and pulled her gently away. "I hope she isn't bothering you."

"Oh my goodness, not at all. She's delightful." Anna turned a radiant smile on the child.

"Do you like children?" Anna turned to Daniel.

"Yes, but I can't imagine having them with Nancy, the girl my parents keep pushing at me, someday if I marry, I do want children."

Their sandwiches arrived, toasted and surrounded by chips. Anna's mouth watered and she consumed the meal with gusto, wiping her lips with a napkin when she finished.

"That little girl we saw reminds me of photos I've seen of my sister, Patsy, at that age. Patsy is so beautiful."

Daniel leaned close. "She can't possibly be more beautiful than you."

"You surely don't honestly believe I'm beautiful?" Anna blinked in astonishment.

"Poppycock, you *are* beautiful. You're a kind, good person and I find you very appealing." Daniel reached for Anna's hand. "I know this might seem fast, but I'm in love with you."

Tears flooded Anna's eyes. "And I love you."

* * *

Outside they held the closed umbrella between them. The rain had ceased. Daniel took her hand and led Anna to St. Augustine's. The church was nearby on a quiet side street. Anna inhaled the fresh scent of grass and trees after a rain.

They ambled along the strategically placed paving stones to the back of the church. It was a tranquil setting, with tall trees and flowering shrubs, still shrouded in that peculiar soft, darkness that comes after a rain.

Anna glanced at the man beside her, he seemed anxious about something. Perhaps he was regretting his recent declaration of love. She shook her head and looked up at him when he halted beneath a chestnut tree.

He took her into his arms. She was careful to not further damage his shoulder. "I know it's too soon, but I feel as if I've known you all my life. Will you please be my wife?"

Anna gazed into hazel eyes and saw nothing save love. Yet she hesitated. If she married Daniel she might never again walk England's quaint streets or smell fish and chips wrapped in newspaper; and her family. How'd she miss her family!

However, living without Daniel would be unbearable. There would be challenges ahead, but with Daniel, she would meet them.

Anna trembled as she smiled up at him. She leaned close and kissed him gently on the lips. "Yes, I will marry you."

Chapter 4

November 4, 1944 dawned stormy with harsh wind and rain. In spite of the weather Anna glowed with joy. Today was her wedding day.

Patsy, maid-of-honour, helped Anna get ready. Patsy looked more ready for a dance club than a wedding in her clinging scarlet dress and black high-heeded shoes. Her long, blonde hair was combed over one eye like Veronica Lake. She looked like a trollop, but Anna loved her sister too much to criticize.

Anna decorated the living room earlier with blue plastic flowers and blue streamers in preparation for the reception. She'd painted a picture of a heart enclosing a couple dancing. It was too cutesy to constitute real art, but Daniel claimed to love it.

Anna sighed with happiness. Even the rain made her smile. She felt safe and warm because she was sheltered within the arms of her family. How could she leave them in a few short months?

The sight of her wedding dress banished any negative thoughts. It was beautiful; a long sheath of white satin with tiny rosettes along the high neckline and long sleeves. Generous Aunt Sophie had loaned it to Anna for her special day. It fit like it was made for her. The hem had been turned down at least two inches to accommodate Anna's longer, leaner frame.

Patsy squirted perfume on Anna's neck. Anna inhaled the marvelous scent, Cinderella, under the care of her fairy godmother.

Patsy spoke through a mouthful of bobby pins as she reached to attach the veil in Anna's hair. "I hope this stays anchored in your fine hair. I wouldn't want you losing your veil when Daniel kisses you. And how about giving some of that perfume to your maid-of-honour?"

Anna passed the perfume to Patsy. "Do your best, big sis. Do your best."

Patsy stepped onto a low stool and placed the veil's luxurious folds over Anna's shoulders. Then she examined her handiwork. "You look marvelous. I'm sure Daniel will want to rip this creation right off you."

Anna gazed with satisfaction at her reflection in the mirror. "He best not. I'm sure Aunt Sophie wants this beautiful dress for her daughters. She was an angel to lend it to me." The dress, her decorations, and much more were the culmination of much planning and preparation.

Daniel had carefully saved the two hundred dollars required before a soldier could marry an English woman. They had both been interviewed by Daniel's commanding officer, Colonel Darling (who was anything but). Staring fiercely at them through his wire-rim glasses and smoking a cigar, the Colonel bluntly asked if they *had* to get married. Anna had turned bright red as Daniel assured him that wasn't the case.

She'd felt like a spy facing interrogation as the man asked her what she knew of Canada. Daniel and Anna read the library book on Canada together, just as they'd planned. However, Anna remained largely ignorant of her future home. Nonetheless, the Colonel nodded his head as she spoke. Her response must have been satisfactory.

Daniel had also filled out Form 1000/110 to prove he could afford to support her when he left the forces, which would be soon. She was also subjected to a blood test and a medical examination. The latter left a nude Anna uncomfortable and embarrassed.

* * *

Anna knew all the preparation had been worth it now her wedding day was here.

Patsy winked with the eye that wasn't covered by hair. "Mom says Daniel is attractive, so that must mean he's *gorgeous*, and I say, great. But, you don't need to marry him. Why don't you just fool around? Then you could stay in England?"

Anna understood her sister's point. She did want to sleep with Daniel. Go to bed with him and all that entailed. However, she also wanted love. "I'm delighted Daniel wants to spend the rest of his life with me. I want our lives entwined forever, not just a slap and tickle." She clasped her hands tight together.

Patsy stepped back from Anna and regarded her with satisfaction. She opened the bedroom door and called to their mother. "Anna looks beautiful. Come and see."

Margaret ignored whatever tasks she was engaged with and entered the room within seconds. She carried the family bible. Anna would carry it in place of a bridal bouquet because of a dearth of flowers in war ravaged London in November. After the ceremony, the large, white, leather-bound bible would be returned to her mother. It contained birth and death information for the whole family.

Margaret gasped and placed a hand over her heart. "You look gorgeous, just gorgeous, an angel escaped from heaven. I think you were right about keeping your hair down. But you need some makeup. I'll go find my lipstick. I remember it makes your whole face glow. Let it be my wedding gift."

Margaret returned with the lipstick, and gave her daughter a big hug. Then, finally, she released Anna. "I'm trying not to be selfish, but you'll be missed. I think maybe Daniel will make you happy, yet this is hard, so damned hard."

It was the first time she'd ever heard her mother swear. Margaret put her face in her hands to hide the tears Anna knew were silently falling.

Tears formed in Anna's eyes and her voice held a plaintive tone. "Mum, I'll miss you, too. You'll never know how much. I love Daniel and I want to be a wife and mother, so like Ruth in the Bible, where my husband goes so do I."

Margaret went out the door, still covering her eyes, too overcome with emotion to speak.

Patsy's angry sneer removed all the prettiness from her face and took Anna by surprise. "So Anna is marrying a Canadian and hurting Mum and Dad in the process. Welcome to the club of people who disappoint their parents. How does it feel?"

Anna bit her lip, trying to ignore the bitterness in her sister's voice. Patsy was prone to sudden mood swings and Anna knew she should have anticipated the jealousy. "Horrible, but also good. I have to look after *my* needs. And Mum said she thinks Daniel will make me happy. That's good. In her own way, she's giving her blessings."

"Yes, I suppose." Patsy sounded noncommittal and dismissive.

* * *

Margaret was just about to awaken Michael from a quick nap, (fathers of the bride being integral to the ceremony); when she was distracted by a loud, urgent knock at the door. Margaret, eyes still tear stained, rushed to answer it. "Now who can that be…Don't worry I'll get rid of them as quickly as possible. Imagine bothering us on your wedding day." She moved rapidly, and in the process her carefully coiffed hair lost some of its splendour.

Anna and Patsy, who came into the room to investigate, peered around their mother. A pompous-looking postman, literally too big for his uniform, filled the entryway holding out a letter.

"I have a special delivery letter for a Miss Anna Marshall? Which one of you would that be?" He spoke in a loud, pretentious voice.

Anna glided past her mother and held out her hand. "That's me." Anna placed her other hand over her busting heart. *Dear God. Let Daniel be alright.*

50

The red-haired postman eyed her attire. "I see you're getting married today. I hope this isn't news from across the channel. It would be a shame to ruin your special day."

Anna doubted he cared; more likely he was a gossip. "Thank you," Anna took the note and closed the door with a thud in the postman's face

She examined the letter. The return address said only, Mr. Charles Harding. The creep! Could she never be rid of him? At least he hadn't come in person.

Probably the letter contained some prattle about her marrying a hick farmer. Nonetheless, her hands shook. "I'm going to go into the bedroom and read this in privacy. I hope you understand. It's from Charles." Anna mustered as much authority as possible.

Both women nodded, their eyes were wide with curiosity. Neither spoke. Anna blushed with embarrassment.

Anna tore at the flimsy envelope as soon as she was alone. She tore open the envelope and yanked the letter out, it was written on soft, delicate paper, light as eiderdown.

My Beloved

I write you this letter because I beseech you not to marry the Canadian soldier. He does not know English ways and he will make your life miserable. I, on the other hand, am the man for you.

Your rejection is impossible for me to bear, so impossible that I am considering taking my life. There is rat poison in my home. I can and will take it if you continue to reject me. I do not want to live if I cannot have you by my side.

You see, my mother rejected me when she ran away from her family. I was only seven years old. I do not know where she is. I re-live this loss daily.

Please don't tell anyone our dirty secret. It is for my father and I, and now you, to share.

My life is in your hands.

Charles

Anna wrapped her arms around her waist and went cold with shock. The letter drifted to the floor from her nerveless fingers.

Like everyone else, Anna believed Mrs. Harding was dead. For years she had pitied poor motherless Charles. Ronald Harding was widely praised for being both mother and father to his son.

This provided an explanation for Charles' persistence in his pursuit of her. It also proved she'd been right to reject him. Not only did Charles not love her, he wanted a mother substitute and used the threat of suicide to incite guilt. She would, of course, keep Charles' secret. But what should she do about her miserable situation? Would Charles really kill himself?

Anna sat down on her bed and proceeded to wring her hands. She *hated* Charles. Hated more than she'd ever hated anyone before. Nonetheless, if Charles really took the rat poison, she would be as good as a murderer. Anna cringed at the thought of Charles dying a tormented death.

She rose from the bed and gazed out the window. She moved quickly with soft footsteps. Outside a dark sky with rain falling in torrents and few people hurrying on the street met her gaze. It even appeared a good day for suicide, as well as a wedding.

She closed her eyes, clasped her hands together and rested them on the thickly painted windowsill. She bowed her head because she couldn't kneel in her wedding dress. *Please God. Show me what to do.* Even in the rubble she hadn't prayed so fervently.

Anna opened her eyes, lifted her head and saw the sky had cleared somewhat. Now a lighter, friendlier rain fell. Her face lit from within when she glimpsed the hint of a rainbow. She had given her problem to a higher power who controlled everything. God had provided her with the answer. Her worry lessened.

Anna curled a strand of hair with her finger, a habitual action when thinking. Charles had a choice. He could find help, possibly from a minister, or he could continue to writhe in agony. She didn't care which. She strove to be kind to others, but she couldn't live for them. She would marry Daniel. She was not responsible for Charles' happiness.

Anna left the window and retrieved the letter. Without re-reading it, she tore it into tiny pieces and threw them into the blue velvet jewel box she'd had since a child. Later, she would throw these pieces into the trash, and when she did so, she would be metaphorically throwing Charles out of her life forever.

Anna, her shoulders straight, exited her bedroom. She moved with purpose. Margaret beamed.

"Are you going to call off the wedding and marry Charles? You can, you know." Her mother obviously believed Charles had offered some last minute incentive so Anna would change her mind about him.

Patsy said nothing, but practically quivered with curiosity. If Charles committed suicide, Patsy and Margaret might guess at the contents of the letter. What if he left an incriminating suicide note? Margaret would blame her and so would her father. *Damn*. Yet her decision came from God. The only decision, the right decision.

"No, no, I'm not calling off the wedding. Charles is a manipulative schemer. I won't fall into his arms, no matter what he says and does. I am entitled to happiness and I will have it with Daniel." She stamped her foot for emphasis.

* * *

The wedding party made the short, albeit damp walk, (the letup of rain only temporary), to the St. Andrews Anglican Church. It was the same church where Anna had been baptized and confirmed, and where she had gone to Sunday school to learn bible stories.

She would be married by Canon George Mathison, a tall, thin man with a shock of white hair and piercing blue eyes. Anna had always liked and respected him. He told Anna how much he would miss her, but nonetheless wished her happiness with her Canadian soldier.

Anna and Michael, huddled under their umbrellas, walked slowly because of Michael's limp. Anna held up her dress so it wouldn't be dragged through the mud. Margaret and Patsy followed. They also moved slowly. Anna was the only one in the family who enjoyed walking.

When they passed Charles' home, Anna peeked out from under her umbrella. Charles stood on the stoop with his head bowed. He was unprotected from the elements and the rain ruined his wool suit and hat. Puddles of water surrounded his feet.

Anna groaned. The guilt reared its head. Then she mentally counted the reasons why she couldn't let the guilt rule her. She didn't love him and he didn't love her. A marriage needed admiration and a sharing of values. It should not be based on pity.

Her head held high, Anna carried on her way without acknowledging Charles.

* * *

Despite their slow pace, the wedding party arrived at the church right on time. They attempted to dry themselves off, albeit unsuccessfully, in the reception room. Patsy peeked into the nave. Many guests were seated and Daniel and his groomsman, Reg, stood in front of the altar. Margaret was seated by Anna's cousin, Tom, who acted as usher. Patsy positioned herself in front of Anna and Michael.

Anna linked her arm through her father's in preparation for the wedding march. The long, red-carpeted aisle stretched forward.

Michael turned to Anna. "I will miss you more than I've ever missed anyone or anything. But I can see Daniel is a fine man, finer than Charles."

My God, was her hearing going? Dad was actually saying something nice about Daniel. Would wonders never cease?

54

Michael's eyes filled with tears. The scene played almost exactly like that with her mother.

However, Anna responded differently. She was scared and it had nothing to do with Charles. In a few short months she'd be leaving everything she knew to journey to a foreign country. She quickly hugged Michael. How could she leave this man? Or her mother? Would there be in-law problems with the religious fanatics? Daniel's shell shock might make him hard to live with. *Oh God. What was she doing?*

In for a penny, in for a pound. It was too late to back out now. Anna straightened her shoulders and smiled at her dad. The organist struck up the opening chords of the wedding march and, she walked slowly down the aisle on her father's arm. She attempted to smile at Daniel but her cheeks felt wooden. His smile loomed huge.

Despite her nerves, Anna found the wedding ceremony, *her* wedding ceremony, short, simple and enchanting. A pretty young soloist sang *Ava Maria* in a high, clear voice. Tears filled Anna's eyes. She failed to hear the rain pounding on the roof and windows.

Margaret also shed tears. Anna suspected they weren't tears of tears of happiness.

Then Anna repeated her vows opposite the man whose life she would soon share. Daniel dazzled in his uniform, and Reg, also in uniform, wore a wide grin.

Daniel's voice came loud and clear. Anna's quivered. Her hands shook when Daniel placed the plain gold wedding band on the third finger of her left hand. She wished she had something special for Daniel.

She was declaring her love for him in front of family and friends. Why must she suffer misgivings?

Then, too soon, the simple ceremony ended; they kissed to applause, signed the register and stood outside in the rain having pictures taken. Anna wondered if her teeth chattered with more than the cold.

* * *

Anna hugged her mother. "Mum, the food looks scrumptious. I don't know how you do it with the rationing, but you always put on a feast. Thank you for this beautiful wedding." Anna's mouth watered as she ogled the ham, homemade buns and peas, carrots and corn. How had Margaret procured all this? For dessert, there'd be chocolate pudding served with tea.

Anna frowned. Shouldn't her mother have passed some of her culinary knowledge onto her daughter? Would she be able to handle the cooking when she got to Canada?

Anna's frown deepened when she noticed Patsy snuggling up to Daniel and squeezing her voluptuous body against him. Patsy's words lingered in the air. "Now aren't you the cute one?" Her lips pursed in a sexy pout.

Daniel rubbed his injured shoulder as he pushed Patsy away. "I just married your sister. What the hell are you trying to prove?"

Anna started to sway from side to side. She was so happy an imaginary orchestra playing a Strauss Waltz rang inside her head. Any doubts she had about marrying Daniel evaporated.

Anna's eyes crinkled with happiness as she and Daniel accepted congratulations from their guests. Some people asked when she planned to leave for Canada. She replied it would be sometime in February.

She was proud to have Daniel at her side. He was friendly, and charmed all their neighbours. He asked the Anderson's how they liked their new prefab house.

Paul Anderson responded, "We love it. It's almost worth being bombed out."

Daniel even got a smile out of staid Janet Meadows when he complimented her on her beautiful new hat.

The only people missing were Ronald and Charles Harding. She hoped to God Charles would still be alive tomorrow.

Michael put the gramophone on and everyone listened to the White Cliffs of Dover. Anna thrilled to Vera Lynn's haunting voice. Michael, with tears in his eyes, started to sing along to the recording in a less than perfect voice. Soon virtually everyone in the room was singing. Michael waved his arms like a conductor. The crowd swayed in time to the music.

Anna also felt unshed tears prick at the back of her eyes. Were they tears of happiness or sadness? Probably both. She would never forget this moment.

Anna approached Julie, stunning in a strikingly beautiful, although obviously well used, navy blue sheath. Anna briefly hugged her friend. "Thank you for coming. It wouldn't be the same without you."

Julie smiled, revealing her perfect teeth. "Thank you." Daniel's groomsman, Reg, rushed to Julie's side and placed an arm around her waist. "I have an announcement to make. Julie has agreed to marry me. We'll go to the altar in three or four months."

Reg and Julie gazed into each other's eyes. Anna knew the rest of the people assembled had disappeared as far as they were concerned. Anna often felt like that with Daniel. It must be the essence of love.

Then the wedding guests cheered and Daniel clapped Reg on the back. "Congratulations, you two are perfect together. I'm sure you'll be as happy as Anna and me. I just wish the four of us could continue to see each other in Canada. Even though it's impossible. Your farm's in Manitoba. Mine's in Alberta. We'll be hundreds of miles apart."

Anna felt sorry as well. It would be wonderful to enjoy Reg and Julie's companionship in Canada. Much would be missed when she moved.

Anna felt a small, warm hand close onto her own. She smiled with pleasure because she felt quite certain it belonged to her nephew, Robert. She bent down and enclosed him in a hug. "I'm so glad you're here. Who brought you all the way from Wales? Oh, never mind. It doesn't matter. I just never want this hug to end."

Anna finally held Robert at arms-length and took a careful look at him. He appeared taller, but otherwise relatively unchanged. His hair still shone a soft blond; his eyes still looked bright blue. His cheeks were as rosy as ever. He must be thriving in Wales.

Robert spoke softly. "Is it true that you are going off with a stranger to Canada?"

"Daniel is hardly a stranger, but yes, I'll be leaving in a short while for Canada. I will miss you terribly. However, I love Daniel and Canada is his home. Someday you'll have a wife, and then you'll understand."

Robert looked like he doubted that would ever happen but he nodded his beautiful head in agreement. "I wish you were my mother. Then I could go with you."

Anna had heard this before. Patsy had been furious and she undoubtedly would be again. However, luckily it looked like Patsy flirted with one of their neighbors and didn't hear the exchange. Anna saw her sister laugh as she tossed her hair over her shoulder.

The first time Anna bought Robert a toy train, which he loved, he called her Mum for weeks. Anna hadn't wanted to cause trouble for Patsy, she simply loved the child. Anna frowned. She wanted children almost as much as food or sleep or life itself. She couldn't understand Patsy's indifference to his son.

However, Anna rarely quarreled with Patsy. She craved harmony and believed it her mission to maintain peace within the family. Was she abandoning this mission by leaving? For an instant her happiness was clouded by guilt before she pushed it away.

* * *

In the taxi on their way from the train to the small quaint inn by the sea Anna and Daniel animatedly related the story of how they met to their driver. The man appeared fascinated by their tale. The honeymoon would last four days. On the fifth, Daniel would begin the return journey to Canada. His parents had written he was needed on the farm. They hadn't said anything about his wife. Anna clutched her queasy stomach. The result of nerves? She feared so. Daniel's parents didn't sound at all welcoming.

Anna delighted in the inn. Even in the rain it looked romantic. She discovered their room contained a fireplace and fine mahogany furniture. A table and two chairs had already been set for the provided breakfast.

A smiling Anna exclaimed, "I don't know when I've seen a more beautiful room. It will be so cozy once we get a fire going in the hearth. I wish I'd brought along my paint box. It would make a beautiful Van Gogh like picture.

Daniel said, "We certainly weren't going to stay with your parents tonight, or in that suffocating room I rent that is filled with men. I need to be all alone with you, Mrs. Armstrong."

Anna glowed. Mrs. Armstrong. How good the words sounded. She had a good, honest, brave husband. Children would follow. She had everything she'd ever wanted.

The fireplace not only warmed the room, but also bathed it in flickering light. Daniel took Anna into his arms and kissed her again and again. Rapture flooded her. They had, of course, kissed before,, but these kisses became more insistent, more passionate.

In the midst of a hot embrace, he unzipped her wedding dress. His big, strong hands felt wonderful on her back and she could feel his male hardness against her body. Anna moaned with pleasure.

Daniel carefully helped her out of the dress. It would remain beautiful for Aunt Sophie's daughters. She placed the dress over the only chair and stood before him in her slip. She quivered with excitement.

"Anna, you are beautiful. So beautiful."

Firelight played on Daniel's handsome face. He became Eros, God of love. Anna was Aphrodite.

She felt beautiful enough to be demanding. Will you take off your uniform? I want to look at you." Anna's voice choked with desire.

"Of course." Daniel slowly began to remove every piece of clothing. Anna moaned. She'd never seen a more fantastic sight. He was gloriously male and as perfectly proportioned as Michelangelo's David. His only flaw were the divots on his shoulder where the shrapnel, or at least much of it, had been removed. Anna decided that the male body was the most beautiful thing she'd ever seen.

"Can I take off your slip?"

"Of course." He pulled the garment over her head and she stood before him in her bra and corset. Her chest was flushed and she felt hot. She was too aroused to be embarrassed, although she had never liked the look of her near-naked body. Daniel easily removed her stockings. Her corset also presented no problem. It had been bought in a large size so it would last longer. He fumbled as he unclasped her brassiere. Her husband appeared as inexperienced as herself. She removed her own knickers.

Daniel sighed. "I'm in heaven." He pulled Anna into his arms. They moved as one to the bed. Soon she had his length and strength and supreme maleness against her. She cried out with desire. He caressed every part of her body. The small breasts and hips she'd never liked felt wonderful under his touch. Anna absently realized she wasn't wearing the blue nightgown her mother had gifted her for the first night of the honeymoon. It didn't matter. There would be plenty of time for the nightgown when Daniel went back to Canada.

Anna groaned when Daniel entered her. It was a groan fueled by desire, not pain. She was in ecstasy. Despite the fact they were both virgins, they found a rhythm and it brought them to climax. Enthusiasm made up for inexperience.

Finally they lay together, spent, in a tangle of body parts. Daniel repeated over and over "I love you." Anna was too overcome for words, but she sighed with pleasure. She was now a woman in every sense of the word.

* * *

It had been the fullest, most exciting day of Anna's life. It was also the most exhausting. Sleep came almost instantly although she wasn't used to sleeping with someone else. A part of her was aware of Daniel's steady breathing and his sexy, musky scent. It mingled with her perfume.

Abruptly, she awoke. Daniel trembled. His whole body was covered in sweat. She felt as if the heat he radiated would burn her flesh. He screamed and she thought she heard, "God. God help me," but couldn't be sure. His voice sounded loud and harsh, nothing like his regular speaking voice. Anna shrank away from him.

He kicked and thrashed so hard she feared he would fall out of bed. He pulled the covers off Anna. *She froze in terror. Oh God, what can I do?* Finally, Daniel quit thrashing about and began to whimper like a lost puppy. Still asleep, he turned towards her, assuming the fetal position. His cries ceased.

"Should I try to wake him??" She was terrified of him like this, but worried he might harm himself, or her, if he remained sleeping. She pulled the covers back over her shoulders because the room had grown cold and propped herself up on one elbow. Her heart pounded. She tentatively touched his good shoulder. "Daniel, wake up. You had a bad dream. You have nothing to fear. You're safe, my love. Soon you'll be back in Canada." She was certain her voice was soothing.

Anna shook almost as much as Daniel. She had suspected something like this might happen ever since she'd noticed the vacant look in his eyes that first night they'd gone dancing. However, it was still horrid.

Daniel awoke. His eyes opened slowly, he appeared wild and crazed. Anna cowered before his gaze. Would he hit her, mistaking her for the enemy? No. In an instant the wildness withdrew. It was replaced by the vacancy Anna recognized from earlier incidents.

A couple of short moments passed with only the vacancy for company. Then Daniel's eyes filled with tears. "Oh God, I'm sorry. Now you know you've married an emotional cripple. I'm broken. I only hinted at my nightmares. I should have said more. It's just that I love you so much." He struggled to stifle a sob.

Anna knew her next words would be crucial so she spoke from her soul. "I will never be sorry I married you. You are a thousand times better than any other man. You are kind and good." Anna jumped when a log crackled in the fireplace.

"Only a cruel man could have gone through what you've seen and not be troubled. I understand. I will always understand." Anna threw her arms around her husband. She felt the pounding of his heart.

Yet, despite her words, Anna wondered if she hadn't made a mistake. What if every night became like this? Interrupted sleep and the anguish derived from loving someone who was sick. It was all made worse because she'd soon be in a strange country. But she loved Daniel. He fulfilled her like no other person. She must do her best to help him. She maneuvered into a cross-legged sitting position on the bed. She looked into Daniel's sad, beautiful eyes. "I have an idea. I think I may know how to fix you. Tell me about your dream. When I was trapped in the rubble I found I became used to the terror after a while. If you relive your experiences I think some of your fears might go away. You'd be confronting them just as your subconscious tries to do in your dreams."

Anna stared at the fire. It had begun to die, but she ignored it. "I read in an article composed by a psychologist that talking about trauma helps get rid of it. So please talk to me. I think you'll begin to feel better."

Anna leaned in close so she could decipher Daniel's hushed tones. "I'm so ashamed. I can't tell you my dream. And I'll never talk to a psychologist. I'm not a nut case." Daniel's hands shook and his face was flushed.

"Please Darling. Please."

Daniel moaned. "I can't. I simply can't."

His face grew red with anger and Anna withdrew rapidly.

"Who says talking helps? You just read something in a silly magazine. What do you know?" He sat upright in bed and buried his face in his hands.

The scent of Chanel No. 5 was cloying. All colour drained from Anna's face while she sought to comfort him. "I most definitely do not think you're insane. But please. If you love me, talk to me."

"I love you Anna, but…" He started to sob.

"Yes, you can tell me. Tell me everything." She reached out and gently touched his arm. His tension surged through her fingertips.

Daniel quit sobbing. She handed him a hankie. He wiped his eyes and blew his nose. "Okay. I'll try. We were assigned to Juno Beach and I commanded a Sherman Firefly tank, and we were hit on the beach." He spoke so softly Anna had to strain to hear him.

He stopped speaking and looked expectantly at Anna, his face still racked with pain.

Please, you didn't tell me enough. Give me details. I know it's painful, but I think it will help. And remember, none of this is your fault. You had an impossible job. I love everything about you. I just want you whole again. What were you feeling?"

"Fear. I've never been so scared. I remember the terrible weather, the seasickness and how the ship reeked of vomit. I couldn't sleep the night before the attack, just as I haven't slept properly every night since." He shrugged, "You see, I'll never be the same again. I was happy and young and stupidly naïve. Now I'm old and broken." He sighed and she winced with his pain.

"I've never been so terrified as when they launched our Sherman Firefly into the rough seas. I heard later some men drowned. Our radios failed because of the seawater. I was with my buddies in the tank, but somehow achingly alone. It was chaos. Dying men were everywhere. The beach was filled with brains and guts and blood, men screaming and crying." Daniel began to shake again.

Anna touched his good shoulder. Her eyes willed him to say more.

"Five infantry mounted themselves on our tank and I worried about them. Not an idle fear. Within minutes, German guns killed them all. Their blood ran down the tank. I still see it. I'd been talking to them only hours before."

Daniel swallowed and Anna feared he might vomit. "My prayers were useless. I may not be particularly religious but I prayed then. I'm sure every man on the beach did. The landing was equally horrific. Our tank buried itself in the sand. It was just like the rubble. I couldn't see a thing and I was supposed to fight."

Suddenly, he stopped talking. He buried his face in his hands. "I *cannot* continue. *Leave me alone.*"

Anna shuddered. It seemed cruel to push him, but she truly believed it was the right thing. "Just a little more. I love you. I would die for you if I could erase your pain."

Suddenly, he slammed his fist down onto the bed with such force both pillows landed on the floor. He roared, "Damn it. I've had enough. This is making me feel worse. You say you love me. So leave me alone." His handsome face was wild with anger. Anna leapt from the bed and landed on the floor in a heap beside the pillows. She feared Daniel might hit her and it wouldn't be his fault. She would never again force him to explain a nightmare.

"As you wish. Remember that I love you." She reached open her arms and Daniel reluctantly moved into them. Despite everything, the warmth from his body soothed her.

* * *

In the morning, the rain ceased and they faced the bright day with sudden optimism. They didn't talk about Daniel's dream, but rather the blood on the stained sheets.

"I hope I didn't hurt you. I love you. I never want to hurt you."

Anna sighed with unexpected happiness "No, you didn't hurt me. Making love with you was even more wonderful than I've ever imagined and it's because of you, Mr. Armstrong. It was beautiful.

He beamed. He took her into his arms and they made love once again."

PART 2
LETHBRIDGE, ALBERTA, CANADA
1945

Chapter 5

Other passengers seated near Anna no doubt thought her serene, and perhaps slightly bored, as she sat with a blanket on her lap in the dim light of the February afternoon. However, inside she churned with excitement. Today she would see Daniel and her new home.

Like many of the women, she attempted to fight the winter cold, which seeped right through to her bones. She couldn't suppress a shiver that made her teeth chatter.

The loud and hauntingly beautiful whistle of the cross-Canada train signaled that shortly her arduous two-week journey would be over and she would be in Daniel's arms. The next stop was Lethbridge, the nearest city to Daniel's farm.

This whole excursion had been an adventure, and Anna definitely believed she must have inherited a yearning for adventure. Her grandfather and great grandfather on her father's side had been sailors, and the latter man had even successfully fought pirates.

This had brought wealth and a certain amount of fame to the family, and left Anna proud of her Marshall genes. Over the years, indolent ancestors had squandered much of the wealth. Anna's father *was* ambitious and his hardware store a success. However, since the war the Marshall's were subject to shortages and rationing just like everyone else.

Anna longed to paint the varied Canadian landscapes that presented themselves. She'd tried to paint on the train, but found the constant movement made the task difficult.

Despite this, she thought travel provided her with a chance to see all life had to offer and at this moment, although frightened, she felt vitally alive.

Anna had almost changed her mind about going off to Canada, and it had nothing to do with Charles, who thankfully, hadn't taken the rat poison.

When the taxi driver knocked on the door of her parent's house, Anna opened it and said to the driver, "Just a moment. This is a time for goodbyes."

Margaret had rushed into her daughter's arms and there was much hugging and kissing and promises that she'd write long letters. Both Anna and Margaret cried.

However, Michael remained rigid and unmoving and Anna knew how much she hurt him. She said in a halting voice, "Goodbye, Dad. I'll always love you."

Tears shone in Michael's eyes, but he made no move toward her.

Anna struggled with her suitcase, packed with family photos, her paints, her clothes and some household linens; a testament to how meager her life had been in England. Then she opened the door.

She had turned to leave when suddenly, despite his limp, Michael was at her side and hugging Anna so hard she had to fight to catch her breath. The taxi driver must have gone back to the car because the horn honked twice.

Then and only then, Michael released her. As Anna hurried to the cab, she called back over her shoulder how much she loved her dad.

Anna had been so overcome with emotion that it took her three tries before the cab driver could discern her destination. It didn't help that a gentle rain fell. It heightened Anna's dismal mood.

* * *

Anna had been too overwrought to feel any excitement about the journey to Southampton, where she boarded the Aquitania for Halifax, Canada.

The ship had been crowded with bunks squeezed in everywhere and Anna had longed for privacy. She decided this must be the case with the women who were in the bunks near her own. Neither woman would do more than say "hello."

She was also plagued with seasickness, and Anna couldn't help but wonder how her grandfathers had made their life on the sea. She couldn't wait for the moment when she could feel firm land under her feet.

Worse still, were the special maneuvers the captain employed to avoid German U-boats in their vicinity. Anna did not wish to die at sea and decided that dodging Germans might well be more frightening than fighting pirates.

She lived an adventure whether or not she wanted it. At times she felt happy, at others, terrified. She would never forget her experiences.

The food on board ship had been excellent with large meat portions, bananas and fluffy white bread, all of which Anna loved, and mealtimes were a delight.

Anna secretly decided, however, that she preferred brown bread, because the white didn't leave her feeling as satisfied. Nonetheless, she would have probably gained some much-needed weight if she hadn't been chronically seasick.

The nausea and its accompanying vomiting finally ended on February 12th at Pier 21 in Halifax, Nova Scotia.

Because of extremely cold weather, the band failed to play The Maple Leaf Forever, the usual custom when a boatload of war brides arrived in Canada.

A disappointed Anna shivered in her thin coat and thought her hands and feet would freeze. She could only think about getting back indoors.

Fortunately, the officials processed Anna rapidly and she soon found herself on this monster of a train, which was nothing like their small, friendly British trains that took patrons only short distances.

However, the train carried her across Canada and she realized how huge a land it was and why it required such a huge train. The Canadian landscape seemed so large and unpopulated Anna decided Charles might be right about his assertion that Canada was a vast wasteland.

There had been trees galore in northern Ontario and now on the prairies there were miles and miles of what appeared to be nothingness. Snow covered the ground almost everywhere and Anna sighed with regret that she would never see England's lush greenness again.

Then Anna wiped a tear from a soot-smudged eye (it being impossible to stay clean on this train) and told herself to brace up. She was married to a good man who would be sure to provide her with handsome, sensitive children. If only Daniel was English.

The train seemed almost as crowded as the Aquitania, and, as usual this morning, she'd had to endure a fifteen minute wait for the loo.

Anna had dressed in her finest clothes, and washed as thoroughly and as quickly, as possible; which was not an easy task in the swaying car. The dirt and soot clung like a second skin.

However, she'd done the best she could and came out feeling at least a little refreshed, and thanks to her Chanel No. 5, smelling sweet.

Anna touched the heart-shaped locket, which contained a picture of her mother and father on their wedding day. It had been a going-away present and Anna doubted she would ever remove it for long.

Amazingly, Anna had a seat by herself and smiled when a beautiful, small, golden-haired girl approached.

Anna smiled. "Amy, come sit beside me. Where is your mother?" Amy didn't answer Anna's question but she sat close beside her. Anna's heart swelled with joy.

She loved children and enjoyed helping Amy's mother, Carole, with her four energetic children during the train journey. Amy was the youngest and Anna's favorite.

Amy said in a high, thin voice, "Is it true you're getting off today? I will miss you." Amy's large green eyes filled with sadness.

Anna realized the girl sounded much like Robert had on her wedding day.

"I'll miss you, too. I will know no one but my husband in Lethbridge. I'm sure to be lonely." Anna realized she talked to herself as much as the child and, as she spoke, she wondered how she would occupy herself on a farm.

"Why don't you stay with us? We're going all the way to Vancouver. Mom says you're a Godsend. What's a Godsend?"

Anna smiled with the child's words and turned to grab a hold of Amy's shoulders and, looked Amy in the eye. "It means she appreciates me. And I appreciate your mother and you children."

When Amy blinked, Anna continued, "However, I'm going to meet my husband and I love him very much. Someday I hope to have children of my own. However, I'll think about you and I will write to your mother. Perhaps she will read my letters out loud."

Anna also planned to write to Julie and tell her all about her journey. She didn't want to lose contact with any old friends and family.

The whistle blew and the conductor shouted, "Lethbridge"

Anna swallowed hard and stood up so she could greet Daniel. In an outbreak of excitement, Anna handed the porter her suitcase and rushed to exit the train. Finally, she would be with Daniel again.

As Anna left the shelter, she cringed before the onslaught of the cold, bitter wind, yet her heart knew warmth.

The porter, a short, thin, balding man, followed Anna at a discreet distance with the suitcase. Anna eagerly leapt onto the platform and searched for Daniel. She looked to the right; then left, and saw only emptiness as great as the landscape.

Her heart skipped a beat as she said, partly to herself and partly to the man following, "It's very cold. Maybe he's waiting inside the station."

Anna doubted the truth of this statement. Daniel would never hide indoors rather than be on the platform to greet her. The wind blew so hard it almost took her breath away.

Several scenarios played out in her mind. The chief one, the most probable one and also the most disheartening one, being Daniel's parents had managed to convince him their marriage was a mistake. She shoved the thought aside, Daniel loved her. He would come.

Nonetheless, despite the fact her legs shook, Anna walked purposely into the station. The porter followed.

She jumped when he tapped her on the shoulder. "I'm sorry. I have to leave you. The train departs immediately. You can wait in the station where it's warm. I'm sure whoever is meeting you will turn up soon. The roads in February can be bad and they may have been held up.

Anna thanked him and let herself into the warmth of the station, settling herself and her suitcase in a convenient chair. Her chin quivered and she clasped her hands to still the trembling. Surely, Daniel would be here soon. Time dragged. Anna was just deciding if she should speak to the ticket agent when suddenly, Anna heard a familiar male voice calling her name. *Daniel!*

She turned around and was struck anew by his good looks. He wore a navy blue suit, white shirt and sky blue tie under what looked like a warm overcoat.

His hands and coat were smudged with grease. Thank God. There must be some excellent explanation for his lateness.

Anna smiled radiantly and nearly tripped on the suitcase as she rushed into his arms. They hugged with Anna careful not to hurt his injured shoulder. He kissed her; right in the station to the amusement of those gathered there. When he finally released her, Daniel kept her at arms-length and clasped his hands on her waist.

"I'm so sorry I'm late. I left home in lots of time but five miles from Lethbridge, five miles from home, the

70

worst possible place; the fan belt went on the car. I walked a mile or so to Ken Johnston's place. He doesn't have a car, but he gave me the fan belt off his tractor."

Daniel once again took Anna into his arms. "Fortunately, I managed to get it to work. I should have left earlier. I should have planned for emergencies."

Anna shed tears of relief.

Daniel's eyes also filled with tears and when he spoke his voice became husky with emotion. "I was so afraid you'd stay on the train, so afraid I'd never see you again. I don't think I could live without you. I need you as much as the crops need rain."

Then Daniel lifted Anna off the ground, and she wrapped her arms around his neck. Despite her precarious position, she relaxed into his strength.

Eventually, Daniel safely deposited Anna back on the floor. "You're shivering. I planned to get you a dozen yellow roses but they would never survive in this cold and speaking of cold, your clothes are totally inadequate for the weather."

He smiled as he said, "You need something much heavier, so it's going to be warm clothes instead of silly flowers. You need a coat and hat and boots. You're almost blue with the cold." He picked up her suitcase. "Come on, let's get you into the car. I left the heater running.

"Oh Daniel, can you afford all this, and what in the world are boots?" Despite her discomfort, Anna's eyes were flashing in merriment.

As they left the station Anna noticed they were alone on the street. The Canadians knew enough to stay indoors. "For your feet, what's the word, yes, of course, galoshes? And yes, I may not be rich now that I'm buying my own land but I can afford to keep my wife warm."

Anna laughed and they hugged and kissed again and Anna lost much of her fear for the future.

Then they walked to Daniel's car, their footsteps crunching in the snow, Daniel easily carrying her heavy suitcase.

71

Anna took in Lethbridge, a small city with very wide mostly-deserted streets, low buildings, and except for the elegant sandstone Post Office building, no interesting architecture.

Snow stuck to the rooftops and on the branches of the few trees and the air felt so dry and cold Anna thought her lungs would explode.

Everywhere Anna looked, she became aware of the huge sky which she found beautiful in an empty kind of way. Nonetheless, Anna knew she'd be homesick for London for a long time.

Within moments, they reached the car. Although old, to Anna's eyes it appeared magnificent.

Daniel said, "It's an old Model A Ford and I hope you like black because that's the only colour Model As came in. If you like, I can show you the new fan belt."

When Anna laughed and shook her head, Daniel continued, "You have to crank this car to start it."

Anna looked on, a bemused expression on her face. As Daniel started to crank, Anna said, "It's beautiful, just beautiful."

The sharp bang of gunfire rang in the frigid air. Anna threw herself to the cold, hard ground because she could see nowhere to take cover. Her heart hammered as loudly as it had in the rubble.

At least she forgot all about the piercing, cold wind.

Daniel laughed and reached to help her up. "Don't be afraid. The car just backfired. It does it all the time so I expect it to happen when I'm cranking the car. You're safe here in Canada, although I must admit, even here, I'm sometimes anxious. Sudden noises trigger the memories."

It pleased Anna to hear Daniel mention his war experiences so casually. Maybe that meant the nightmares would stop. He hadn't awoken her the last two nights of their honeymoon, although he'd admitted to frightening dreams.

He'd said to her on the last day they'd had together, "I'm so glad I didn't awaken you these past two nights. I didn't want to worry you."

Anna had almost cried in sympathy. Daniel was so kind, so considerate, and so broken. She'd found that she could do nothing but take Daniel into her arms and hold him close.

But, now they were safe in Lethbridge and, within moments, riding in the car.

Anna enjoyed riding up so high and being in the front seat, a new experience, because she'd previously only ridden in the backseat of taxis.

Daniel turned the car's heater on full and they were protected from the wind, so being inside the car felt significantly more comfortable than outside.

Daniel drove Anna all around Lethbridge. He told her Lethbridge had a beautiful high-level bridge, but it was too icy to show it to her today because of the rather steep coulees it sat nestled in.

Anna had no idea what a coulee was. So Daniel carefully explained. "Coulees are gorges produced by our Old Man River. I find them beautiful. I sometimes climbed and explored them when I was a kid."

Daniel drove slowly and applied the brakes even more slowly. He obviously knew how to drive in ice and snow.

Although the weather caused her to miss the bridge, she saw the supermarket, Safeway, where Daniel said she'd only find a few goods rationed, and from which they would shop once a week for much of their food; a sharp contrast to London where her mother frequented a grocer's, a butcher's, a baker's, and numerous other shops daily.

She would miss London's many quaint shops and its indoor bathrooms, and, of course, the pubs. Apparently women weren't allowed in Canada's beer parlours.

Lethbridge also had a hardware store, which reminded Anna of her father and she felt a twinge of homesickness; a Woolworth; and a larger Canadian department store, Eaton's.

Daniel expertly angle parked the car in front of this store and Anna didn't even have time to get cold, the walk inside being so short.

Eaton's, a small store when compared to Harrods or Marks and Spencer's, contained a variety of merchandise nicely presented; and blessedly, not queues or the need for rationing. Anna felt like she had arrived in heaven.

They soon found the rack of winter coats, which Anna enjoyed examining. The coats looked stylish and warm. She practically vibrated with excitement. She hadn't had new clothes in years.

Daniel spoke tentatively, "Mom shops at the Imperial Ladies Store and I'd like for you to shop there too. You're a beautiful woman and I want you to have the best. And you will, I just can't afford it right now."

Daniel refused to make eye contact. "Eaton's is a great store and very popular."

Anna began to reply, "These coats are beauti…"

Daniel interrupted her in mid-sentence, "I've purchased land, 160 acres, it's good land and sure to provide me with a good living but I'm still paying for it…"

Daniel looked at Anna's nose and continued breathlessly in a harsh voice, "I have to tell you, Dad won't help me financially so I can't afford to put a house on the land right now. At least they've agreed to let us live with them until I can get on my feet.

"It's certainly not what you deserve, but we'll have to live with Mom and Dad for a while. I'm so sorry." A crestfallen Daniel continued to avoid his wife's gaze.

Daniel's words filled Anna with despair. She feared Daniel's parents wouldn't like her no matter how hard she tried to please them. They might be worse than her parents were to Daniel and she'd be in their home where she couldn't ignore them.

However, she was determined to make the best of things. "It will be okay. I'm sure it won't be for too long." She tried hard to keep the resignation out of her voice.

Daniel breathed a sigh of what Anna suspected was relief. "And you won't have to meet Mom and Dad until tomorrow at a party that's going to be held in your honour."

The idea of a party scared Anna. How many people would she have to meet? There was no opportunity to voice her concerns because Daniel rapidly continued. "I've arranged for us to stay at a hotel tonight. I want you all to myself. Thank you, for being so good about things. You're a good woman."

They entered Eaton's and Anna reflected on what a roller coaster of a day it had been.. A tall, elegant, red-haired woman asked if she could help Anna try on the coats.

Anna beamed. "Yes, please." She may have to live with miserable in-laws but she had a car to ride in and a new coat and boots. Her smile grew wide.

Daniel explained to the clerk Anna came all the way from London, England and this was her first day in Lethbridge. The charming woman smiled and wished Anna happiness in her new home.

Then Anna tried on every coat they had in her size and she enjoyed the experience more than anything in a long time. Contenders were a gray coat that looked beautiful on the rack, but overwhelmed Anna's thin frame; a purple coat that washed out her complexion, and finally a black one with a wide collar and a narrow belt.

Daniel clapped his hands when he saw Anna in the coat. "You look magnificent. You remind me of a rose. Let's get that one. That is, if you like it." The happiness reached Daniel's eyes.

Anna laughed. "Yes, this is the one. I love it. Thank you." Anna had rarely owned a garment she felt so right in.

When the sales clerk asked her if she wanted to wear the coat, Anna nodded. "Yes. It's freezing outside. I need something to combat that cold wind."

As the pleasant woman wrapped up Anna's old coat, she said, "I've never seen that coat look so good. You do things for it that no one else can. I enjoyed serving you." She had a warm, genuine smile.

Anna quickly replied, "You did an excellent job of showing the coats. I hope that everyone in Canada will be so kind and helpful." Anna doubted very much that they would be, thinking of her unmet in-laws.

They also went to the shoe department where they soon found a pair of fur-lined boots and a warm hat and gloves. The warmth felt wonderful. Despite the unwelcome news about living with Daniel's parents,, Anna couldn't help but be happy.

As soon as they purchased the clothes, Daniel smiled. "So Mrs. Armstrong, are you hungry? I'm famished."

* * *

They entered the restaurant of a fine, old hotel where they would have dinner. The clean, elegantly furnished restaurant featured a dark wooden floor, red velvet chairs and even red velvet curtains framing the large windows.

Their table also looked beautiful with white dishes, red napkins and heavy and ornate silverware. Daniel did all this for her. It felt wonderful to be loved.

As they seated themselves Daniel said, "We eat our big meal at noon. I hope that's okay."

Anna smiled. "It sounds great to me. This restaurant is beautiful."

She glanced around the elegant room. Everyone had shed their winter coats and Anna noticed the men all wore suits; although she knew they must be farmers, with the occasional banker or lawyer added.

It must be their day to go into town. The women wore dresses and hats. There was no sign of the ugly trousers women wore in England, or at least not in this restaurant.

Anna felt like everyone was taking her measure, the stranger in town with the odd way of speaking. She hated being the centre of attention. Daniel also seemed to be searching the room, perhaps for someone he knew.

Forsaking the other diners, Anna and Daniel turned their attention to the menu. Daniel decided on veal cutlets and Anna decided to try them as well.

The waitress, a diminutive strawberry blonde with big, dark freckles, took Anna's order with a smile. "You can't be from around here with that lovely accent. I'd say British or Scottish."

Anna smiled. "English." She wondered how anyone could not know the difference between Scottish and English speech.

Daniel opened his arms wide, and smiled. "Soon she'll sound as Canadian as we do. She's a war bride. My war bride. Meet Mrs. Armstrong, she's come all the way from London."

When their meal arrived Anna enjoyed not only the veal cutlets, but also the mashed potatoes and carrots. She'd never had more tender meat or more delicious vegetables.

Anna ate until she was satisfied, something she hadn't been able to do in years because of all the rationing in England.

As soon as Anna finished eating, she smiled. "This food is scrumptious and there's so much of it. I love it. I just hope I don't get fat." She took the napkin from her lap and wiped her mouth.

"You'll never be fat. You're not the type. Lucky for you, I like thin women, of course, but it wouldn't hurt if you gained a few pounds." He winked at her.

Anna agreed.

As they waited for dessert, apple pie smothered in ice cream, Daniel said, "I hope you like it here." His handsome face filled with expectation.

While Anna enjoyed the food, she wasn't sure she liked Lethbridge's vastness and its complete lack of trees, or the piercing cold.

However, she lied, "I like it already. It's just so different. I feel like I've left earth and landed on the moon."

Secretly, Anna wondered if she would ever get used to Canada. Perhaps she would like it more if she attempted to paint it. But how does one paint such nothingness? Nonetheless, she must try to find some beauty in this barren wasteland. It must be there. Daniel had seen London and he'd still longed for Canada.

* * *

77

When they emerged from the restaurant, Anna experienced a surprise so great, it felt almost like shock.

In the hour or so while they ate the weather had changed.

The snow melted and the sun warmed Anna. Water ran all over the sidewalks and made a merry sound in the process. The wind still blew strong, but now it felt warm. Her new coat suddenly became too hot.

Daniel laughed at his wife's shocked expression. "A Chinook must have blown in while we were in the restaurant. They come fast like this sometimes. Chinooks are warm winds that blow in from the Pacific Ocean."

Daniel reminded Anna of her high school science teacher. "They leave their moisture over the mountains and the result in Alberta is a warm, dry wind. How do you like your first Chinook?"

Daniel's hazel eyes grew merry with laughter.

Anna's face wore an incredulous expression. "Wow, I can't believe it. I think I like Chinooks a lot. I'll have lots to tell in my first letter home. There's nothing like this in England. I wanted adventure and now I'm getting it."

For the first time Anna decided that she might just get to like Canada.

* * *

It was still relatively early when they checked into their room but Anna longed for a bath and, of course, they both wanted to make love.

However, as she stepped over the threshold into their small yet elegant room, decorated much like the restaurant downstairs, Anna suddenly became shy. She hadn't been with Daniel for a long time.

Fortunately, the bath came before the lovemaking and she knew she would scrub and scrub until she removed all the soot and grime that had accumulated from that monster of a train.

She removed the locket and carefully cleaned it.

The hotel provided a strong fragrant soap and bubble bath and Anna decided that bathing might be as much fun as shopping.

While Anna toweled off and once again applied perfume, Daniel decided to have a bath as well. "It's not so easy on the farm having a bath. We are lacking so much. I'm sorry. It might take some doing for you to get used to rural Canada."

Anna's replied immediately. "I've lived in war-torn London. I can live anywhere. I'll be okay." Anna hoped she spoke the truth.

Then they went to bed and Anna immediately grew aroused with any unease surrounding her husband forgotten. Their lovemaking was more tender than passionate and Anna felt supremely loved.

* * *

Daniel soon fell asleep but in the early morning hours, as often the case, the vicious dreams assaulted him.

He was in the Sherman Firefly with the noise of artilleries all around him; his fear so great he couldn't stop himself losing control of his bladder.

Men fell all around them who didn't have the security of the tank. When he saw other tanks being hit his fear changed to sheer terror.

He wanted to lash out physically at the Germans even though he knew it would do no good. He clenched his fist and struck out.

* * *

Anna also dreamed; a happy dream. She walked beside a beautiful child of about five years, obviously one of the children that she would have with Daniel.

They strolled in a delicately scented flower-filled meadow. The sun caressed Anna's arms and legs. The exquisite child told Anna how much she loved her.

Then, quite suddenly; a sharp pain in her left arm made her jump and touch the injury in hurt surprise.

The little girl changed, now vicious and cruel she threw a stone at her mother. A surprised, and frightened Anna fled as the child threw more stones. In her fear, Anna willed herself awake.

When Anna awoke, she saw Daniel sitting up in bed, rubbing his right hand, which he'd clasped into a fist with a puzzled expression on his face.

When he saw Anna was awake and staring at him he cursed under his breath.

"My God, your arm. Did I do that? I've had a nightmare and I must have lashed out at you." He wiped tears with back of his hand.

His voice shook. "Oh God, I'm so sorry. I'm a wife beater, a cruel, horrible wife beater. You should never have married me. I'm dangerous. The war has ruined me. I'll understand if you can't forgive me." Daniel's face was almost as white as the snow outside.

Anna examined her sore arm. It was tender, but not serious. "I'll be okay. I know you would never hit me intentionally."

Despite her words and the fact she meant them, Anna was afraid. Daniel could very possibly cause her serious injury, or, if he hit her hard enough in the right place, even death.

Anna thought of women whose husbands beat them regularly. Daniel wasn't like that but she sympathized with them all the same. Anna couldn't help but sigh.

Daniel used the top sheet to wipe his tears. He spoke through sobs. "I'll do anything if you'll just forgive me."

"Daniel, I forgive you. You are probably the finest man on earth, and I love you unconditionally. I just wish you'd agree to see a psychologist. I'm sure that a lot of returning soldiers must have these problems."

Daniel slumped down under the covers. "I would if I thought it would help, but I know it won't. Nothing helps. I'm sorry Anna." He would not look into her eyes.

Anna couldn't suppress another sigh. Daniel might never get better, and she feared pushing him further. She was a casualty of the war as much as Daniel, something she would have to accept.

So, because she knew of nothing more she could do, she reached for Daniel, grabbed his cold right hand, and kissed.it. "I think you've had enough sleep for one afternoon. It's time to get up. Let's get dressed and walk or drive around Lethbridge. I want to see more of my new home."

To her surprise, Daniel responded as if the previous conversation had never happened. "We can see more by driving. It will be safe to see the bridge now the ice and snow are melting. And I'll show you the countryside. You can meet my family tomorrow." Daniel paused and looked tenderly at his wife. "I love you Anna."

Anna melted into her husband's arms

Chapter 6

The next day, the day of the party, came all too fast. Soon she would have to meet Daniel's family and neighbors.

Apparently, whenever someone new arrived, the community held a party. It was a practice Anna wished didn't exist. She'd be exposed to so many new and curious people and examined as if under a microscope. Of course, there'd been gatherings before in her honour, such as her birthday party and wedding. However, then she'd known all the guests. Now she was a stranger and expected to fit into a community that was alien to her.

The weather certainly didn't match her pensive mood. It hardly seemed possible, yet the Chinook day was even more perfect than the day before. Abundant sunshine with more melting temperatures met her gaze, and, rare for southern Alberta, next to no wind.

Daniel pointed out the Chinook arch in the sky. She learned that it meant tomorrow would also be beautiful.

Too soon they approached the gleaming white school where the party would be held.

It was a well-cared for small building with a couple of swings and a slide for the children to play on.

The parking lot, if you could call it that, appeared almost full; not only with cars, but also a few horses and buggies.

The animals appeared to be waiting patiently for their humans to return, although one large black gelding shied when Daniel and Anna passed.

Anna leapt out of the way of its huge hooves. She was normally comfortable around horses, but her nerves were getting the best of her today.

Myriad voices floated out to Anna as she entered the coatroom. No one appeared to have noticed their arrival with the din emanating from the auditorium.

Anna had a moment to steady her nerves. She smoothed down her hair and dress. She needed to look her best.

The small room overflowed with coats and boots and Anna and Daniel had to pile their coverings on top of others. Anna laughed nervously when a mink coat slid onto the floor. She couldn't resist the temptation to run her hand over the soft, luxurious black fur as she returned it to the pile. She was relieved none of the mud from the floor clung to the coat. Daniel said, "That's Mother's. My parents don't stint themselves, but they can be tight with it when their sons don't obey them." His face was dark with anger.

Anna swallowed; their marriage was the cause of Daniel's money woes and it left her feeling like a burden.

* * *

They slipped unnoticed into the small, smoke-filled hall. Anna took the opportunity to survey the assembled crowd.

Everyone appeared dressed up, the men in suits and shirts and ties and the women in dresses and silk stockings. Anna detected the scents of many perfumes and shaving lotions.

She estimated there must be at least fifty adults, all laughing, and talking and smoking. A hoard of children played games, which produced shrieks of joy as well as tears. Anna wished she could play with them, but decided it wouldn't be appropriate at the moment.

Anna smiled. It would be pleasant to be part of this community if they could accept her. Gatherings were rarely this large back home.

The small room was filled to capacity with partiers. A long row of tables moaned under the weight of food. Anna's mouth watered in anticipation.

Daniel had mentioned that sugar and flour were rationed in Canada. Yet what she saw before her would be unthinkable with England's war restrictions.

There was roast beef, cabbage rolls, preserves, buns, butter and, surprisingly; delicious desserts. Pretty dishes and silverware graced the table. Anna sighed with pleasure. She felt like visiting royalty. *Imagine, all this splendour was because of her!*

Anna and Daniel moved further into the room. The clamour lessened as people noticed them. Anna blushed in embarrassment with the attention and wished she were more confident.

She should be plumper and more stylishly dressed, and prettier. She couldn't believe Daniel actually thought her beautiful.

Anna felt like a specimen under a microscope. Surely everyone must be comparing her to Nancy and she feared she wasn't coming out well in the appraisal. *Oh Lord, is Nancy here? Please, don't let her be here.*

Her discomfort passed when many people in the hall linked their arms, formed a circle around her, and began singing, "For She's a Jolly Good Fellow."

Anna didn't know who anybody was and it didn't bother her that many sang off key. She saw smiling faces, young, old, mostly kind, mostly happy. Some people substituted woman for fellow. Anna appreciated their intention.

Her nervousness almost abated. Anna didn't, at that moment, concern herself with those who hadn't joined in her tribute.

The singing reminded her of their wedding when Michael led everyone in "The White Cliffs of Dover." Suddenly, homesickness engulfed her. She wanted to kiss her mum and dad and throw her arms around Patsy and Robert. She feared she would be homesick for a long time.

She committed the scene to memory so she could share it with her parents in her next letter home.

Should she go on too long about the abundance of food? It would be almost cruel to do so when things were so short back home. And they'd be missing her contribution to the household expenses. She turned her attention back to the celebration. Time enough to worry about what to include in the letter later.

* * *

Daniel led Anna to a tall, slender, austere woman. She was one of the people who hadn't participated in the singing. The woman was very beautiful, with particularly striking, yet very cold, hazel eyes. They reminded Anna of a piece of ice.

Daniel's eyes, she realized with a start, but while his were warm, this woman's were just the opposite.

"I would like you to meet my mother, Grace." Daniel flushed with nervousness and stumbled over the words.

Anna decided her mother-in-law was aptly named. She was regally graceful, an impression heightened by an elegant black dress and long strand of pearls. Anna extended her hand and Grace briefly clasped it in her cold one.

Grace's first words took Anna aback. She couldn't seem to tear her gaze from the woman's very white teeth.

"Have you taken the Lord Jesus as your Savior?" Grace's voice was so cold and challenging Anna suppressed a shiver. How was one supposed to respond to a question like that?

"Yes, I guess so." The words sounded tentative, even to her.

She had no intention of informing her mother-in-law, the woman she would be living with, that she didn't completely believe in organized religion. There was no point in antagonizing the woman.

Anna did believe in God, especially when He had inspired her not to call off her wedding. She attended

85

church faithfully as a child and young woman. But, religion wasn't her whole life and she didn't believe God wanted it to be.

Grace appeared angry and unpleased with her new daughter-in-law's response. "I'll expect you to join us for prayers, Anna. We worship before each meal and we have evening devotionals."

Grace straightened her shoulders and moved closer to Anna. "We, along with the Bartlett's, Smyth's and Brown's, have established our own religious order. We started with only three families and now we have a congregation of over fifty happy souls."

The muted rattle of cutlery reminded Anna of the sound of sabres rattling.

"It is called the True Religion Church and it's aptly named. We have found the true path to salvation. Once when we were baptizing down at the river, a most holy site, I saw Christ standing in the water. Can anyone else attest to that?"

Grace's entire face glowed with fervor. Anna worried she detected a touch of madness.

Daniel's words from the rubble came back to haunt her. "My parents have established a church. It's almost cult-like," he had said. Now Grace confirmed her son's words.

Anna's stomach tightened in fear and apprehension. She fought back the urge to look away, she hadn't said anything wrong. How could she live with this woman? What was she supposed to call them? Surely not Mother or Father, and Christian names were too familiar.

Grace answered the unspoken question. "Until we get to know each other better, you may call me Mrs. Armstrong."

Anna nodded, "You can call me Anna." It would be ridiculous to have two Mrs. Armstrong's in the same house. She tried to smile but her mouth was stiff. She knew Grace would never like nor respect her.

Why didn't Daniel say something to make this easier? She glanced at her silent husband. He didn't speak but did take her hand in his. Grace turned away in obvious dismissal.

Daniel took her toward a tall, well-built man with sandy hair, gray eyes and a weathered, ruddy complexion. She supposed this must be George, her father-in-law. He inhaled on his cigarette and blew smoke in Anna's face. She managed not to cough.

"Dad, this is Anna, my wife," Daniel introduced her.

The man appeared slightly more welcoming than his wife. "Welcome to the Lethbridge area." He even smiled.

The scent of cabbage rolls distracted her from the seriousness of the meeting. She was starving in spite of herself and forced herself to listen to George.

"Although there are only a few True Religion believers, our faith has brought us bounty and prosperity. We have two hundred forty aces of rich, irrigated land and it provides us with a good living. If you believe in God then your life will be rich and fulfilled. We drive a new car and we have the finest house in the area."

Anna suppressed the urge to inform him that God didn't always provide for those who worshipped Him. Some very religious people in England lost their houses to German bombs. Perhaps God tested them like Job. More likely, He just wanted to see what would happen in times of adversity.

At least George had welcomed her and she didn't fear him as much as his wife.

Anna was introduced to a bevy of friendly, well-dressed neighbours. They were eager to learn about life in wartime England and sympathetic when she described the danger she'd lived with. She began to feel a little better.

Many of the women claimed to be in awe of her "peaches and cream" complexion. The result, no doubt, of London's many cloudy days. *Maybe she was pretty enough to be Daniel's bride.*

A handsome man in an impeccably tailored gray suit grabbed Anna by the waist and held her close. She gazed into a face characterized by large, wide set eyes, a cleft chin and otherwise perfectly elegant features.

"Hi. I'm Peter, Daniel's younger brother." "You are as beautiful as Daniel said. I'm certain you're sorry you married that brother of mine now that you've met me." A grin materialized on Peter's tanned face. The scent of his shaving cream made her nose twitch, and a nervous laugh escaped Anna. She didn't find Peter at all amusing.

"Daniel is a wonderful man. I'll stick with what I've got. Thank you." Anna squirmed out of Peter's embrace. She didn't care if she sounded prissy.

She was spared Peter's reply because another farmer came up to Peter and asked him if he planned on a crop of wheat next spring. The man requiring advice wore an old suit with fraying cuffs. Not all the people here had money.

Peter dismissed Anna, turning his back to her. "Yes, I had a good crop last year and I'm hoping for a good crop again next year. Besides that, the market is good for wheat right now. I think it will hold."

Peter stood erect with his left hand in his suit pocket. He brought out a cigarette and lit it with an expensive-looking lighter.

The farmer, a short, wiry, red-faced man smiled widely, exposing a mouth of rotten teeth, "Your opinion is good enough for me. You're the best farmer in the whole district."

Anna forgot Peter as a large, stout, wrinkled woman approached her and began asking questions about England. Anna knew she had met her but she couldn't remember her name. She decided not to mention her lapse of memory.

Anna stammered a bit as she tried to maintain the conversation when she overheard a shrill-voiced woman speaking to Peter.

"What were you doing with that English tart?"

Anna couldn't help herself. She turned away from the friendly neighbour to see who had spoken.

The woman was short and stocky, almost as wide as she was tall. Her blue sheath dress with capped sleeves revealed arms and legs like tree trunks. Like Grace, she wore her hair in a bun. Unlike Grace, she didn't look elegant.

Surely this plain, nasty woman couldn't be the handsome Peter's wife? Then Anna remembered Daniel told her Peter and Charlotte had to get married.

Peter swiftly replied, "Now Lottie, you're always getting your shorts in a knot over nothing. It's you, and only you, I love."

Lottie snorted. The argument became loud and a number of people gathered to watch the quarreling couple.

Lottie swung her attention to Anna and stalked over to her. "Stay away from my husband, or you'll be sorry." Her beady eyes looked bloodshot.

Anna's temper flared. How dare this woman call her a tart when it was Peter who was the flirt? Her frustration overflowed her restraint. "Peter approached me. It wasn't the other way around, so don't blame me."

Anna tried to keep her voice down but several people looked in alarm in her direction. Lord, Daniel had the worst family on the planet.

Lottie glared and stomped off, the flesh on her legs quivering with each step.

Suddenly, Anna's anger evaporated and she filled with regret. Arguing in public with her sister-in-law didn't seem like a good start. Yet what else could she have done?

Unfortunately, she now had another enemy in a new country where she knew no one, and all because Peter thought he was God's gift to women. How did Lottie attract the handsome Peter in the first place?

Considering his familiar behavior Peter must have had many past indiscretions. Lottie probably had reason to be suspicious of him. Nonetheless, Anna doubted she and Lottie could ever be close. It saddened her.

"I see you've met my flirtatious brother-in-law. Lottie is always jealous and blames the woman, not her husband." The woman at her elbow spoke in a pleasant, lilting voice into Anna's ear.

Anna sighed with relief; it seemed that someone understood her predicament. Anna turned and caught her breath. The woman was beautiful and stunning, with dark brown hair, brilliant blue eyes and full lips. "She's convinced I'm having an affair with Peter. She's wrong, of course. I love my Jim. He's a much finer man than his brother. Although I have to admit Peter is an excellent farmer."

Anna smiled and extended her hand. "Thank you for your understanding words. I appreciate them more than you can imagine… You must be Maisy. Daniel thinks the world of you."

Maisy returned the smile. "And I think the world of Daniel."

Anna didn't want her first friend in Canada to leave her side so did her best to prolong the conversation. "Maisy, what a pretty name. It reminds me of a beautiful, sunny day walking in a meadow."

Maisy laughed at the colourful language, but Anna could sense her pleasure.

"Thank you and welcome to Canada. It's a great country in the summer and after a while you'll get used to the conditions on a farm. However, you'll probably miss electricity and indoor plumbing."

Anna felt the need to confide in someone and Maisy seemed perfect. "I'm sure I'll manage, but I'm more than a little concerned about Daniel's parents. His mother especially, is cold and hostile. She told me to call her Mrs. Armstrong," Anna spoke as softly as possible and she believed that no one save Maisy heard this exchange.

Maisy rolled her blue eyes. "I know. It's too bad you have to live with them. They're strict True Religionists and much too devout for my taste. Don't let them get you down and come to visit us whenever you can."

"Thank you so much. It means a lot to me." Anna felt tears of happiness spring into her eyes. Even in the midst of angst, goodness could be found.

Daniel joined them and took Anna's elbow. "Come meet Maisy's husband; my brother, Jim." He beckoned for Maisy to follow them.

They worked their way through the crowded, smoky room over to where a tall, lanky, freckle-faced man laughed with friends. Like most of the men in the room, his face appeared weathered. He wasn't as handsome as Daniel or Peter, but oozed integrity. Anna smiled with pleasure as she shook his large, warm hand.

Jim leaned toward Anna, an earnest expression on his face. "The army rejected me. They said they needed farmers. Daniel's done more for his country than any of us. Sometimes my brave brother makes me feel inadequate."

Daniel put a hand on his brother's arm. "It isn't your fault, Jim. So don't feel guilty."

Anna impulsively took Jim's hand again. "You're a good man. Daniel doesn't blame you for what happened to him, or for staying on the farm."

Maisy attempted to lighten the mood. "Anna, you have such a beautiful complexion. You're the proverbial English rose. I hope our harsher weather won't ruin it."

"Thank you. I can't help but love this fresh, bright sunlight." Much of the tension eased. The rest of the conversation centred on farming.

* * *

Anna met the remainder of Daniel's friends and relatives, including their children who ran about laughing and playing.

Most everyone except Grace and George seemed friendly and welcoming. Anna and Daniel repeated the story of how they met over and over again and Anna suspected it would soon be all over the community and well on its way to becoming legend.

The room grew warm and hazy. Many of the men took off their jackets and ties and rolled up their shirtsleeves. Some of the women fanned themselves with napkins from the tables. Anna almost choked on all the smoke, yet people still lit up.

The moment Anna anticipated finally arrived. It was time for the delicious supper laid out in unprecedented, (by English standards) quantities.

They served themselves buffet-style and then sat down at long tables. Everyone insisted Anna serve herself first.

Her hands shook when she helped herself to the feast, dizzy with excitement over the amount and variety of food offered.

She joined her husband and settled into her chair with Daniel on her left and Maisy on her right. Situated between these two friendly bodies, Anna enjoyed the grand meal. She made a mental note to thank the women for all their preparations.

All conversation stopped when a handsome, young man with dark, wavy hair and blue eyes pulled out his violin and began to play.

Anna sat in rapture. His rendition of *Greensleeves* sounded so beautiful she was left near tears. The playing appeared to have the same effect on Maisy.

However, it also made her homesick. *Greensleeves* originated in the British Isles. If only her mother and father lived here instead of the icy Grace and insensitive George.

* * *

The concert ended and it was time for Anna and Daniel to say goodbyes. They spoke to each of the guests in turn. Anna was beginning to enjoy herself when a small, thin shapeless woman strode into the room. All conversation stopped and Anna's stomach clenched with apprehension. *Now what?*

The woman reminded Anna of a mouse. Her brown eyes were small in her pale, pinched face and the shapeless, brown dress hung on her boyish figure.

Daniel stiffened beside her and Anna realized the woman must be Nancy. Nancy rushed up to Daniel and threw her arms about him. He flinched and brushed her thin, stringy hair off his face.

"I'm so glad you survived and came home to me." Her husky voice was loud and filled the room.

Daniel pushed her away. When she tried to throw herself at him again, he held her back. "Nancy, you know I'm married, don't you?"

Nancy hung her head. "I heard, but I don't care. You're home and that's all that matters. God answered my prayers." Nancy looked tiny and fragile.

Keeping a firm grip on the woman's elbow Daniel pulled her over to Anna who stood open-mouthed. Nancy resisted for a moment and then allowed herself to be towed behind him.

"This is Nancy. She wants to meet you," Daniel said grimly.

Anna suspected falser words had never been spoken.

Nancy's face was dark as a rain cloud, but Anna forced a smile.

"Hello, Nancy." She didn't extend her hand.

"Pleased to make your acquaintance, M'am." The words were polite but the delivery was sarcastic and cold. Anna had never felt older.

Grace and George appeared at Nancy's side. Her mother-in-law's face softened as she gazed lovingly at Nancy. Grace placed her hand on Nancy's shoulder. "It's so nice to see you again, dear. How have you been?"

Anna almost envied Nancy. She wrapped her fingers around her parent's locket for comfort. Grace hated her, Anna just knew it.

* * *

The room was hushed as everyone took in every detail of the encounter while trying to appear as if they hadn't noticed anything. Anna sighed. Her welcome party would provide fodder for gossip for years to come.

A few of the guests greeted Nancy (probably fellow True Religionists). The rest said their good byes to Daniel and Anna. Some of her neighbours' faces looked sympathetic. For some strange reason Anna felt ashamed and dirty.

Maisy hugged Anna. "Remember you have friends."

Anna clung to Maisy for a long moment, grateful for the support.

Eventually, the food was cleared and the tables and chairs stored. Daniel and Anna were alone in the empty hall.

Daniel looked tired and pale. "If they could just accept the fact I have the right to marry the woman I choose. They're so damned unfair…" He slammed his right fist into his left hand. "You're my wife and I love you more than anyone. I've brought you into a bad situation. I thought they'd be more accepting once they met you. You don't know how sorry I am."

He reached out to Anna, took her into his arms and kissed her gently on the lips. He reluctantly released her. "Mrs. Armstrong, what say we stay in the hotel for another night? You've had enough to deal with for one day."

His tone suggested that he was resigned to accept the situation. Anna wondered if she could.

Anna nodded her head in silent agreement. However, procrastination wouldn't solve the problem. Tomorrow would come and she would have to face it. It was too late to turn back now.

Chapter 7

The following day the weather dawned as lovely as the Chinook arch had predicted.

However, Anna was filled with dread. Today she was going to move into the formidable Grace and the bragging George's home. Would she be able to cope?

Last night it'd been Anna, not Daniel, who'd had the nightmares. She'd awoken drenched in sweat and clinging to her feather pillow.

She'd dreamed Grace forced her to swim in a deep irrigation ditch, and she'd almost drowned.

Daniel appeared equally unhappy. His expression sagged with sadness, devoid of emotion, and he cut himself twice while shaving.

Anna pushed her breakfast around her plate, but couldn't bring herself to eat anything.

"Don't worry. It won't be as bad as you imagine. We'll spend time with Maisy and Jim and we'll go into town every second day," Daniel attempted to reassure her.

Daniel blew on his coffee and then swallowed. "I love my parents, but sometimes I don't particularly like them. They spout religion, but they can be very unkind. I remember when our neighbours, the Brown's, lost their farm. Mom and Dad always have money for the church, yet they didn't give a single cent to the people who'd lived on an adjacent farm for years."

Daniel jumped when a tray of dishes crashed to the floor by the kitchen door. "I was only thirteen, too young to help, but I was ashamed of my parents. Steve and Edna Brown moved into town and they got jobs in the flour mill.

Their kids got into all kinds of trouble because there was no one at home to look after them."

The pretty brunette waitress re-filled Daniel's coffee cup.

"Of course, I have to admit there are reasons for Mom and Dad's devotion to God. Mom suffered abuse as a child. She's turned to religion to compensate. Dad lets Mom tell him what to do, how to think. He grew up the second youngest of twelve children. He got used to being bossed around," Daniel spoke softly so they wouldn't be overheard.

He leaned in even closer to his wife and whispered in her ear. "In many ways he's weak. Though, I've also seen him strong and I admire him at those times. I want to be strong as well."

Anna nodded and forced a smile. She appreciated the insight into her in-laws. However, she still felt almost frozen in fear, and wrapped her cold shaking hands around the welcome warmth of her coffee cup.

* * *

Anna's heart thudded like a beating drum. Yet, somehow she managed to enjoy traveling in the fine old car. It was so different from anything she'd known in England. Much older and noisier.

She'd already become accustomed to having the passenger seat on the right hand side of the car and driving on what had at first appeared to be the wrong side of the road.

They drove down a dusty, gravel road when they left Lethbridge. It was wide by English standards and bordered by crop fields. It pleased her that the gravel forced them to go slow. She wanted to take as long as possible to reach their destination.

She saw wide, snow-dotted empty fields, it being winter, and cattle grazing. Most of the cattle had red bodies and white faces. Daniel called them Herefords and explained they had originally come from England. Anna thought them quite beautiful. They looked placid and content chewing their cuds.

Anna saw more than one haystack. These bundles of hay piled high helped feed the cattle.

The car stopped abruptly and they skidded on the gravel when Daniel swerved to miss a tumble weed the wind had blown across the road. Anna had never seen tumbleweeds back home. She knew what they were from the book she'd read on the train.

Apparently they'd been particularly prevalent in Canada during the depression of the 1930's. This decade had been dubbed "The Dirty Thirties," at least partly because of all the dust piled in the fields during that dry, jobless era.

Daniel laughed. "I thought it was a gopher. Of course, that's ridiculous, they hibernate during the winter. They stand up on their back legs and are cute as the dickens. I could never kill one. I won't kill unless I have to. I saw too much killing in the war."

The somber mood continued when they passed a prisoner-of-war camp. Surprisingly, it looked less desolate in the February sunshine than Anna expected.

The buildings were clean and well cared for and the men working outside appeared strong and healthy, healthier than many of the inhabitants of London. Anna knew it wasn't at all like the concentration camps in Germany.

Nonetheless, she felt sorry for the men. They must be lonely being so far away from home. The prisoners looked like clones in their ill-fitting clothes. She sighed, the war ruined both Allied and German lives. Why did God let men like Hitler exist?

In what felt like only minutes but actually took over half an hour, Anna and Daniel approached the Armstrong homestead.

It was beautiful. The house was a large, white two-story with a veranda. A trimmed hedge of cotoneasters and an iron gate constituted the landscaping. Behind the house a number of out buildings were visible, all red with white roofs.

* * *

The homestead was set in a picturesque valley. Despite herself, Anna couldn't wait to paint the scene. She would try to do so at dusk when the light would be particularly soft and beautiful.

Once they entered the yard and exited the car, Anna forgot the beauty of the scene and followed Daniel on legs that shook so much she could hardly walk.

A large, tan and black dog barked as he rushed up to them. Daniel stopped the animal and scratched behind its ears, "Now Sooty, this is one fine lady. I want you to be friendly to her. We call him Sooty because his nose is black as night."

Sooty wagged his tail and stood beside Anna. She reached down and petted him. His hair was thick and soft. She relaxed when Sooty licked her hand. Thank God at least the dog liked her.

Too quickly, they were on the doorstep and Daniel led his bride into the elegant home. Anna wiped her feet on the welcome mat and recognized the irony in doing so.

The inside of the house revealed its owners wealth. Lace curtains framed large windows and a Persian-inspired rug partially covered wooden floors. The furniture appeared strong and well-built. In more welcoming circumstances Anna would have exclaimed over the beauty of her surroundings.

George Armstrong came to greet his new daughter-in-law. He wore gray overalls and a red plaid shirt and a forced smile on his face. "Welcome, daughter. This will be your new home until Daniel can get settled on his farm. I'm sure you'll be here for at least a year."

He cleared his throat. "You seem a little frightened of us and I want you to know you have no reason to. We're kind, God-fearing people and assume you are too. You have taken the Lord as your Savior, have you not?"

Oh no, thought Anna, not this again. She stuttered, "Yes."

Daniel came to her aid. "Anna is a good, Christian woman."

George nodded. "None of our sons are as devout as we'd like. But you can exert a powerful influence. Promise me you'll try."

"I will try." Anna spoke in a flat voice. Her tone suggested a lack of conviction.

Anna believed religion often did more bad than good. There'd been the violence of the crusades, the battles between Protestants and Catholics in Ireland, and now the atrocities in Germany with regard to the Jewish nation. Why couldn't people just quietly believe in God?

Grace's entrance into the room interrupted Anna's thoughts. She wore an unadorned black housedress covered by a starched, white apron. Her hair was styled in its usual severe bun. She looked as elegant as ever.

She strode to Daniel and kissed him lightly on the cheek.

"Darling, it's wonderful to have you back. I missed you when you stayed in town. Of course, I missed you even more when you went to war. I prayed every day you would come home. My prayers were answered. God is good."

Grace hugged Daniel close. "You should never have gone to war. The Armstrong's are pacifists and that is the right way in God's eyes." Grace turned to Anna. "I hope you agree."

Anna didn't agree so she said nothing. The tension in the air grew thick as the smoke from George's recently lit cigar.

Grace directed her attention to Anna. "Do you pray, dear?"

Grace's eyes looked just as cold as they had yesterday and her full lips remained unsmiling. She obviously surmised the answer to her question would be a negative.

"Yes, I pray," She spoke with honesty. Anna stepped back from her mother-in-law, repelled by the hatred in the beautiful face. Anna wished Grace would look at her as she had looked at Nancy yesterday; with affection and complete warmth.

She didn't want to become a True Religionist. Although she had to admit the concept of starting a new life, a new existence, after being saved must be appealing to a great number of people. Anna was an Anglican and she would feel like a hypocrite if she professed to believe in something she did not.

"We both prayed a lot when we were trapped in rubble in London. And I prayed when I was in a tank in Normandy. Yet, bad as the war was, I still don't believe in pacifism. Sometimes it's necessary to fight for what you believe," Daniel said in her defence.

Daniel ended the conversation by grabbing Anna's suitcase and marching up the stairs to their bedroom. He handled the heavy piece of luggage as if it was as light as a tiny overnight bag. Anna followed close behind.

* * *

Daniel stayed in the bedroom, ostensibly to help unpack Anna's things. Anna appreciated his presence and began to relax a little.

Their bedroom was as beautiful as the living room. The deep bay window looked out over the vegetable garden. The walls were covered with delicate blue paper. A beautiful brass bed with a blue coverlet dominated the room. It had been Daniel's and his brothers' childhood room. Now there was nothing within it to suggest boyhood.

Daniel's voice interrupted Anna's thoughts. "Dad wants me to go to an auction with him, if that's all right with you. You can get to know Mother. When she's not on about Nancy and religion, she's actually very nice. So I guess I'll see you at supper?"

Anna suppressed a sigh. Her husband must be eager to get away. It bothered her that she would now have to share Daniel with his parents. She felt abandoned. Anna nodded her head and forced a smile.

* * *

She lingered over the task of unpacking. However, too soon she finished. She had no choice but to go downstairs. She walked down the wooden stairs as slowly as possible. She was filled with dread. *Imagine, hours alone with her mother-in-law.*

Grace's smile was false when Anna entered the living room. "I trust you find your accommodations comfortable and might like to be assigned a task. Am I right?"

Anna nodded. Grace led her to the kitchen. Like the rest of the house, she found it beautiful, with a large number of white cupboards, a pump that loomed over a large sink and lace curtains over a window that overlooked a peaceful, tranquil pasture. Despite this, Anna missed bombed out London where she'd been loved and accepted.

Grace's eyes shone. "I planned on making bread today, and then I thought you might like to do it instead. I'll show you where all the ingredients are kept. We have some fine white flour."

Anna gulped. "Yes, I would like to make the bread. I'll just need a recipe."

Grace smiled icily. "I thought you'd know a recipe by heart. You can cook, can't you?"

"Yes, a little." She knew it to be very little and suspected Grace realized this. Anna silently cursed her own mother for keeping her out of the kitchen.

Grace produced the ingredients. They included flour, yeast, sugar, eggs, and lemon juice. Then she showed Anna how to pump water from the well.

Besides plentiful cupboards, the room contained a pantry, an icebox, and a large coal stove. Grace showed Anna how to go about heating the coals.

Anna could see no indication of how to discern the oven's temperature. However, since she wanted to appear competent, she said nothing.

Sunlight poured into the kitchen from the large window and Anna couldn't help but appreciate the room's beauty. It was far more spacious and finely furnished than the kitchen Anna had grown up with.

Anna found herself imagining what it would be like to be the owner of this house, rather than just a reluctant guest.

Grace produced the recipe and announced she was going upstairs to take a nap. Her tone suggested she didn't want to be disturbed. Anna stared at Grace's elegant, straight back as her mother-in-law climbed up the equally elegant staircase.

Anna returned to the kitchen. The ingredients, the recipe, the stove all looked formidable. Anna read the recipe and realized bread making was a highly complicated, time-consuming process.

Yet she forced herself not to panic. After all, how difficult could baking be?

Anna set to work. She put the yeast into warm water with sugar, (at least she knew how to fill a kettle). After enough time had elapsed, she combined all the ingredients and kneaded them into a ball. It proved hard work and her arms ached. She was reminded of her job at the munitions factory.

She picked up a Ladies Home Journal magazine Grace had left on the coffee table, and waited for the dough to rise. She found the articles interesting and the pictures of fashions fascinating. Yet she didn't allow herself to become too engrossed in the magazine. She had a monumental task at hand.

Time passed. A pleased Anna saw the dough had risen. *She could do this.*

Finally, she had four loaves that were ready to be baked. *Oh no!* The loaves weren't all the same size. One was so large it spilled out of the pan and another so small it looked like it needed more time to rise. Two appeared about right. Anna decided she would volunteer to eat the small loaf.

She did her best to get the monstrosity of a stove ready for baking, but had no idea if the temperature of the oven would yield satisfactory results.

However, since Grace remained upstairs she shrugged and slid the bread pans onto the oven racks.

She said a short, silent prayer that her first attempt at baking would be a success. She suddenly had an urgent need for the outhouse. Daniel had pointed it out to her, so she put on her coat and galoshes and went down the path to the toilet, a structure as beautifully painted as all the other buildings.

However, despite the Chinook's warmth, she found the biffy freezing cold and it smelt terrible. Anna rushed through her business. She used a portion of an Eaton's catalogue for wiping. She'd have liked time to examine all the displayed merchandise. But didn't linger because she was freezing and she wanted to get back to her bread.

She opened the outhouse door and discovered a large red and white spotted animal standing nearby. A cow. It didn't appear frightened of her. Rather it watched her and chewed its cud. Weren't cows supposed to be docile?

Anna put her shaking hands on her pounding heart. Would it chase her? What should she do? She could see no one else about.

Several seconds elapsed and Anna told herself not to be frightened. Anna walked past the cow and squeaked in fear when it followed her. Dear God, it was chasing her!

Anna ran as fast as her legs would take her, fearing a goring by sharp horns She just missed thundering hooves as she slammed the gate to the house's yard.

She stared back at the cow and found she now seemed engrossed with eating. The animal's behavior surprised Anna. Daniel had told her only the bulls needed to be avoided.

Anna decided to abstain from all liquids after 7 pm so she wouldn't need to go to the bathroom in the middle of the night.

* * *

Anna entered the house and discovered the kitchen had filled with smoke. Could this day get any worse? Had she been gone too long? No, probably not. The oven temperature must be wrong.

Anna rushed to the stove and yanked it open. Her bread was burned beyond recovery. Anna grabbed potholders, and pulled out the ruined loaves, choking on tears and the scent of burnt bread.

Grace rushed into the room, her nap obviously over, and took in the scene. She started to laugh. "I thought you said you could cook. This is a disaster. Don't worry, I'll just whip up some baking powder biscuits for our supper tonight. Tomorrow, *I'll* make the bread."

Suddenly Anna felt her face go hot with rage and embarrassment. A cow had chased her, she'd been given a difficult task with no instruction and then she'd been laughed at. "How in God's name am I supposed to know what temperature the oven is at?"

For the first time, Anna saw warmth in Grace's eyes. It must be because they had filled with laughter at her expense. However, the coldness immediately returned. "It's something you learn, sort of by intuition."

Grace waved her arms in an effort to disperse the smoke. "Anna, never ever again speak the Lord's name in vain. God is my salvation. It is because of my belief in God that I live a good, honourable life.

"When I was a child, my parents would lock me in a closet for hours. I didn't have to have done anything wrong. I never mistreated my children. God freed me from cruelty."

Anna appreciated Grace's disclosure and felt she had gained a greater understanding of her mother-in-law. She almost summoned pity. She nonetheless believed there was more than one form of cruelty.

Grace hated her simply because she held a different belief system. Religion made her intolerant of any other views. Still, Anna was pleased Grace had explained the reason for her religious fervor. Maybe there was a chance they could become friends.

Grace asked Anna to set the table, her expression and tone suggesting she doubted Anna could carry out the task without a disaster.

The Armstrong's owned a beautiful white linen tablecloth that had obviously been starched and ironed, cloth napkins, real silverware and Blue Willow patterned dishes.

Anna couldn't contain her awe. "These are the most beautiful dishes I've ever seen. I hope someday Daniel and I have dishes so fine." She ran her hand over the rim of one of the plates. She became so entranced she momentarily lost her fear of Grace.

Grace's face softened and she smiled with genuine warmth. "You probably will someday. Daniel's a hard worker and he's generous."

Maybe the ice queen would thaw after all.

* * *

Within fifteen minutes, Daniel and George returned. Both men looked relaxed and happy. Anna envied them.

Anna rushed into her husband's arms glad to be near him in spite of the fact she had to confess her difficulties with baking. "I had a problem today. I made bread and the stove burned it all." She felt justified in blaming the stove. "I'm sorry."

Daniel held Anna close. "It is no big deal. You'll soon get used to how things work around here. You were brave to attempt to bake something."

Anna failed to tell him it had all been Grace's idea.

George also seemed unconcerned. "Don't worry. Soon you'll be making bread as well as the gals around here. Why Nancy, for instance, makes delicious bread and even angel food cake. It's light as a feather. That girl can do anything, anything at all."

Daniel cast a sharp look in his father's direction. However, it appeared to have no effect, George didn't seem to realize his comment might hurt Anna's feelings. Anna sighed. Would she be negatively compared to Nancy for the rest of her life?

The Armstrong's ate supper at six p.m. sharp. Anna was starving by the time supper was ready, she'd been too nervous to eat breakfast so she'd had almost nothing all day.

Anna snatched her hand back from her fork when she realized belatedly the rest of the family had folded their hands and bowed their heads.

Grace said, "Anna, would you like to thank the Lord for this bounty?" She gave her daughter-in-law a sharp look that said she'd noticed Anna's faux pas.

Anna gulped. Her family had never much bothered with grace so nothing suitable came readily to hand. Grace was certain to want something elaborate.

However, she nodded and said in a soft, high voice, "Dear God, thank you for this food we eat. Amen." She looked up in hopeful expectation.

Grace's eyes seemed even colder than normal and her voice sent chills up Anna's back. "We expect something more heartfelt and profound at our table. It might be acceptable to you Anglicans, but such a blessing is not what is expected here. I will say the prayer."

Grace began and the prayer went on for a good ten minutes. Anna worried the delicious food would grow cold and she hated cold food. It could be worse she supposed.

Anna mumbled 'amen' when the prayer finally came to a conclusion. Although somewhat chilled, Anna found the food delicious. But no one spoke throughout the meal of pork chops, mashed potatoes and baking powder biscuits. Anna longed for England and her family. She brightened a little when Grace served chocolate pudding for dessert.

Anna helped Grace with the dishes, although she longed for the security of her bedroom. The two women were once again alone and it appeared Grace wanted to continue the interrogation. "Anna, what is your favorite Bible verse?"

Grace's tone suggested companionship but Anna fretted. No matter what she said, it would likely be the wrong thing. However, she forced a smile, and scanned her brain for something familiar. "I would say the 23rd psalm."

Grace's eyes lost some of their ice. "Yes, it's lovely. My favorite is John 3:16. It sums up all of what believing in Christ can do for a person. It is the creed our church lives by."

Grace handed a bowl to Anna. "We are true Christians. I thought you might like to read the Bible verses to us tonight. But I've changed my mind. You might stumble over the unfamiliar words. Perhaps you can read another time, when you are more used to our ways. We observe evening devotionals in this home."

Anna was overwhelmed by Grace's veiled venom. She knew the psalms. She knew the Bible stories. However, Anna held her tongue. What could she say?

Grace unstopped the sink and the dishwasher poured down the drain.

* * *

Due to the short February days, bedtime came early which was a welcome relief to Anna. It provided a reason to escape the poisonous atmosphere in the living room.

She undressed and slipped into her beautiful, new bridal nightgown. She was too troubled to savour the exquisiteness of the garment. "Daniel, I don't think I'll ever be accepted by your mother. All she can think about is religion and I want to enjoy life now, not with a constant eye to a future eternity."

Daniel hung up his green work shirt. "I understand where you're coming from and I feel so bad I'm putting you through all this. I just don't see any other options."

Daniel stroked Anna's hair, "Your hair is so soft and blonde. I love it. I love you. Can we make love tonight?"

"Of course."

Anna was just drifting into sleep when she overheard Grace and George talking in the next room.

Daniel had started to softly snore but Anna could hear George's words when she lay on her back and strained her ears. "He's got a fine woman crying over him and he just doesn't care." He's married a woman from a different

107

country, a different religion. I fear this marriage will end in disaster."

Anna vowed to prove George wrong. However, despite her love for Daniel, she felt trapped as surely as she had in the rubble.

* * *

The days stretched on, each like the last. Anna grew to almost hate Grace.

Grace hadn't liked a demure yellow dress Daniel had purchased for Anna on one of their frequent outings into Lethbridge simply because of its colour.

"You're not going to go to heaven dressed in bright colours. I always wear black. It is understated and modest."

Anna thought it also suited the woman's colouring, but not her own. She kept her thoughts to herself. However, one evening over supper she mentioned the exchange to Daniel who leapt to her defence.

"Anna is my wife and a grown woman. She can make her own decisions about what to wear. Personally, I love that yellow dress and want her to wear it." Anna hid a triumphant smile from Grace.

Her mother-in-law also objected to Anna's painting. "You can't go all over the countryside like some harlot," she declared.

Anna's temper flared. On this she wasn't backing down. "I can't tolerate being stuck indoors all day. I *will* go outside and enjoy myself." She'd grabbed her paints and run out the door, narrowly resisting the temptation to kick the hated stove. Sooty followed her and his loyalty brought her to tears.

Despite the fact she'd once again managed to antagonize the red-spotted cow, whose name she now knew was Dolly, Anna managed to paint the homestead. She figured out if she faced Dolly and stood her ground, the animal would retreat.

She believed the painting was her finest work ever. Sooty saw it first because the loyal animal stayed by her side throughout the pleasant afternoon.

Anna lived for the nights when she found herself wrapped in Daniel's arms in the big, moonlit room. Of course, Daniel still had nightmares and Anna could think of no way to help him.

It surprised Anna that George and Grace blamed her. Grace even had the audacity to ask her what she was doing to cause Daniel's nightmares.

Anna snapped back. "It's not me. It's the war. He hasn't told me everything. But what he went through was terrible."

Grace shut her mouth in a thin line and said nothing more on the subject.

Anna discovered that when she stood up to Grace, the older woman often backed down. However, Anna hated conflict and after a confrontation, she often found herself unhappier than ever.

Anna enjoyed writing to her parents. She relished composing these letters and she filled them with descriptions of Canada. They enjoyed hearing about Dolly, the ferocious cow, as well as other amusing anecdotes.

Somehow she managed to write optimistically and focused on what her life would be like when she and Daniel could afford to build on their own farm.

The letters Anna received back were also optimistic and Anna doubted her parents were telling her the whole truth either. After all, the war still went on.

Anna loved visiting Maisy's and Jim's farm. Maisy understood her predicament and proved kind and empathic.

As time went on, Anna took over household jobs that Grace didn't like, such as the laundry and sewing. She even learned how to use the stove. She enjoyed these tasks, but wished she was in a home of her own where she could escape her mother-in-law's scrutiny.

Anna cherished Sunday mornings because she wasn't invited to go to church. At first, it had bothered her to be excluded. However, when she learned she could spend her time reading or painting she took advantage of the situation.

Daniel, still not dressed in his suit, had once expressed a desire to stay home with Anna.

Grace had been furious. "If you stay home Nancy will be asking about you. I will not have a son of mine missing church."

"Yes, you will. Anna is my wife and I want to be with her."

Grace had burst into sobs and even Anna felt sorry for her. "The woman you've married is ruining your chances for a life with our eternal Savior."

Grace bowed slightly with hands clasped before her son. "Please, please come with us. I ask it as the mother who loves you and cares about you."

All of this happened in front of Anna and she stood silent, pitying Grace. No one should be that consumed with anything.

"Go ahead Daniel. I'm okay here alone."

Reluctantly, Daniel had given in.

Sometimes, as she sat reading on a Sunday, she longed for England and held back bitter tears of resentment for what she'd given up. Canada was empty and lonely, and, except when Chinook winds blew, cold. Anna had doubted if spring would ever come.

* * *

However, spring did come. One beautiful May Sunday when the air was warm, the sunshine abundant, and songbirds trilling their beautiful tunes, Grace asked a surprised Anna to attend church with them.

Anna agreed because she couldn't think of any way to tactfully say she would prefer to stay at home. Wouldn't it be grand if Grace was finally going to accept her?

Perhaps out of spite, although she hadn't made a conscious decision, Anna wore her yellow dress. She and Daniel held hands as they sat close together in the back seat of George's black Cadillac.

They drove along an unfamiliar gravel road. Grace kept up a constant stream of conversation.

"Nancy Smyth is going to teach two classes of Sunday school. Apparently, they're having a hard time finding teachers. You could take a class if you were baptized. Teaching would show you are a woman of faith. Open your heart to Him now. Perhaps you will see Jesus as I have seen Jesus. I would hate for you to go to hell."

Daniel gripped Anna's hand, but he said nothing. Actually, Anna would have liked to teach Sunday school. She loved children and she imagined herself giving beautiful little girls gold stars because they learned a bible verse. Anna didn't know why, but she always dreamed of little girls rather than little boys.

However, Anna would never teach in a cultish church. The poor little innocents would probably have nightmares about hell with the lessons she'd be forced to give. She didn't believe in fire and brimstone.

Grace turned in her seat so she could look at Anna. "If you were baptized, any children you and Daniel have will go to heaven. We like you, Anna, and we want to accept you. But you make it so difficult." Her tone dripped with insincerity.

Anna was astounded; she'd done everything she could think of to make her in-laws like her without compromising her own religious beliefs. Surely a person was allowed to follow their heart?

"I am baptized. I was baptized as a child in the Anglican Church near my home. Despite your beliefs, I am going to heaven. Actually, our religions aren't that different. We're all Protestants and the Anglican God is the same God as yours," Anna's voice shook with suppressed anger.

Anna clenched her teeth and compressed her lips into a tight line.

Grace's face grew pink with religious fervour. "If you only embraced something besides the Anglican Church; historically, many religions broke away from the Anglicans.

111

"Can't you just take the Lord as your Savior and follow our faith?" Grace's voice revealed her exasperation.

Anna wanted to scream in frustration but she forced herself to speak calmly. "I can't do something my conscience says is hypocritical. It would be so easy, but I can't. I'll go to church with you once a week in order to keep peace in the house. I think that should be sufficient."

Anna wanted to be accepted by Grace and George, but she couldn't profess to something she thought foolish. Grace obviously believed if she just kept talking Anna would give in.

"We don't believe baptism is for everyone and we don't believe in baptizing infants. We only baptize after an individual has taken Jesus as their Savior."

Anna was not only angry at Grace. Daniel hadn't said a word; he just sat staring blankly straight ahead as if the conversation between his wife and his mother had nothing to do with him. She pulled her hand out of his and moved as far away from her husband as possible.

Her action appeared to bring Daniel back to the present. "Leave Anna alone. She's entitled to her beliefs the same as you are," Daniel shouted.

Grace swiveled in her seat so rapidly that a piece of hair came out of her bun. She stared straight ahead, her back and head so rigid Anna grew frightened. The woman was as unforgiving as stone.

Finally, they reached their destination. The church sat in what appeared to be a pasture, with a gravel road leading up to it. The building was small, humble and plain. Not the edifice of Anna's imaginings.

Nancy came out to greet them. She looked as mousy as ever, despite the fact she wore a rather pretty navy and white print dress and a navy bow in her stringy hair. Her smile revealed huge gaps in her teeth.

Why was Nancy greeting her? And with warmth? There was none of the formality of their only previous meeting. Anna tried, unsuccessfully, to smile. She suspected a hidden agenda.

* * *

Because Sunday school classes had ended, Nancy sat with the Armstrong's in an uncomfortable pew in the second row.

A woman in the seat ahead wore cloying perfume. Anna stifled the urge to cough.

The conversation in the car left Anna so distraught she found it impossible to concentrate on the sermon. She had no idea what had been said. She wished she'd been permitted to stay at home.

* * *

They came out into the sunshine and Anna met several fellow members of the congregation. She found everyone to be pleasant and friendly and welcoming.

She decided any one of the older women would make a wonderful mother-in-law. Why did she have to be stuck with Grace?

Some people remembered her from the party in her honour. One woman asked her where she'd found her beautiful dress.

Several people expressed surprise that they hadn't seen Anna at church before. Anna said, as matter-of-factly as possible, she'd been busy at home. She received some surprised looks.

Soon everyone but the Armstrong's and Nancy left. Anna walked a little ways into the pasture, enjoying the sunshine.

Grace followed her and grabbed Anna by the elbow. She towed her towards Nancy. Anna's suspicions of a hidden agenda were confirmed.

"Nancy would like to speak to you." Grace sounded like a Nazi SS Officer.

Grace stepped back. Suddenly Nancy stood uncomfortably close, her face inches from Anna's nose.

"Repent, Anna, repent or you will go to a fiery hell. First, it will be your feet, then your legs; finally your whole body and it will never end. You will burn for all eternity." Nancy raised her arms high as she shouted the words.

Behind the raving woman Daniel stood open mouthed. Obviously this performance was a surprise to him, but he left Anna to fend for herself instead of coming to her aid. Anna threw him a wild look of betrayal before she turned and ran as fast as she could away from the church. Daniel finally sprang into action and followed. Her dress caught between her legs and she tripped over a gopher hole but she scrambled up off her knees and kept running. She never wanted to stop.

She felt as if she'd run at least a mile before Daniel finally caught up to her. He pulled her to a stop and gathered her against his heaving chest.

Anna cried and screamed as best she could in her winded state. "Your parents, they're terrible. I can't live with them any longer. That Nancy is a nutter and she scares me. Your mother holds her up as a shining example and I'll never measure up in their eyes and I don't want to." Anna squirmed out of Daniel's arms and continued to rant. "I'm leaving. I love you. I'll always love you. But I can't take this. I'm going back to England where people are sane and they actually like me. Anything is better than the hell I'm living."

Anna meant every word, although she didn't know how she would execute her plans.

Daniel threw back his head and howled in protest; the piercing cry seemed to fill the vast prairie. Anna shrank away.

"Anna, please don't go. I can't live without you." His voice was savage.

"You don't stand up for me with your parents. I can't go on. I simply can't go on." Anna's face was wet with tears and she wrung her hands as she spoke.

Daniel hung his head. "You're right. I've been a first-class jackass. But I'll change. If necessary, I'll get a job in the city."

He roughly pulled Anna into his arms. "I love farming and I love the land, but I love you more. Please stay. I'll make it better." His eyes pleaded with his wife.

* * *

They returned to the car where his parents waited. Nancy was nowhere in sight. No one spoke on the journey home.

Once they returned to the house, Daniel asked Anna to go up to their bedroom. He needed to speak to his parents alone.

She heard every word. Grace shouting, "She doesn't love God. You married an English heathen. Nancy waited for you. She's a good Christian woman. Send Anna back to England where she belongs. We'll pay for her passage."

Then Daniel's voice, loud and firm. "You're wrong, Mother; dead wrong. I love Anna, not Nancy. And I am leaving here, whether you help me or not. I'm going out tomorrow to look for work in town. Then we're renting a room or something. I've stood by and said nothing while you've undermined my wife but that is going to change, starting now."

Grace's hysterical sobs carried clearly up the stairs. Then she heard George's voice, strong and clear, "You don't need to quit farming, son. I can see you and Anna love each other. And, I know you feel married before God."

"George, our church does *not* recognize Anglican marriages. You know this." Grace's voice was shrill.

"Maybe not. But Daniel is our son and we have no right to keep him from the woman he loves. Over time, Anna may come to believe as we do. I hope so. In the meantime, Jim and Peter and I will build you a house on your land. Mind you, it won't be anything fancy. But it will be yours. I don't think Anna is the kind to mind." *Thank God. George had discovered a spine.*

Anna took a good, long breath and almost managed to smile. Finally, she would have a home of her own.

Chapter 8

On July 15th, the house was ready for Daniel and Anna to move in. Anna danced with happiness.

She no longer had to carefully edit her letters to her parents. She had nothing to hide now. Consequently, she filled her posts home with colourful descriptions of the house and anecdotes about Daniel's kindness and consideration.

George had been right, the home wasn't fancy, but Anna loved it.

It consisted of only three rooms; a small sitting room, an equally small bedroom and a kitchen. Although small, the kitchen had white cupboards and adequate counter space.

A wire fence surrounded the house but they had no vegetables, flowers or trees to protect. It would all happen next year. This year she had enough to do.

Anna didn't mind that the house was small and plain. Except when she'd lived with Daniel's parents, she'd never experienced luxurious surroundings. She was extremely happy. She could now do whatever she wanted, whenever she wanted, freed from her in-laws and the miserable job at a munitions factory in England.

She taught herself to cook from both recipes and careful instructions from Maisy. After the fiasco with the bread, Grace had limited Anna's attempts in the kitchen. She also sewed curtains and kept the house as clean as possible.

Now mid-summer, Anna enjoyed the southern Alberta weather. There were glorious sunny days, even though strong winds seemed to dry Anna from the inside out.

She also had to co-exist with mosquitoes, creatures neither Anna nor Daniel minded killing. These incredibly aggressive insects left itching welts on Anna's arms and legs and interrupted her enjoyment of the welcome cool of the evening.

Already people ceased to comment favourably on her complexion. And she noticed small, faint freckles starting to appear on her arms and hands.

However, she'd begun to gain weight and that pleased her. Anna believed good food brought good health. She felt strong and energetic. Daniel said she glowed.

Setting up their home and farm had been exciting, but also frightening. It had been fun to purchase furniture and household goods and Anna had enjoyed the almost daily trips into town. However, she knew Daniel's bank account grew dangerously low. His disability pension helped, but it wasn't sufficient to cover all the new expenses.

Anna blamed herself for their financial situation and she filled with guilt. If Daniel had married Nancy he'd have all his parents' backing and it would be considerable.

Anna often wondered if she shouldn't have stuck it out with her in-laws. However, she knew in her heart she'd taken all she could tolerate.

Anna had established boundaries with regards to visits from Grace and George. They would only see Daniel's parents once every two weeks, every second Sunday. Anna and Daniel would not attend the True Religion Church.

Daniel accepted her conditions without complaint, although he sometimes went to a machinery auction with his father. She knew her husband enjoyed these outings and Anna hated distancing Daniel from his parents, but felt she had no choice.

Grace and George seemed to accept the situation. Nothing further was said about Anna's salvation or Nancy's virtues. Anna thought her in-laws wanted to see her as infrequently as possible.

Grace's manner remained stonily polite and George remained unchanged. Fortunately, since the installation of the new rules Anna had no difficulty accepting their flaws.

No matter what the circumstances, Anna vowed to never again live with her in-laws. She would return to England if Daniel tried to force that issue again.

* * *

Each morning Anna awoke to the crowing of Fancypants, the multi-coloured rooster who serviced the fifteen hens.

Besides the chickens, they had fourteen cows (none of which proved as fearsome as the rambunctious Dolly), five pigs, and two horses to help with the plowing. The horses were Princess and Duchess. Anna liked them both. Prince was a large bay gelding, and Duchess a small, all-black mare. They made a good team, although Duchess was the harder-working horse.

Anna didn't ride Prince or Duchess, although Daniel would occasionally take one of them out. He had learned to ride as a child. He'd had to ride five miles to and from school as a young boy. Anna liked all the animals and agreed with Daniel's assessment they would be profitable.

Anna laughed whenever Daniel told her not to discount the thousand or so head of gophers. Anna thought them cute, just as Daniel had predicted. However the holes they dug in their pasture and crop land could be dangerous.

Despite his financial worries, Daniel was content. He told Anna he no longer cared about material things like he had before the war, a trait he'd shared with his father.

"I don't care about driving a Cadillac. When you've seen killing, you realize just how lucky you are to be alive. The things I used to think were important are trivial in comparison, now I just want to be free from pain." He still had nightmares. Otherwise he was a joy to be around. He didn't dominate her, as her father had her mother. In fact, he let Anna do as she pleased even when he thought the idea ridiculous.

Anna insisted they name their property. "Everyone does so in England. It's only right to have a place with a name. Why not call it Whispering Gables? The wind whispers around the house."

Daniel laughed at the flowery name. "The wind around Lethbridge is more like a bellow."

Nonetheless, he agreed to let his wife paint a sign for the farm gate. Whispering Gables, it proclaimed.

Anna found time to paint more than just signs and Daniel praised her work. She presented him with one of a sunset and waited for his reaction.

Daniel said, "It's beautiful. I love it. You are definitely talented."

Anna gave Maisy one of a meadowlark, Anna's favorite Canadian songbird. She loved the birds' beautiful trill and gorgeous yellow colour.

The two women also exchanged books. Maisy had loaned her *Oliver Twist* and Anna had secured a couple of special books for Maisy. They always discussed the books after they'd read them.

Anna regularly wrote to Reg and Julie. She and Julie reminisced about England. They both missed their native homeland. The bond between Anna and Julie was as strong as their husbands', Daniel and Reg.

Anna hoped she'd found a kindred spirit in Lethbridge when she met another war bride. Tall, buxom Mildred lived nearby.

Maisy disapproved. "Mildred's face is round as a pudding. She even colours her hair. Are you sure she's not a prostitute?"

However, Anna wished for instant friendship. Mildred would understand why Anna missed England's quaint beauty, and what it felt like to be far from home and family.

"It's a pleasure to meet another war bride. Which part of the U.K. do you come from?"

Mildred sharply retorted, "Ireland. I'm not much of a one for small talk. I hope you understand." She frowned fiercely.

119

"Yes, of course." However, Anna didn't understand and she gave up on pursuing the friendship.

* * *

The day started out beautifully on August 15th, 1945. For one thing, the dog returned and Anna loved dogs. This was the third time he'd shown up on their doorstep. It had taken them awhile to track down his owner. Their neighbour, Van Johnson. Van had appeared unconcerned with his dog's whereabouts. Anna feared he didn't love the animal. A pity.

The dog seemed to like them better than his owner. Possibly because they petted him and fed him delicious table scraps.

Wolfie, as Daniel called the nameless animal, was a one hundred fifty pound mixed breed. He was black and brown with a huge head. His long hair made him look shaggy.

When Anna saw him she ran outside with a large bowl of water and another of leftovers. Wolfie rapidly devoured them. When he finished eating, he placed his large head under Anna's hand. It was warm and comforting.

Anna thought Wolfie a wonderful replacement for Sooty. He was the only thing she missed from the Armstrong homestead.

Daniel watched the interchange with amusement and soon he was scratching behind the animal's ears. In response, Wolfie leaned into Daniel's thigh.

"Maybe I should run over to Van Johnson's house and tell him where Wolfie is," he spoke tentatively. Anna hoped Daniel could be talked into keeping Wolfie. She knew Daniel also missed Sooty.

Anna reached down and buried her hand in Wolfie's soft, dense hair. "I wouldn't bother. Wolfie will probably just come back as he has in the past. I think we should plan on keeping him. We don't want Van chaining him up to keep him at home. He's a nice dog and he'll make a good watch dog. He can't be happy there or he wouldn't keep coming here."

Anna held her breath as she waited for her husband's reply. If Daniel agreed, they could keep the dog. If not, she might not see him again. Anna wanted a dog almost as much as she wanted children. She continued to stroke the adoring Wolfie.

Daniel smiled and Anna exhaled. "Yes, Mrs. Armstrong, I like him too. He's a fine dog and it appears he likes us. If we don't hear from Van, we've got a dog. I hope we don't hear anything. Van does nothing more than feed him."

Anna wrapped her arms around Wolfie's neck. Then she embraced her husband and he kissed her under the beautiful, bright, blue sky. A meadowlark sang in the pasture.

Wolfie followed Anna as she went about her outdoor chores. She found herself talking to the animal like a companion.

However, she knew enough to keep him from the chicken coop when she went to gather the eggs. "Stay, Wolfie."

Wolfie sat, tongue lolling while he waited.

"Good dog." She would have to do little to train him.

Anna didn't mind gathering the eggs, although she often received a sharp peck from a hen. She must leave some to incubate, she thought. Just thinking of the soft balls of yellow fluff made Anna smile.

However, Anna noticed one old hen had long ceased producing eggs. She would have to be killed for her meat. If she didn't lay eggs, if she didn't meet her purpose any longer, there could be no reason to keep her.

Anna sighed. Neither she nor Daniel relished killing.

However, practicality won out. After all, they were hardly rich. Anna picked up the old hen, a gentle bird that nestled against Anna's chest.

The bird clucked softly as Anna reluctantly carried her out of the hen house and towards Daniel. Wolfie followed.

Anna, feeling like the worst kind of scum, found Daniel taking a smoke break from fixing the pig pen. A board had come loose and the pigs were eager to escape. Both Daniel and Anna hated rounding up pigs. Daniel blew smoke through his nose. He looked the essence of contentment. He smiled at his wife.

Anna didn't waste time on a greeting. "This hen hasn't been laying. But she's a dear old soul. Perhaps we should let her die of natural causes."

As with the dog, Anna hoped Daniel would come around to her way of thinking. Fortunately, Daniel appeared to be in a good mood. The gentle bird rested her head on Anna's arm.

Daniel immediately straightened and Anna could detect his intent.

"Gosh, how long has it been?"

Anna stroked the hen. "A couple of weeks or so. I don't think her meat will be very good. She is obviously very old."

Anna could think of no other words to prolong the life of this dear chicken. She continued to stroke the clucking bird.

Daniel hastily placed the hammer he'd been using on the ground, his face red. "Those crooks in town told me all the hens were young and just starting to produce. I was lied to. I'm afraid we're just going to have to eat her. We can't run a retirement home for chickens. The dog is going to cost us enough in food."

Anna sighed. Life could be cruel. "I suppose you're right. However, she is a dear old soul." Anna hated this moment as much as any in her life.

"I can see that. Sometimes killing is necessary, you know that. I wish to God it wasn't mandatory, then or now."

Daniel went to get the axe. He moved slowly, reluctant to carry out the task.

Anna continued to stroke the bird, although she wanted to release it. Let it escape the bite of the axe.

She couldn't do it, Daniel would be angry and they really couldn't afford to feed a non-producing hen. Why did God make life such a struggle?

* * *

Daniel fought back tears as he took the hen from Anna and placed her on the ground. He'd never killed a chicken. All of the slaughtering had been done by his father when he'd been growing up.

The dear hen sat still. Poor tired old thing. Daniel felt like a murderer. He held the chicken still while he swung the sharp axe as hard as he could so the chicken would suffer as little as possible. Thankfully, the bird's head severed easily, blood spurted onto Daniel's pants and shirt. He fought back the bile rising in his throat.

The decapitated bird ran wildly in circles and he stifled a cry of distress. He turned from the headless bird's wild gyrations. Wolfie grabbed the head and Daniel stifled a strangled cry. At that moment, Daniel almost hated the dog, although Wolfie was just following his instincts.

Death was terrible and grotesque. Except for the lucky few who managed to die peaceably in their sleep. The old hen produced a great deal of blood, more than he expected.

Without warning, Daniel found himself back in the Sherman Firefly tank on the beach, the thunder of guns and screams of the wounded beating down on him. They'd suffered a direct hit and even in the dim light the bodies of his unit were strewn about grotesquely twisted in death. A scream of rage and despair burst from him, why was he spared when everyone else was dead?

The blood and other bits of the men under his command littered the inside of the tank and stuck to his uniform. His throat closed with the acrid scent of fuel and bowels loosened in death.

Daniel's shoulder was odd and wouldn't move; he looked down and was surprised to see blood staining his shirt. Death surrounded him and Daniel couldn't seem to tear his gaze away from his fallen friends. Easy-going

Randy slumped over his gun, Frank with his brain blown apart, Sam sprawled across the floor blocking Daniel's escape, young Ken who'd lied about his age, curled up on the floor looking like he was sleeping.

God, if only he'd conquered his fear and opened the hatch to survey the battleground he might have been able to take evasive action even in the cloying sand. He closed his eyes and willed himself to be anywhere else.

A gust of wind rattled the cottonwood leaves above him. Daniel shook his head and opened his eyes to the familiar barnyard. Weak with relief he almost dropped to his knees. The old hen lay still some feet away from him. Poor old thing, he hated taking her life, even though practicality decreed it was the best thing to do.

Blood dripped from the axe he still held clenched in his fist. With a cry of horror he flung it away from him and collapsed in a heap sobbing as if his heart would break. Death; so much death. Would it never stop?

* * *

Anna avoided the killing. Poor old hen. She caught her bottom lip in her teeth when her husband stood trancelike with the beheaded creature spinning around him. Anna gave a cry of dismay as Daniel threw the axe and crumpled to the ground. She ran to him and gathered the sobbing man in her arms. "Daniel, Daniel, hush now. It's okay. Hush now." She stroked his hair and tried to ease the shuddering of his body. It scared her how frail he seemed in her arms. Wolfie came and leaned against them, offering his protection and comfort.

Eventually the tremors eased and Daniel raised his head. "Anna, I can't talk about it. Leave me for a bit. Can you do something with that dead bird, please? I can't look at it…"

Anna hugged him and kissed his forehead before getting to her feet. Gingerly, she picked up the chicken and took it to a sheltered spot beside the house. The kettle was already on the stove, she'd need hot water to help remove the feathers. Despite the fact she hated the messy job, she toiled as rapidly and efficiently as possible.

The smell of wet feathers made her stomach clench in protest, and the eviscerating would be worse. Anna hated the feel of the internal organs, still warm from the recently departed life. A shiver ran over her skin. This was woman's work, Grace had insisted when she first showed Anna how to prepare the chicken earlier in the marriage when they still lived with her in-laws. Men slaughtered the animals and the women took care of the rest, except for the heavy work of butchering cattle and swine.

* * *

At supper Anna forced herself to eat, there was no excuse for wasting food Daniel declared, although he only picked at the meal too.

The old bird was surprisingly tasty especially accompanied by the dumplings Anna put together. They ate in silence.

After supper, Anna softly hummed a lullaby as she cleaned up the leftovers and washed and dried the dishes. Hers may not be the beautiful Blue Willow pattern of her in-laws, but she loved the simple, inexpensive dishes they'd purchased at Safeway. They belonged to her and Daniel.

She changed into her nightgown, and noticed an unopened box of Kotex in her underwear drawer. She found the sanitary pads a vast improvement over the tissues employed by women in wartime London.

It occurred to her she hadn't had her period in the last five weeks, and she was usually as regular as clockwork. There had also been some slight nausea in the mornings.

Could it be possible? Would her greatest dream come true? Might she really and truly be pregnant? Anna forgot all about the chicken and Daniel's breakdown. She danced about the room.

She ran out to where Daniel sat reading the Free Press. She was so excited she could hardly talk. "Darling, I think I'm pregnant."

125

Daniel slowly and carefully folded the paper, eyes shiny with tears when he looked up at her. "I know it's something you want…I just don't know if I can trust myself with a child."

He looked down at his large hands and Anna wondered if he saw them covered in blood his face was so white.

Anna knelt beside him and took his hands in hers. "Despite your war experiences, you are the kindest, gentlest man I know. You'll make an excellent father." Anna gently kissed her husband on the cheek.

Daniel gave a great shuddering breath and his body relaxed against her. He pulled Anna into his arms and kissed her on the neck. "I love you. We'll be wonderful parents, I know it."

PART 3

LETHBRIDGE, ALBERTA, CANADA
1951 – 1952

Chapter 9

Anna sang out one of her favorite songs, Bing Crosby's *Swinging on a Star*, as she prepared four loaves of bread.

She was now an excellent cook and knew exactly what temperature in which to bake bread. The incident in her in-laws' home would never be forgotten. Yet now it only brought comfort because her situation had changed so much.

Her bread in the oven, Anna began to wash up the bowls and wooden spoon she'd been using. She should have done this earlier but had neglected the task because she'd been too engrossed in her grooming. She'd just bathed, and felt fresh in a pink and white flowered sleeveless dress Daniel loved.

Washing dishes would never be a favoured task. However, Anna did find something comforting about it. Like her mother, she enjoyed most household chores.

Anna stared out the window at her two beautiful daughters, saucy Amber and gentle Crystal. They played with their cute little dog, Chocolate, a fine Cocker/Springer spaniel cross. His coat glowed a rich dark brown.

Because of his small size he didn't make a good watch dog like his predecessor, Wolfie, who had died of old age. But the girls adored him.

Anna smiled as a robin flew past her window. Robins, with their red breasts, were beautiful birds. As beautiful as the meadowlark Anna had painted for Maisy.

Numerous birds nested on the farm because Anna and Daniel had planted and conscientiously watered numerous trees around their house. Anna also tended a large vegetable garden, and even a few rosebushes.

Along with gardening, Anna cared for her children and cooked and cleaned. She'd become a very busy person and felt as if she fulfilled her destiny through the work. She was contented.

Each evening, Anna said a gentle, personal, silent prayer of thanks to a God other than True Religionist. She was especially thankful for her healthy, happy children. There'd been no post-partum depression for her. She enjoyed motherhood even more than she'd imagined.

Five-year old Amber, her eldest, resembled Daniel. She had his cleft chin and hazel eyes. Anna knew she would grow into a beautiful woman.

When she'd been born, Anna had been certain Amber's blue eyes would turn to hazel. She'd been right. Her child had been aptly named. In a certain light, those eyes glowed like a piece of amber.

From the cries of delight emanating into the house, Anna discerned her eldest child had jumped off the roof of the chicken coop into strategically placed straw bales. It pleased Anna her daughter enjoyed herself. She just hoped Amber's gymnastics wouldn't stop the hens from laying. So far, it hadn't.

Three year old Crystal had sat contentedly playing with her toes for hours when she was an infant. Even now she remained quieter and less active than her sister.

However, like her sister, Crystal looked like her name. She bore a resemblance to a rare jewel. She had long, pale blonde hair, blue eyes and a delicate frame. She had inherited her mother's love of drawing.

Except for the occasional fight, the two girls played well together. Anna wished her parents could meet Amber and Crystal. Mum and Dad would adore them.

Anna constantly thought about her parents. They never aged or changed in her mind from the day she left them.

She still missed England itself. Now the war had ended London would be filled with fine shops and beautiful flowers. Far more beautiful than anything she could cultivate on a farm near dry, windy Lethbridge.

Nonetheless, Canada had become home because it housed her husband and children.

Anna heard the faint, haunting sound of a train whistle and sighed with pleasure. The train had brought her to Daniel. She had forgotten how dirty the train had been. Or how she'd arrived to find the station platform empty.

The sound lingered in the crisp September air. September was beautiful in southern Alberta with crisp, cool mornings and evenings; and hot, sunny days. And, blissfully, at that time of year, little of the roaring wind.

Unfortunately, the month of golden leaves did contribute to an abundance of flies. They inevitably made their way into the house. The house was fitted with a screen door, but neither Crystal nor Amber, nor even Daniel could be moved to close it. So Anna swatted flies. The flyswatter was almost as necessary as the refrigerator or stove.

Nonetheless, Anna adored the fall season even though a harsh, cold winter would certainly follow. She knew the beauty of September would give her the strength to endure the upcoming winter season.

Anna had just finished sweeping the floor when Amber and Crystal came in, followed by Chocolate. Chocolate was allowed in the house, although Wolfie had not.

Both girls wore matching sleeveless, pink frocks trimmed with white lace, and white socks with brown oxfords. Daniel insisted on sensible shoes. Each child's hair was tied with a pink ribbon.

Both Amber and Crystal liked dressing up. Only Amber also liked daredevil activities like standing on the teeter totter. She fell and hurt herself on more than one occasion, though it hadn't ended her need for excitement.

Crystal carried a confection of dirt and water covered in wildflowers. It was yet another mud pie. Anna hoped her daughter wouldn't drop it all over her clean floor.

"We tried to give it to the king, Chocolate. We are the royal bakers for His Majesty. He seems to like his other food more." Amber's soft, childish voice sounded perplexed.

Anna laughed. Her children had vivid imaginations.

She bent down to pick up the cake. "Thank you, girls. It's lovely. I'll leave it on the windowsill to dry. You can play with it whenever you like. I don't think it's proper food for Chocolate." As she spoke, she patted Chocolate on the head. He responded by licking Anna's hand.

"Why don't you pick me some more bouquets of dandelions? You know how much I like them." Anna, of course, didn't really want a vase full of dandelions or another mud pie. However, she graciously accepted them as proof of her children's love.

"We will, Mommy," said Crystal, her eyes wide with excitement.

However, Amber had other thoughts. "Mom, when the crop comes in, Dad says we'll be rich. Can I have a bicycle? My friend, Tammy, has a bicycle. She has great fun."

"If it's okay with Dad, then it's okay with me. However, you'll have to let Crystal ride it too."

Crystal's wide-set blue eyes grew wide in anticipation and Anna hoped she wouldn't fear the bicycle. Crystal was a cautious child.

Amber simultaneously jumped and clapped her hands. "I can't wait. I'm so happy."

* * *

Anna grabbed the woven picnic basket containing the lunch she'd prepared earlier that morning, and went outside. Daniel couldn't leave the back pasture, he needed

130

to prevent water from leaking onto the crop. The combine would arrive later today. She'd take the lunch out to him.

She immediately found her children. They picked dandelions, just as she'd told them to. Anna thought they looked like little angels as they bent toward their task.

Crystal particularly, at that moment, looked like something out of a painting. Her hair shone golden in the sunshine. She screamed with joy. "This one's so pretty. Mommy will love it." However, Crystal looked less angelic when Anna noticed yellow stains on her soft, white hands.

"Come girls, I've made us a lunch of egg salad sandwiches with my own baked bread. We'll also have apples, and there'll be biscuits for dessert. We're going to take the lunch out to Dad. I've made enough for all of us so we can have a picnic." Anna spoke as commandingly as possible. Both her children hated to be interrupted when intent on a task. A trait inherited from Daniel.

Amber and Crystal both looked up in expectation. "You can bring the flowers with you and show them to your father."

Amber said, "Oh goodie, a picnic. I can't wait. I like egg salad sandwiches. Can't we have one now?"

"No, we're going to eat with Dad. So come along. The faster you move, the sooner you'll be able to eat." Anna clapped her hands. She was relieved when her daughters stopped picking and proceeded to follow her.

The trio moved slowly across the field of grass, avoiding cow paddies in the process. The time passed quickly for Anna listening to the girls' constant chatter.

Chocolate sniffed individual blades of grass as he followed. Anna knew dogs had an incredible sense of smell.

Amber, in a voice filled with excitement, said, "I want a pink bicycle with a basket on the front to put stuff in."

Before Anna could reply, Amber said, "Mom, why are dandelions called weeds?"

Crystal interrupted the conversation. "Why can't Chocolate sleep with us? I've never seen a flea on him."

Anna answered all their questions as quickly and succinctly as possible. She loved their incessant conversation.

Soon, in another year, Amber would be starting school. Days such as this with the three of them together would pass. She wasn't one of those mothers who couldn't wait for her children to start school. She could honestly say she thoroughly enjoyed her children's company.

Finally, they reached the long, narrow, fence-lined lane separating the top pasture from the bottom pasture. Anna loved this path. It reminded her of lanes in England. The soil underneath her feet felt hard and worn.

Anna had once tried to paint the scene she now enjoyed. However, she hadn't been able to do it justice. Maybe in better light it might be possible. Like today's. The sky was an intense shade of blue.

The trees showed a touch of frost, beginning to glow with colour. The result was incredibly beautiful, almost as lovely as England.

Anna marveled at the seeming contentment of the cows as they chewed their cuds and flicked their tails across their backs. She had no fear of these cows like she had the rambunctious Dolly on her in-laws farm many years ago. She'd come to love these animals. It horrified her whenever Daniel suggested they sell one of them.

Suddenly, a large, brown rabbit ran across their path. Chocolate let out a quick bark and excitedly gave chase. He ran as fast as his four short legs would take him. But at no time did the rabbit have any need for fear.

Anna and the girls laughed at their pet's antics.

Chocolate often made them laugh. Whenever they came home he chased all the birds, including those in the air, out of the yard. It was all in splendid preparation for their arrival. He also buried bones all over the pasture and caught garter snakes and salamanders.

They left the lane and entered a grove of trees. The girls spotted Daniel and broke into a run.

"Daddy, Daddy, we came with lunch. We're having egg salad. We picked dandelions for Mom, but we'll give them to you."

Daniel put down his shovel and scooped his daughters into his arms. "It's good to see you. I feel a bit lonely out here by myself. And it couldn't be better timing. I'd just begun to think about lunch."

He looked into Anna's eyes. "And Mommy, I missed her too." Daniel reached past the girls and pulled Anna into his arms. The dandelions scattered at their feet while Anna raised her face for Daniel's kiss.

Stepping back, Anna looked around for a level piece of pasture and then set down a red and white checkered, plastic tablecloth. She placed a thermos of tea on the tablecloth. "I've brought lots. We're going to have lunch together."

Daniel motioned toward the ground. "Girls, come sit down. This looks like the best kind of picnic and I'm glad you brought lots of food. I'll be combining all afternoon and into the evening so I won't eat supper until very late."

Fortunately, no ants appeared. Anna noticed Crystal gave most of her sandwich to Chocolate. She decided not to say anything. The day was too perfect for any sort of conflict.

Anna shifted position, careful to avoid a thistle. They looked pretty, but touching them brought discomfort at best. Bleeding at worst.

Daniel was also happy. "It's a wonderful day. The crops are swollen with ripeness and the combine's coming this afternoon. It's much more efficient than Prince and Duchess and faster too." Anna knew what Daniel said was true, but she sometimes missed the horses.

Daniel leaned over so he could kiss Anna on the cheek. "You know, Mrs. Armstrong, I'm a happy man. I have you and the children and I'm doing work I like. Life doesn't get any better than this.."

Anna met his gaze. The previous night Daniel had experienced a nightmare so bad she awoke to find he had pinned her arms to the bed. She'd had to scream to rouse him. Amazingly, the children didn't stir. Thank God they were both sound sleepers. Thank God it was now daylight. Perhaps living a life he loved would help him overcome the emotional scars left by the war.

* * *

They finished the picnic and Anna and the girls gathered up the remains. Basket on her arm, she kissed Daniel farewell before taking the girls back to the house. It was a pleasant stroll, despite their slow pace.

Anna viewed her home anew and noticed the many changes they'd made over the years. They'd added a small bedroom complete with twin beds for the girls, and electricity. A Godsend. Anna hated kerosene lamps. She remembered how excited she'd been when the power pole went up in the yard. Her kitchen now contained an electric range. How she loved it after years of fighting with the ancient coal stove. She loved the refrigerator that replaced the icebox even more.

They'd also installed a telephone. It dominated one wall. They were the sixth member of a party line; their signal consisted of one long ring and five short. Anna had learned to be careful of what she said over the telephone. "Listening in" by others on the party line was a popular activity.

In response, Anna and Maisy developed a sort of code to describe George, Grace, Peter and Lottie. They laughed about it and made up more codes on the rye whiskey and laughter-fueled evenings they spent playing cards.

Anna hoped they'd be able to add a veranda onto the house this year. It was a realistic plan because the crop appeared bountiful. Anna couldn't wait to sit outside on the veranda come spring with a coffee and a magazine.

* * *

Anna heard the sound of a car in the driveway. It was probably George's new, maroon Cadillac. He bought a new car each year.

Amber and Crystal shrieked with delight and ran outside. They quite predictably failed to shut the door.

Anna's ears had not misled her. She came out the door to greet the impeccably dressed Grace and George. They both exited the automobile, revealing as they did so the swank, black interior of their car.

They greeted Anna stiffly, but hugged their grandchildren, and gave each of them a large dime chocolate bar.

Grace's eyes lost all their coldness as she gazed at her granddaughters. She might have been looking at Nancy, the woman both Grace and George preferred over Anna.

Anna's smile was genuine as she addressed George, the least formidable of the pair, "My goodness, this is so kind of you. Thank you so much. What do you say, girls?"

"Thank you," said Amber, her face covered in chocolate.

After some hesitation, Crystal also said, "Thank you. Hey, this is the same colour as our dog." Her face looked clean but a streak of brown marred her pretty dress.

All three adults laughed.

"That's why he's called Chocolate, dummy," said Amber.

Suddenly, the happy moment passed. Grace's eyes grew cold as snow. "Well, we've got to be getting home. We just wanted to see the girls."

Her back remained rigid as she walked toward the car.

George followed his wife, then turned back and smiled. "We're expecting you for supper on Sunday. We'll be having roast beef and Yorkshire pudding. We didn't see you last week." George referred, of course, to Anna's proclamation they only visit George and Grace once every fortnight.

Anna forced a smile. "Yes, of course. We'll be there. Thank you for the invitation."

Sometimes, she almost felt sorry for Grace and George, for they quite clearly adored Amber and Crystal, their only granddaughters. Jim and Peter had only sired boys.

However, Anna knew Grace would revert to her miserable coldness if given the slightest opportunity. She loved her granddaughters but would never accept their mother.

Anna sighed with relief when George and Grace reached their car. The Cadillac sprayed gravel as it left the yard.

* * *

Daniel's face glowed with happiness as he climbed into the cab of the shiny, new, red combine. To Daniel, right now, it was the most wonderful thing he'd ever seen.

The crop was perfect. The heads of wheat were so swollen the grain lay almost flat on the ground. There had been just the right amount of rain, just the right amount of sunshine.

With this bumper crop, he and Anna would be able to afford some luxuries. One of these included a trip to England. A plan Daniel had kept to himself because he wanted to surprise Anna. If the wheat prices would just hold, it could all come true.

Daniel had only advanced down the first row of the main field when a cold wind blew from out of seemingly nowhere. Within seconds thunder roared overhead followed by an almost immediate flash of lightning. Horribly, impossibly, hailstones thudded on the bent wheat heads and pinged off the combine. At first only small stones stung his back. He carried on, determined to finish the job. *"Please stop the hail. Please God."*

The prayer went unanswered. Within seconds the hailstones became larger, more ferocious. Daniel took cover under the combine, bruised and battered by the ferocity of the sudden storm. The crash and clang of the

136

hail striking the metal became the sounds of the anti-tank shells bombarding his Firefly.

Shells pierced the tank and he cowered. The men in his keeping, all lay dead. His heart pounded. His brain was almost numb with shock.

He had to get out. Now! They called the Sherman a Ronson. Like the lighter, it lit every time. And took only three seconds to burn. He scrambled to the hatch.

He clung to the undercarriage of the combine only vaguely aware of what he held, while his gaze turned inward.

Free of the tank, he crawled through the carnage, guns thundering, bombs flashing, blinding him. He heard again the bellow of his tank bursting into flames. Desperation drove him on. A trench, he'd fallen into a trench. He bit his lip so hard it bled. The trench full of dead men. He burrowed in among them, frantic to hide from the Germans he heard approaching. Cold, wet, fear, exhaustion. Then the welcome sound of Canadian soldiers bringing him struggling to his knees to call for help.

* * *

The hail lessened and turned to rain. Daniel dragged himself upright, leaning on the combine and gasping for breath. He wiped rain from his eyes and cursed at the devastation before him. The heavy beads of wheat were bent, broken and shattered as far as he could see. "Why God? Why?" he whispered between numb lips.

He kicked himself for not having hail insurance, it had seemed an unnecessary expense at the time. Without the money from the crop he couldn't pay the mortgage. He fought back bitterness, his parents would say it was punishment for not attending church, honouring God as he should. Anna would no doubt say God was just testing them. "Testing us, punishing us...cursed is what I am...cursed." There would be no money for home improvements, or a car, and no trip to England for Anna.

The hail storm would be sure to put a strain on his relationship with Anna. When he found a job in Lethbridge, Anna would have to do some of the farm chores. She had enough to do already. Fortunately, Anna didn't need luxury, but she and the girls did require a certain amount of money to live.

Daniel wondered how many others had been hailed out. Probably not Peter. Everything he touched turned to gold, just like Midas.

* * *

Daniel searched for a job. He tried speaking to other farmers. He devoured the want ads in the newspaper. He dropped into businesses around town. He grew busier than ever before. Searching for a job exhausted him.

Yet, he found nothing. The weeks and months went by, and soon November came. Still Daniel had no job. He felt as trapped as he had in the tank.

George surprised Daniel and Anna with a visit one particularly cold, blustery day. Anna stirred soup from a ham bone. It was the cheapest food she could find at the grocery store. Daniel perused the want ads.

Daniel happily admitted his father, ignoring the tension that existed whenever George and Anna occupied the same room. "Dad, it's good to see you. Come on in." He reached out and shook his father's cold, calloused hand. He motioned to a chair, but George remained standing.

George was alone, which was odd. Grace cherished trips into town. This obviously wasn't a pleasure visit. His face was dusty and he still wore gum boots and a red plaid shirt under his overalls.

"Girls, Grampa's here," Anna called the girls from their play in the bedroom.

The two beautiful children ran out, their little dog followed. "Grampa, Grampa," cried Crystal.

George's face lit up as he held out his arms to Crystal and then Amber for a hug. Chocolate jumped up and rested

138

his paws on George's knees, an indication he wished to be petted. George absentmindedly complied.

Suddenly, his joy faded. His voice grew stern. "Actually, this isn't a pleasure visit. I need to have a word with you, Daniel."

Anna said, "Girls, take Chocolate and go play in your room." Her tone was commanding and the children automatically obeyed. Fortunately, neither child said anything about chocolate bars. However, they looked disappointed as they filed out of the room.

Anna played the hostess. "Can I get you some tea? It'll only take a moment to get the kettle boiling. I've got real cream from our cow for it."

"No, thank you," said George.

Surprisingly, George remained standing. Daniel said, "Have a chair, Dad." He pointed to the best seat in their home, a comfortable brown rocking chair.

George slowly lowered himself into it. He'd recently developed arthritis in his knees. Once seated, he folded his hands together, an uncharacteristic gesture. He didn't look at all relaxed.

In contrast to the scene in the living room, laughter emanated from the bedroom where the girls played.

Daniel caught a gleam of satisfaction in his father's eyes. "I'll come right to the point. They're hiring dock workers in Vancouver. There's good pay and free transportation and accommodation provided. You'd have to stay at least six months but you'll make enough to cover your mortgage and then some."

Daniel clenched his jaw. His father wouldn't offer any financial support, although he could well afford to do so.

Nonetheless, this new development came as a jolt. Daniel stalled for time to think. "Dad, how did you hear about this?"

"You know Edwin Waters. Well, he's got family out there. It's probably heavy work, but you've never been afraid of heavy work." George leaned forward in his chair, earnest now.

Daniel nodded his acceptance, although he didn't know how much his shoulder could take. "The thing is, it's going to be hard to leave all this." He gestured toward the window. He believed his father would realize he meant the trees, garden, and fields. That was something George could understand.

However, George shut his mouth tight, in a gesture similar to his wife and said nothing more. Daniel refused to come any closer to asking for help. He would have to accept his fate. The unspoken words lay between father and son. This wouldn't be happening if he'd married Nancy Smyth, instead of Anna.

From the back pocket of his overalls, George produced an application form. His hands shook as he handed it to his son. However, his voice never wavered. "Just fill this out and sign it. According to Edwin, you're as good as hired."

Daniel swallowed his pride; at least it was a job. "Thank you, Dad. I won't forget this." The irony of the statement choked him.

George got up quickly, avoiding Daniel's gaze. "I'll be going now." He stomped out of the house.

Daniel didn't immediately say anything to Anna as he contemplated the situation. He must leave his beautiful land and even more beautiful wife and children and take up residence in Vancouver for at least the next six months. Possibly longer.

Finally, he spoke. "Anna, what do you think? What should I do? I hate the thought of leaving you and the children, and you're going to be stuck with way too much work to do. We'll both be lonelier than either of us can imagine. Yet, damn it. I can't think of any other solution. I'm sorry."

Anna sighed and she looked as if she'd aged ten years. "You're right. There's no other choice. I'll manage." She forced a smile. "And we'll write to each other at least once a week. It won't be as bad as you think."

He'd never been to Vancouver and he knew no one there. But the job was his for the asking. He must take it.

Chapter 10

The day began better than yesterday. The worst since Daniel left. It had begun with the laundry, a task Anna normally enjoyed. However, cold weather made it almost impossible.

Amber and Crystal had been inside all day and constantly underfoot. Anna worked around them as she went through the intricacies of heating water and applying soap, then rinsing and finally putting all the clothes and sheets through the wringer. Anna kept an eye on Crystal, worried she might get her small arm caught in the wringer. The small house had filled with an almost suffocating humidity.

Anna struggled to put the sweaters, dresses, stockings and underwear out in bitter, early January temperatures. Her wet fingers almost froze as she tried to pin the garments to the clothesline.

Worse still, the wet clothes froze. Anna brought them inside where they ceased to seem like mere clothes and almost took on personalities.

The girls had shrieked with laughter and played with the life-like garments while Anna strung lines across the kitchen to hang them. In their excitement, the girls managed to tear and ruin some of the garments. Anna bit her lip. There was no money to replace what was lost.

Amber and Crystal developed head colds. Anna, with great difficulty, forced them to lie down in their bedroom. She tried steaming them with a kettle containing recently boiled water. It didn't seem to help either child, it just made them irritable.

They developed hacking, persistent coughs. Anna had a sore throat and felt weak.

Anna knew her daughters' suffered from more than head colds. Amber and Crystal both missed Daniel and constantly asked, "Where is Daddy? Isn't he coming back?" And the worst question of all. "Doesn't he love us anymore?"

With tear stained eyes and a voice thick with emotion Anna reached out to her children and pulled them close. She crowded them both onto her lap. "Your father loves you very, very much but he had to go away because we need the money he's earning." She had kissed each child on the cheek.

Amber quite predictably asked what they needed money for. "We need money to live. It gives us almost everything we need. Our clothes, our home, and much of our food. I'm sorry but it will be a long time before Dad is back. It will be months. Many, many sleeps. But he'll be back. I promise you."

Amber said nothing more, but looked at her mother with sad eyes. Finally, she started to play with some wooden blocks.

It wouldn't be long until Amber or Crystal, or both of them, asked when Daniel would return.

The house chores were only part of Anna's problems. She also had the pigs, chickens and cattle to attend to, an exhausting job. Last night, when Anna went out to check on the cattle, she found one cow in labour. It was immediately apparent the birth wasn't going well.

Anna stayed with the cow, Spot, a gentle black animal with a white mark on her forehead. Anna, surrounded by bales of hay and the scent of manure, almost felt like a true farmer. Until she realized she didn't know how to help the poor, bawling cow.

She wanted to call in a veterinarian, but there was no money for that. Daniel regularly sent money and it helped, but they had accrued many debts while Daniel looked for work.

If the cow and calf both died, she would have to live with the consequences. And she had no idea how to dispose of the dead bodies. And that was only part of it. She actually loved Spot and would miss her if she died.

Fortunately, the calf, a large bull with a white spot on his forehead; finally arrived, and both the cow and calf lived.

Anna's elation was short lived. She didn't get to bed until four o'clock in the morning. She had to be up by six to do the milking.

Yet she'd survived and today appeared to be a little better.

Daniel also struggled. He wrote how he hated life in the barracks and was shunned because his nightmares kept his bunkmates awake. He was terrified he'd be fired.

He related how the foreman, a tall, lanky, red-haired man, put his hand on Daniel's good shoulder and told him he understood his predicament. He could stay. All the other men received ear plugs. After that, Daniel was accepted.

Anna lived for Daniel's letters. She felt his presence beside her whenever she read one of them. She always replied immediately and made her letters as cheerful as she could. She described how Jim helped with the chores and even drove her into town once a week. She also told him Peter and Lottie had been over.

She didn't tell him that when Peter and Jim had first come to repair the fencing, Anna had expressed her thanks with a simple, "I wish I had some way to repay you." The day had been crisp and clear. Anna had almost been blinded by the sun shining on the snow.

"That's not necessary," Jim had said with his characteristic grin.

"I can think of a way," said Peter and he'd reached out to his sister-in-law and held her close. He'd even kissed her neck. His arms were strong as iron and she had to admit a part of her wanted to respond to him she was so lonely.

Anna shoved him away and moved a couple of feet away from him so he couldn't grab her again. "Peter, I don't want you to come over unless you bring Lottie and the boys. I could never be unfaithful to Daniel. Leave me alone."

Anna was surprised when the next day Peter actually showed up with Lottie and their youngest boy, Sam, a handsome boy who resembled his father. Sam's older brother, Kyle, was in school.

Surprisingly, Anna and Lottie actually developed a friendship. It wasn't as deep a friendship as with Maisy. But it became a satisfying relationship. Because of it, Anna felt a little less lonely.

To Anna's surprise, one day while they sipped tea, Lottie confided in her. "I was jealous of you because I know Peter finds you attractive. I wish I could be pretty. I feel so inadequate beside you and Maisy. I can't help but like you because you are so nice." Beads of liquid had formed on Lottie's thin lips. Her close-set eyes brimmed with emotion.

"My goodness, Lottie. You surprise me. First of all, I don't think I'm at all pretty. My face is too thin. In fact, my whole body is too thin and angular. And my nose is too long."

Amber and Crystal, followed by Sam and Chocolate, raced into the house and demanded water. Anna got them some from a pitcher in the refrigerator. Then she told them to "scram." She wanted to continue her conversation with Lottie.

"But a great looking guy like Daniel loves me and wanted to marry me. It's what we are inside that counts, not how we look. I think everyone is at least a little bit pretty, including you."

Anna paused for a moment and eyed Lottie appraisingly. "I think you'd be even prettier if you wore your hair down."

Anna tentatively reached out her hand and gently touched Lottie's hair. "May I loosen it?"

Lottie held her breath but she nodded her acceptance. So Anna freed Lottie's fine, soft hair. It fell in waves around Lottie's plain face.

Anna smiled. "Yes, you're definitely pretty. I'll go get a mirror."

Lottie almost purred with pleasure when she saw the result. "Oh Anna, you are a true friend. I'm going to have Peter drive me over even when he doesn't work on your farm."

Tears of joy entered Anna's eyes. She reached out to clasp Lottie's free hand. The key to friendship contained empathy and a bit of ingenuity. "Thank you so much. I appreciate your friendship. It's difficult having Daniel gone."

It was an understatement. Despite Lottie, despite Maisy, despite Jim and Peter, Anna found herself desperately lonely.

She told herself to be strong. In order to do so she developed a strategy. She forced herself to live one day at a time. To not think about the past and certainly not the future. Only the present.

When she got through a day, she marked it off on the calendar and looked only to the next day. She tried not to plan nor worry.

* * *

Yes, today seemed better. She'd managed to finish the laundry. She would do the ironing tomorrow. It was a relatively simple task.

A Chinook had blown in and the girls could finally play outside. The plentiful sunshine seemed to help their colds. Anna's own throat no longer felt sore. Anna swelled with gentle pride. She'd survived.

* * *

By mid-morning Anna began to think that, with luck, she might have time for a cup of tea. Since the girls played outside, she had a few precious moments to herself. Only Chocolate remained. He'd be no bother.

145

However, before making it, she decided to lie down on the bed for just a moment and rest her weary eyes. She went into the bedroom and immediately dropped down onto the bed with all her clothes on, even her slippers. She fell instantly to sleep. She was exhausted by the events of last night.

Too soon she was awakened by an insistent banging on her door. This surprised her because Jim and Peter usually telephoned before they came over. Perhaps the caller represented one of those religious sects who advertised their faith. If so, she wouldn't buy one of their pamphlets. She didn't have money for things she didn't want.

It wouldn't be Amber and Crystal. They'd just charge in like they always did. *Would the caller scare the girls? Or maybe even hurt them? She'd better get to the door. Pronto.*

A curious Anna, still groggy with sleep, answered the door. The sun filled her with light and warmth. She squinted into the strangest pair of orbs she'd ever seen. The right eye was blue. The left brown. They belonged to a tall, lanky man with narrow shoulders. In that sense, she was reminded of Charles.

He wore shabby, ill-fitting clothes. Anna felt sorry for the stranger. She remembered her own lack of new clothing during the war years. Anna tried to peer around the man. She could see no sign of Amber and Crystal. *Oh God. Keep them safe.*

He shifted nervously. "My name is Willy Jones. Glad to make your acquaintance." He offered his bony, dusty hand and Anna shook it as gingerly as she could. Her pity rose higher. He was thin. Too thin. He needed a good meal.

"A man in town told me you might be looking for a hired man, considering your husband being gone and all. I walked all the way out here lookin' for work. That's all I want from you, M'am." His voice was hoarse.

Willy looked like the kind who'd stay for a while, do a mostly adequate job and then leave. Exactly the kind of person she needed. However, she couldn't hire him. "I'm sorry. It's impossible. I barely have enough money to feed myself and my children. I also can't offer you a place to sleep in the house." She didn't say it would be very bad for her reputation to have him staying without a chaperone. But it was certainly the case.

Willy's plain face fell. Anna suppressed a pang of guilt. "I'm sorry. I simply can't help you." She decided to offer him something to eat as soon as she found the girls. *God, where were they?*

Willy's face darkened and twisted as he shouted, "You bitch, you hopeless, ugly bitch." He grabbed the collar of Anna's dress and with one ferocious tug, ripped it down the front. Anna trembled in horror at the noise of the tearing fabric and the violence of his assault. She screamed and made an attempt to cover herself with her hands.

Chocolate began to bark and growl and nip at Willy's heels. Anna felt some hope. Maybe the little dog's attack would frighten Willy off.

"You miserable excuse for a dog." Willy's boot connected with Chocolate's rear and sent him sprawling into the kitchen. The loyal little dog yelped in pain but continued to bark. Carefully watching Willy's boots as he did so. *If only Wolfie could be reincarnated.*

Anna, her heart pounding and with adrenalin surging through her veins, ran into the bedroom. She hoped she could get the door closed before Willy entered the room.

He shoved the door hard and Anna almost instantly found herself lying on her back sprawled out on the bed. Willy flung himself on top of her, tearing at her underwear. Anna tried to fight him. She wanted to kick him in the groin. But he was too strong. He pinned her arms above her head and held her legs down with his knees. Anna struggled uselessly. Anna had always found Charles repulsive. Willy was all that times ten.

Willy held Anna's two hands with his right hand while his left tore at Anna's thin knickers. Soon they were little more than threads. He tried unsuccessfully to pull off her bra. "There's nothing there, anyway. They're not worth worrying about." Anna stared at his mismatched eyes as he spoke.

Willy shoved her thighs apart and forced himself inside her. The pain blinded her, the weight of his body almost crushed her. His stinking breath made her gag. She cried out in pained agony.

No one came. She wished herself dead. But she couldn't die. She had Daniel and the girls and her parents. *The girls. He could have molested them. He could have killed them.*

She could do nothing. Finally, she let the shock of the assault take her from reality and she hovered in a safe place in her mind.

"I walked ten miles to see you. To ask you for work, nothing more. And you sent me away. You deserve this, you fucking bitch."

Anna shook her head wordlessly.

Finally Willy finished, sticky fluid coated her thighs as he withdrew. He slapped Anna's face hard. "There, I'm finished with you. Now get out of my sight."

Anna was too scared to move. She lay where he left her, choking on her sobs.

The face disappeared from her sight and heavy footsteps echoed in the house, followed by the slamming of the door. The house was empty.

Anna let her anger push back the despair and pain. She willed herself to get off that bed and follow Willy. *No one could attack her and get by with it.* First, she must find Amber and Crystal. *Oh let them be all right.*

Without stopping for a coat and still just in bedroom slippers and tattered clothes, she grabbed the rifle from the hook on the wall of the porch. She didn't stop to see if it was loaded. She simply went after Willy.

She saw him walking down the road. She couldn't see anything of Amber or Cystal. Should she look for the girls or follow Willy? She would follow Willy. She *must frighten him off for good.* She'd know from his face if he'd harmed the children.

The gun weighed heavily in her right hand. Daniel kept it in case he needed to kill a coyote who ventured too close to the hen house. Anna had never shot a gun in her life, but she knew how. If Willy didn't promise to leave her alone, she would kill him, regardless of any legal consequences.

Despite the almost overwhelming pain, Anna moved quickly. She caught up with Willy where the property intersected their neighbours. Anna hoped no one would pass by and witness her bedraggled state, pointing a gun at a man. Fortunately, she remained alone with Willy. She could hear sparrows chirping. The gentle sound made herself and everything around her, surreal.

Almost out of breath, Anna managed to shout, "Where are my children? I'll kill you if you don't stop walking. I'll shoot you dozens of times if you harm my girls or ever try to rape me again." The gun shook in her hands. She was almost as afraid as she'd been during the rape. *Could she pull the trigger? See Willy collapse? See his blood?* God would never blame her if she shot Willy. Neither would the law. She'd be acting in self defense.

Anna stood up straight, tall and proud. She would never be a victim again.

Willy's face was twisted with fear. He reminded her of someone who'd received an electric shock. He hadn't expected her to follow him. His obvious fear fueled not only Anna's anger, but also her curiosity.

"I planned to offer you food. I felt sorry for you. You're evil. It's wrong to take your frustrations out on someone weaker or smaller." The gun suddenly felt heavy in her hands, but she continued to point it at Willy. "This gun makes me stronger and I'll use it."

Willy looked down at the ground and said nothing.

Anna bellowed, ""Talk to me or die."

Willy finally spoke; his voice low and forced and filled with fright. "I'm sorry. I'm sorry. I never saw any kids. What are you talking about?" He held up his hands in surrender.

Anna slowly lowered the gun.

The man took her action as capitulation. "You couldn't please your man so he deserted you. Desertion isn't good enough for the likes of you. You deserved a good screwing, so don't be so uppity."

149

Anna raised the gun with renewed anger. She heard the sounds of running feet and heavy breathing. Amber and Crystal followed by Chocolate, who remained wary of Willy, arrived. Anna was so glad to see them she had to stifle a cry of delight. They appeared unharmed. Nonetheless, she shuddered. The timing was bad. *Would she be able to protect them?*

Both girls were dirty and covered in hay. They carried their dolls dangling by one leg. Anna presumed they'd stopped their game and gone up to the house looking for her. They'd obviously run to the field when they couldn't find her.

The girls hugged Anna's legs. Anna hoped she wouldn't lose her balance or the grip on the rifle. She longed to scoop her daughters into her arms. She knew it was a futile wish. The gun was her lifeline.

Amber was the first to spot Willy. "Mummy, who's that man? And why do you have the gun out? You're bleeding and your clothes are torn. What's the matter?" Tears of anxiety filled her beautiful, hazel eyes.

Anna forced herself to appear calm. She still held the shaking gun, "Yes darling, this man hurt me. But I'm going to be all right." She stood as tall and straight as possible. *She was invincible.*

Anna's voice shook almost as much as her hands. "He's a bad man. Stay away from him. Not all men are good like your dad. If you see him, run and tell me. I'll get the gun and shoot him."

Willy seemed planted on his spot in the field. His eyes widened with fear at her last words. His fear gave Anna renewed confidence.

Amber looked confused as well as frightened. "I thought Dad said we had the gun just for coyotes."

Anna glared at Willy, "Usually, but we'll make an exception in this man's case. Now, go and don't come back."

She pointed the gun to the ground. Willy turned away and walked rapidly down the field, and then onto the gravel road.

His worn boots crunched loud on the gravel. Anna hoped he'd get blisters. She knew she'd scared him. She hoped it'd been enough to keep him away.

And she'd thought today would be better than yesterday.

* * *

Anna asked Amber and Crystal if they could please play in their room while Mummy had a bath. They seemed eager to comply. *They were rightly frightened by the "bad man."* Amber, particularly, was old enough to reason if he'd hurt Mummy, he might also hurt her and Crystal.

Anna placed a chair in front of the door so Willy wouldn't be able to gain entrance to her home a second time. Then she prepared to boil water for a bath.

The water warmed. Anna poured it into her small, galvanized tub. She found her Ivory soap and crawled in. She let the water soothe her sores. She washed the memory of the slap off her face. The bath helped. *Would she be able to make love to Daniel when he returned? She doubted it. She was too dirty and, by association, evil.*

Anna savoured the privacy of her bath, and decided Daniel must never know about the rape. Even though a small part of her wanted Daniel to find Willy, and beat him up. Hurt Willy as much as he had hurt her.

Of course, the bath water eventually grew cold and Anna knew she would have to get out. She grabbed her favorite towel, and realized she was still nervous and frightened. She vowed to secure a lock for her door. The gun aside, Willy might return while she slept.

For the sake of her children Anna knew she would have to act as normal as possible. So she disposed of the bath water and began to efficiently prepare their noon-time dinner, usually their biggest meal of the day. She forced herself to act as if nothing had happened as she and the girls consumed pork chops, mashed potatoes, and apple sauce.

However, Amber had a long memory. "Why did that bad man come?"

"He came to hurt me. But he won't be back. I'll see to it." Sudden tears filled Anna's eyes and her knife and fork shook in her hands, "Don't forget to tell me if the bad man comes back."

They finished their meal and Anna realized she had eaten very little. Crystal quite predictably wanted to help with the dishes. Anna lifted her onto a chair and let her assist with the drying. "Now, please be careful. You don't want to break anything." She said this although many of the dishes were made of metal and unbreakable.

Anna found it relaxing to be around her gentle youngest child. The dish washing was the happiest moment of this most miserable day.

* * *

Time passed and Anna saw no further evidence of Willy. She believed with reasonable certainty she had scared him off. Nonetheless, she was as nervous as a deer in hunting season.

She slept badly. Just before Anna fell into slumber each night she felt his presence. Her heart would pound and she'd find herself sweating. The days were less stressful than the nights because of her extreme busyness. However, she no longer played the radio. She wanted to hear if Willy or some other violent person approached. Consequently, she had no knowledge of current events. She fervently hoped no war had been declared.

At great expense, she'd had a locksmith out and he'd installed the best lock money could buy. Jock Edwards turned out to be a big, strong man who frightened Anna. He had the potential to hurt her even more than Willy. She was so afraid she avoided shaking the hand he offered. Before the rape, she would've found him attractive.

Jock sensed her fear. "Mrs. Armstrong, I believe someone has hurt you. I'm sorry it happened. You seem like a nice woman. You might feel safer if you call the police."

Anna looked at the floor as she mumbled, "I'll be all right now that I have a good lock."

Finally, she looked up and met his small but friendly brown eyes. "Thank you very much." She was still too afraid to shake hands.

Without any further word Jock walked out the door and headed to his car. Anna tested the lock and found it worked perfectly. She relaxed a bit when she heard Jock's car speed down the gravel driveway.

Nonetheless, as the days passed, Anna continued to experience persistent anxiety. Nothing would relieve it.

Her appetite dwindled to the point where she ate next to nothing. She grew thin everywhere except her belly. She tried to force herself to eat but she found she choked on her food.

She couldn't help but feel responsible for what had happened. She shouldn't have so freely opened the door. She should have greeted him with her gun in her hand. The rape had been her fault.

* * *

Anna didn't know when she realized she must be pregnant but there were many signs. She hadn't had her period for two months. She was often nauseous in the morning. And, thin as she was, her breasts and stomach expanded. She'd had similar signs with both Amber and Crystal, but they hadn't been as intense. Willy's child was sure to be troublesome.

Anna railed at life's unfairness. She'd had sex with Willy once. Only once and it had been rape.

How she hated the man. He had not only wounded her both physically and psychologically but would also almost certainly ruin her marriage.

She'd never be able to convince Daniel she'd been raped. He'd be certain to think she went looking for it. He would hate her and almost certainly send her back to

153

England in disgrace. And what would Grace and George have to say?

And what if Daniel didn't allow her to take Amber and Crystal with her? Even more unthinkable, she felt as doomed as an animal caught in a steel trap.

She thought about jumping into the water-filled dugout where the cattle quenched their thirst. She couldn't swim and would drown. Or perhaps she could use the ladder to climb up to the barn roof and jump off. The fall might not cause death, but it should be enough to cause her to miscarry.

Of course, like with drowning, she might die. Her own life wasn't worth a farthing, but she had her darling children and all the farm animals dependent on her. *She must live this hell.*

* * *

The days passed, the weeks passed and Anna felt more and more desperate. As she began to show, she took to wearing her coat even in these warm days of April.

Yet it didn't help. Her condition revealed itself and she could see herself growing larger daily. It was not lost on her in-laws. Grace, George and Peter arrived at her door early one morning. Not surprisingly, Grace led the charge. There were no pleasantries. Grace looked colder than Siberia. "It's obvious you're pregnant. It's equally obvious Daniel cannot be the father. You're ungodly." She pointed her finger as if brandishing a gun. "We hereby excommunicate you from our family. We hope to never see your face again." The trio turned and piled into George's Cadillac without a backward glance.

Anna sighed and tears filled her eyes as she went to the barn to do the milking. She asked herself, "What did you expect?" She realized it was exactly what she'd just experienced. She was pleased Jim and Maisy and Lottie hadn't been a party to what she'd just witnessed. Not all the Armstrong's were rigid and dogmatic.

She anticipated Daniel's return with fear and dread. However, she continued to write to him twice a week. She said nothing about the rape or her condition. It wasn't something she could explain in a letter. Thank God she was the only person who knew Daniel's address in Vancouver.

Two days later, Anna had just started to clean up the breakfast dishes when Jim called to ask if Maisy could come over this afternoon for a visit. Anna could hear the breath of someone listening in on the party line but she didn't care about the lack of privacy.

She felt happier than she'd been since she'd realized her predicament. Finally she'd be able to be alone with her dearest friend. Maisy would help her forget her humiliation. Hopefully, she'd also be able to explain. Anna spent the rest of the morning cleaning, something she hadn't done in over a month. She'd been too busy and too distraught to keep up with all the work. Sometimes she felt as if she could just curl up and sleep until she could sleep no more.

When bedtime came, Anna still couldn't rest. Despite the lock on the door, she feared intruders. She also imagined Daniel's angry face when he returned home and found her pregnant with a child that couldn't be his.

Nonetheless, Anna found the act of cleaning satisfying. For a moment, she had control, even if only over her surroundings. So she swept and washed the floor, wiped down the white cupboards, and scoured the stove and refrigerator. For today, at least, the house felt less like the locked prison she usually saw it as, and more like the house she loved.

Anna washed her hair with Breck shampoo and the result pleased her. Washing her hair seemed almost as emotionally cleansing as having a bath. However, she'd felt vulnerable with her head in the sink. Willy or some other rapist would be able to attack her from behind.

Yet, I have the gun and if necessary, I will use it.

Anna could hear her daughters' giggles from outside the house. She could tell from the nearby proximity to the sound of laughter that they likely played on the teeter totter just outside the door.

155

Even now, their laughter made her joyous. However, she hoped Amber wouldn't stand on the teeter totter instead of sit. She'd fallen off and broken her head open on more than one occasion in the past. Anna didn't like cleaning up head wounds.

Neither Amber nor Crystal appeared haunted by images of the "bad man" Anna had threatened with the gun. It must be wonderful to be so young and innocent.

* * *

Right on time, to a chorus of barking from Chocolate, Maisy appeared at her doorstep. Anna unlocked the door and reached out and hugged her friend. The human contact felt wonderful. Anna hadn't seen Maisy in almost a month, an unusual occurrence as they usually visited frequently. Anna had worn her loose coat whenever Jim dropped off groceries. Lately, she'd avoided going into Lethbridge.

Maisy smelled of Ivory soap and lemon oil. Anna sighed with happiness. *Finally, there would be someone to lighten her miserable mood.*

Amber and Crystal played outside. Maisy's boys were in school. *She had her friend all to herself.*

Maisy, as usual, looked beautiful. As beautiful as the birds outside Anna longed to paint. She wore a pink flowered skirt that emphasized her narrow waist and a soft long-sleeved cream sweater that complemented the colour in her cheeks. Anna felt plain in comparison.

Anna wore a baggy dress. It was not only shapeless, but also in a drab brown colour that did nothing for her complexion. The dress managed to make both her arms and legs look gangly and awkward.

In her previous pregnancies, she'd been told not only by Daniel but also by several acquaintances she'd never looked more beautiful. This was certainly not the case now. Circumstance affected everything.

Maisy seated herself on the sofa.

"I've got Earl Grey tea and a packet of chocolate-chip biscuits. I mean cookies." Anna stopped for a breath. "They're store bought. I didn't have time to bake. Would you like one?"

"That would be great and you can call the cookies whatever you like," Maisy leaned forward. "It's so good to see you." Her eyes smiled.

Anna put the kettle on and added loose tea leaves to her Brown Betty teapot. She placed the cookies onto a plate. She used her best cups and saucers and was happier than she'd been since the rape.

Anna seated herself across from Maisy so they could talk. She picked up a cookie but knew better than to try to eat it in Maisy's presence. She didn't want her friend to see her choking on her food. Something she now did regularly. Just yesterday, Amber had asked, "Mummy, why do you choke?"

Anna dismissed it as just something mothers sometimes do. Yet Anna knew, of course, the choking was the result of nerves. She'd tried extra hard to appear happy and relaxed throughout the rest of the meal. *Please God. Don't let me frighten my children.*

Maisy immediately recognized Anna's failure to eat. She reached across the small kitchen table and put her hand on her friend's shoulder. "Anna, eat your cookie. In fact, have several of these cookies. You're so thin. Thinner even than when you came over from England. I love you like a sister and know you're unhappy. What's the matter?" Maisy put down her cookie, stood up, and opened her arms wide to Anna.

Maisy had eyes, and George and Grace would be blabbing all over the countryside about her condition. Maisy knew what was the matter. She wanted to be told. She wanted to hear Anna's explanation. *Finally, someone cared.*

Anna remained seated because she felt tears enter her eyes. Her friend's love left her brimming with emotion.

She spoke slowly at first and then the words came out faster and faster until they created a virtual torrent. Her

157

confession completed, Anna began to sob. She sat with her head bent so low it almost reached her lap. She attempted to catch the tears with her hands.

Maisy wrapped her arms around Anna's shoulders, and held her close. Maisy ignored Anna's tears soaking her sweater and skirt. Oh Anna, I'm sorry. So sorry."

Finally, Anna ceased sobbing. She blew her nose on the one very inadequate handkerchief that she kept in her pocket.

Maisy shook her head back and forth. She was almost as overwhelmed as Anna. "I think you should call the police. This guy shouldn't get away with this."

"No," screamed Anna, "I could never do that. I don't want to tell a man I don't know what happened to me. I would be too embarrassed. Besides, Willy is a drifter. I'll probably never see him again. At least I hope I never see him again. Anyway, the police won't care. Without Willy, they won't be able to lay charges. I'll just be a silly woman with a story." Anna once again began to weep.

Anna felt much better with the telling; it was a relief to share her burden with a special friend who cared and understood.

Anna trembled with pent-up relief and fear. "Maisy, please don't tell anyone about this. I'm too frightened and embarrassed. I just want to forget the whole thing. But I can't. Oh Maisy, I don't know what to do."

Maisy's beautiful eyes filled with tears of understanding. She spoke in a whisper. Although with the children outside, no one would hear their conversation. "It's too late for abortion, and since it's illegal, the doctors who perform them are often incompetent. You might consider putting the baby up for adoption. Daniel loves your purity. He would never accept another man's child. Hopefully, the child will arrive before Daniel. There'll be talk but things might go better without evidence. It's what I would do in your place." Maisy reached out and put her hand over Anna's very cold one.

Anna took a sip of tea gone cold as she took in what Maisy said. Maisy did have a solution. Anna had hope. Her future needn't be so terrible. She'd have to bear the child of rape but she wouldn't have to keep it.

Willy undoubtedly had "bad genes." His child would be difficult to raise, and become a troubled adult. However, this child also had her genes. It may, in fact, turn out to be kind and loving. Could she give up this unique human being, this part of herself who was going to become her child just like Amber and Crystal? *She feared she couldn't.*

Anna began to wring her hands. "Oh Maisy, I don't know. I don't know if I could give up a child of mine. Even though that would be the simplest thing."

Anna heard the chirping of sparrows. "I guess I'm like my sister, Patsy, who had a child out of wedlock she kept. Robert is a great kid. Mine might be too.

"Keeping the child would cast shame upon both me and Daniel and my two older children. Keeping it is not sensible. Still, I don't think I can give it up. I'm already starting to love this child in my womb." Her face was red from crying.

Anna stood up, went to the sink and pumped some water into a glass. Her hands shook as she drank a small portion of it.

"I love you Anna. I'll always be your friend." Maisy would never again speak of adoption.

The months passed. Jim seeded her crops. Anna knew he did so against their father's wishes. Anna grew larger and larger. She could no longer hope to disguise her pregnancy. She suffered more and more for her morality.

One bright day in June, when the humidity felt wonderful after a spring rain and a rainbow graced the sky, Amber rushed into the house. "Why don't Granny and Grampa stop by anymore and give us chocolate bars? I saw their car go by and Crystal and I waved like crazy. But they didn't stop, although I think Granny spotted us. Don't they love us anymore? Amber's pretty face was filled with anguish.

She looked especially lovely in a white cotton dress that flattered her tanned skin. *How could anyone shun her?*

Anna knelt down and pulled her daughter into her arms. She smelt of the fresh air and grass. Anna felt nothing but love. "They're just busy, that's all. They love you. They'll always love you. I'll always love you." She kissed Amber's cheek. *How could two supposedly God-fearing people be so cruel?*

* * *

Two days later, Jim and Maisy took Anna into Lethbridge to pick up some groceries and other supplies.

Anna always felt some misgivings when she went to town. More and more, she would hear laughter and whispers as she passed people on the street. She couldn't help but wish she lived near a larger community where she wasn't known by so many people. A place like London. Well, she'd be back there in disgrace soon enough.

At least she knew she would always have her parents' unconditional love. *Would they believe she'd been raped? Yes, she decided, they would.*

Despite everything, Anna enjoyed the drive into Lethbridge. She couldn't help but be delighted about riding in an automobile in late June with the birds singing, the air warm and fresh and the crops bursting with new life. Even the wind had abated.

Anna felt like painting a picture. It would be of the five of them, all in their best clothes, traveling in Jim's beautiful new green Chevrolet.

They spoke about the pleasant weather, and their children, even though Amber and Crystal came along. Also their dogs. Maisy and Jim had a fine mongrel named Jake. They discussed the news. And they gossiped. Anna knew she created much of the latter within the community. Nonetheless, it was great to speak to adults once again.

Since Anna's confession to Maisy, neither she nor Jim had said anything about her condition. They were two of the kindest, most empathic people on the planet.

160

Anna was anxious as she walked alone on the sidewalk in front of Eaton's store. She didn't want to meet anyone. Thus, she grew frightened when she encountered her neighbor, Ned. She'd always liked Ned, and so did Daniel. He had dancing brown eyes and a happy grin. She'd always found him friendly and considerate.

Ned tipped his hat to her, a custom Anna had always liked. It appeared he wanted to chat. "How'd it go with that drifter...what's his name? Yes, Willy Jones."

Anna tried to make her voice calm, tried to keep her heart from pounding instead of just beating, "Actually, I didn't have enough money at the time to pay him. So he travelled on."

Anna twisted her wedding band. "Thanks for thinking of me, though."

Ned nodded. She saw him glance at her body. A look of distress crossed his pleasant face.

Anna felt as vulnerable as if she was naked. She could think of nothing further to say or do.

Ned tipped his hat to her again and carried on. Anna knew she couldn't blame Ned. He thought he did her a favour when he sent Willy Jones out to her farm. He didn't realize the trouble he caused her.

Anna soon realized her fears for her reputation were not baseless. She entered Woolworth's by herself. Jim, Maisy, Amber and Crystal were at the butcher shop. She was just starting to accustom herself to Woolworth's distinctive smell and crowded aisles when she spotted a woman she knew. Mrs. Edith McPhail.

Edith had always been friendly and openly admired Anna's accent. Today she dressed in a form fitting red dress, a red hat and even matching red shoes. She appeared to have gained weight, which suited her. Anna noticed Edith talked to a woman in blue Anna didn't know.

Anna hoped she hadn't been seen. She ducked behind a column of shelves stocked with cosmetics and beauty accessories.

Edith's voice carried. "I feel Daniel made a big mistake getting that English wife. Nancy Smyth says

161

Daniel hasn't been home in months and that woman is pregnant. No one knows who the father is. Furthermore, the Armstrongs are devout, and evidently Anna has taken Daniel away from the church. I wonder what he'll do when he comes home."

Anna felt her cheeks burn red with shame. A package of bobby pins fell at Anna's feet and she realized she had, in her misery, knocked them off the display. She was too embarrassed to pick them up.

Despite this disruption, the gossiping women didn't bother to see who stood behind the shelves and continued talking. They remained, despite Anna's clumsiness, oblivious to her presence.

The older woman in blue, tall and full-chested, with frizzy pin-curled hair, continued the conversation. "Apparently, George Armstrong says she's no longer their daughter-in-law. She has their son hoodwinked. George believes Daniel only imagines he's in love with her." Her voice carried even more than Edith's.

Anna stamped her foot down hard. She'd had more than she could handle. She left the protection of the shelves and showed herself to the two gossiping women. "Things aren't always as they seem. I'm a good person. A moral person. Perhaps too moral."

Anna turned and left the store. She forgot all about the things she needed.

The women stared after her open-mouthed.

Chapter 11

Daniel arrived in Lethbridge on a beautiful late September day. The skies were blue. The sunshine abundant. It was a day just as beautiful as over a year ago when the hailstorm had caused such destruction.

Daniel was proud of himself. He'd made good money and Anna's letters had told him the harvest had been bountiful. This year shouldn't be a repeat of last.

He'd been gone more than the requisite six months, but he'd made good money. He would now be free of debt.

Daniel's shoulder ached after all the hard work he'd done on the docks. However, he managed to ignore the pain. Today he would once again see beautiful, gentle Anna. And, of course, his daughters.

Together he and Anna had decided not to have any more children. It would be nice to have a boy, but Amber and Crystal made them a happy family.

He lived for Anna's letters. Now he'd be there in person to experience all he'd been missing.

The train ride home had been much like the train ride to Vancouver. And much like the journey back to Canada from England. They were experiences he would always remember.

Anna's journey had probably been dreadful. He knew war brides were subjected to dirty, unsanitary conditions, and extreme crowding. That meant no privacy and lots of crying children. However, she'd made it and he now had a perfect, loving wife.

He'd found the trip through the mountains exhilarating. He'd seen bears and deer and mountain goats.

The mountains were majestic and the air fresher even than on his farm.

There'd been fields of golden wheat on the prairies. He loved his beautiful country.

The docks where he'd worked had been putrid with rotting fish. Nonetheless, Vancouver was a gorgeous city. There were massive, beautiful flowers such as hydrangeas, and forests of grand oak trees.

On his one day off a week, he usually went to Stanley Park and never failed to find the experience restorative. He enjoyed the zoo and the many walking trails. His favorite paths snaked by the ocean.

Daniel knew Anna would love to paint Vancouver. It would remind her of England. In his opinion, Vancouver was the more magnificent because of its mountains and woodlands.

Daniel's co-workers told him Victoria on Vancouver Island was also a beautiful, charming city. But Daniel never had time to go there. He vowed to take Anna out to the west coast someday soon. He hoped they'd arrive on one of the few sunny days in summer. He hated the many winter days of dreary drizzle.

The barracks he'd stayed in were similar to those in the army. There was little privacy. But he'd somehow managed to grow used to the stench of hard working male bodies. And a part of him enjoyed being somewhere different.

Like a prisoner, Daniel had marked off the days on his calendar until when he could come home. He missed his family, of course. But he also missed Alberta's bright sunshine, even in winter, and the quiet beauty of his land.

He'd made some friends amongst his fellow workers and he told them all about Anna. He missed her with all his being. He wasn't entirely whole without her at his side. It was as if he'd lost an arm or leg. He'd rubbed her picture so much it'd grown worn and bent.

He became good friends with Percy Johnston, a handsome man with curly brown hair and blue eyes. Percy had grown up near Vancouver and introduced Daniel to

Stanley Park. He'd never been out west. Daniel extended a warm invitation to come out and visit.

Percy had also been in the forces and been wounded in Normandy. He'd been in the infantry, near the front lines, but somehow managed to survive. He'd suffered a shattered leg that thankfully took a very long time to heal.

Over beers one Monday evening, they'd exchanged stories. Daniel failed to share how he still felt consumed with guilt because he'd failed to look out of the hatch of his Firefly.

Neither Percy nor Daniel had anything to do with the prostitutes many of the other men visited on pay days. Daniel not only needed to save his money, he also wanted to remain true to Anna. Although single, Percy feared syphilis or gonorrhea.

Together Daniel and Percy would play cards when many of the other men left the barracks. They both enjoyed crib.

* * *

Daniel heard the conductor call in a loud, singsong voice. "Lethbridge." He touched his hand onto his rapidly beating heart and stared out his window at the familiar city. It seemed small and vacant after Vancouver.

He waited patiently for the female passengers to exit. This seemed to take longer than necessary, despite the fact he helped many of these women with their luggage.

His chivalry resulted in several invitations to dinner from the single ladies. One slender redhead with a very full bust line told him he was the handsomest man she'd ever met.

Despite all this, Daniel managed to be the first male out the door. Nothing would keep him from Anna.

He hardly noticed the weight of his own suitcase, although it was the large, heavy bag Anna had brought over from England. It weighed at least fifty pounds. Besides his clothes and personal effects, he'd packed it with gifts for Anna and the children.

He knew he was now even stronger than he'd been during the war. He could feel his suit jacket straining at his back, shoulders, and arms.

Finally, he stood on the station platform. He took a deep breath of fresh, dry air. He also revelled in the wide sky. He searched for a taxi and almost immediately found one. He hadn't told anyone when he would return. Of course, he could call Peter, or Jim, or even George. He didn't want anyone around when he greeted Anna. He wanted to surprise her. He imagined the look of delight that would brighten her beautiful features.

He believed the cab driver would appreciate the large fare. He decided as well to leave a tip.

Daniel was about to enter the cab when he noticed two thin, bearded men smoking cigarettes and gossiping. Both wore old, faded jackets and pants. One leaned against the station building. The other stood up right beside his friend.

Daniel heard one of the men say, "I guess he couldn't satisfy his woman. She had to look elsewhere." Daniel absently wondered who they were talking about and decided gossips came in both sexes.

Daniel settled himself into the backseat of the large, black cab. He smiled with contentment as he revelled in the wide, familiar streets. The cab driver had a thick Dutch accent. He didn't speak except to ask Daniel for directions. Daniel freely enjoyed the scenery.

They left the city and he noticed many of the crops had been harvested. The landscape was beautiful in its austerity. His eyes moistened when he passed by the homes of their friends and neighbours. He knew then just how homesick he'd been.

* * *

Finally, he told the driver to "turn here." They were approaching his driveway. He smiled as he surveyed his house, barn and outbuildings. He'd have to paint them soon. *Thank God, the crop was harvested.*

166

Chocolate ran around in circles and barked. He'd be embarrassed when he saw who'd arrived. Daniel's eyes filled with tears of happiness. He'd waited for this moment for months.

He paid the driver, a short, thin man with pale blond hair and thin features, and grabbed his suitcase from what Anna called the boot of the car.

She had lost much of her accent, but sometimes he still didn't know what she referred to. This thought caused the smile of anticipation on his face to broaden.

The next thing he knew Chocolate yipped with joy. He placed his front paws on Daniel's trousers. Daniel scratched Chocolate behind the ears and looked for Amber and Crystal. He found no sign of them. He was relieved. He loved his children but wanted time alone with Anna before he greeted his daughters. He desperately hoped Anna would be at home.

Daniel made his way to the door, scattering some chickens who'd escaped the coop. He was surprised to see the expensive lock on what had always been an unlocked door. Anna must have been nervous without him. He experienced a pang of guilt.

He knocked and heard Anna call, "Who is it?"

He said, "Daniel, your loving husband."

Anna said nothing more but he heard the lock turn and then he stared down into the tired, line-etched face of the woman he loved.

Anna's once beautiful skin had become mottled and colourless and she looked as surprised as he'd expected, but without the joy. Daniel surmised all the work she had to do must have been too much for her. The guilt returned.

Finally, he looked down at her body. He understood much. Too much. He couldn't breathe. It was as if he'd been hit with a hammer.

Anna, with her tired face and too skinny, swelling body had lost not only her purity but also her beauty.

It had been him who'd been laughed at in town. He was an obvious fool. Everything he'd believed to be true was actually false.

For a long moment, neither Daniel nor Anna spoke. Finally he said, "When were you going to tell me?" His voice contained both pain and sarcasm. He choked back the bile that'd entered his throat.

Anna wrung her hands. "I couldn't put it in a letter. I just couldn't." She looked pathetic.

He was obviously no judge of character. He'd fallen in love with the wrong woman. He felt like a punctured balloon as the love oozed out of him.

Suddenly, it was all clear. "Why couldn't you stay away from my philandering brother? I know he chases everything in a skirt. But I thought you knew better."

Daniel clenched and unclenched his fists. However, he would never hit a woman. Certainly not one obviously pregnant. To do that made a man lower than someone too afraid to open the hatch on his tank. Having it out with his brother would be another matter.

Anna's eyes grew wild with fright. "Peter never came without Lottie. I wouldn't allow it. I'm the victim of a horrible rape."

Then, through tears, Anna described a tale of rape by a drifter named Willy Jones who'd walked all the way from Lethbridge. It was a silly, fantastical story. He didn't believe a word of it.

Her words left him feeling even more like a fool. This woman had become nothing like the girl he'd fallen in love with.

Daniel grabbed Anna by the shoulders, and shook her hard enough to make her teeth rattle. "Now stop your silly crying and tell me the truth. I believe this Willy Jones may be the father. I don't believe your tale of rape." He screeched the words.

His lowered his voice an octave. "If you were raped, you'd have called the police. They'd have a record of your complaint." Daniel heard the wind whispering in the trees as he spoke. "We could call them now."

Anna just shook her head.

"Why didn't you say anything in your letters? You're missing your calling. You should write wild stories rather

168

than paint pretty pictures. You're not pure or innocent or good."

Daniel could feel vomit rising in his throat. He found this to be, in many ways, more painful than Normandy. His trust and love lay in ashes at his feet.

Anna became paler than he'd ever seen her. "Maisy suggested I give up the child for adoption. It wouldn't solve everything, but at least you wouldn't have to be around it all the time. I'm not sure I want to do that. Strangely enough, I've come to love this child inside me. Even if it's a child of rape. It's not the baby's fault."

Daniel could hear his daughters playing on the teeter totter. He fervently hoped they wouldn't stop their game and enter the house.

"And Daniel, I'm telling the truth about this child's conception. Believe me. I would never intentionally be unfaithful. I was too embarrassed and humiliated to call the police." Anna wrung her hands.

Daniel had to admit it. She sounded like she was telling the truth. But he doubted her ridiculous tale. Almost as much as he hated being the buffoon everyone laughed at.

"How do you expect me to believe such nonsense? Was this guy more attractive than me? With a bigger dick?" He felt his face grow red with rage.

Anna wrung her hands again and her voice revealed her fear. "Of course not, I hated the whole thing. Being with him was awful. Not like being with you, which is wonderful. Believe me, I was raped."

Daniel realized he wanted to believe her. He loved her that much. A man's love could be as strong as the mother's love she'd described.

Yet he found he couldn't. The story was too preposterous. He felt his heart pounding. And the bile entered his throat again.

Anna started to cry when Daniel pushed her into a chair and demanded she give details of the rape. He asked her again and again and her story remained the same. She couldn't be telling the truth, so she must be the best liar he'd ever met.

As she spoke, he saw a vision of a fluffy, beautiful white cloud disintegrating. It was followed by an ugly black cloud. The hallucinatory cloud formed at a spot just above Anna's head. It told him his life with Anna was disintegrating.

Finally, Daniel clapped his hands. "I've had enough of these lies. I can't stand the sight of you." He spit onto the floor, narrowly missing Anna's foot. She didn't flinch.

Anna's tears fell down her cheek and landed upon her shapeless dress. She appeared to have no handkerchief. "I've expected this. You can send me and the girls back to England."

"No, you can't take the girls. They'll stay with me and my parents." His voice was harsh.

He grabbed a kitchen chair and swung it wildly. "I'll go back and live with my parents. The three of us will raise the girls. George and Grace adore them."

Abruptly, Daniel set the chair down. "My parents may be overly religious, but neither one of them is promiscuous. And they are both obviously a better judge of character than I am." Despite his words, Daniel realized how much he hated the future he presented to Anna. He didn't see how he could manage the farm and the girls without help from his parents. He'd never let her take Amber and Crystal away from him.

About one thing he felt certain. He would never marry Nancy Smyth.

His children would have to grow up without a mother. He didn't know how he could explain all this to the girls.

Daniel didn't believe Anna could grow any paler. But somehow she did. "No Daniel. I can't live without my children. Young children need their mothers. I beg you; please don't send me away without them."

She made an attempt to bow before him but her bloated belly made the attempt ridiculous. She resembled a white-faced clown.

"You have the child in your belly. That should be enough." His voice was icy cold.

He knew his daughters would be miserable without Anna. And he didn't really want them raised in an overly puritanical environment as he'd been. Yet he remained rigid and cold.

He wanted to hurt Anna as much as she'd hurt him. She had ridiculed their life together. She would pay.

Conversation stopped when Amber and Crystal entered the house. They both smelled of the outdoors with their pretty dresses covered with straw and caked in mud, but he'd never seen anything more precious or beautiful.

They both ran yelling, "Daddy, Daddy." He kneeled down and pulled them into his arms. He was filled with love. *How could he send them away? Yet young children, especially girls, needed their mother. The situation was impossible.*

Crystal said, "Mommy said you'd come. She was right." Daniel kissed her and held her even tighter.

Daniel had a thought. Maybe his daughters would remember the "bad man" Anna had threatened to shoot. They might be able to corroborate their mother's story.

He realized a part of him, not a small part, still wanted to believe her. All so he could continue to love her. *Was he weak? Probably.*

It hurt him to think of someone else's arms around Anna. Someone pressing her slender body onto his chest, and then ultimately going through the intimate act of intercourse. Why had she brought this upon him?

When he questioned his children, Amber said, "Yes, Mommy called him a bad man. He tore her clothes and I saw blood." Amber held her head high and her voice was clear.

Amber stopped speaking, Daniel probed, "Tell me more."

"We're supposed to tell her if he comes back. So she can shoot him. Isn't it bad to shoot people? I thought the gun was just for coyotes?" Daniel failed to answer Amber's query. He decided she sounded rehearsed. It was obvious Anna had gotten the children to lie.

"Did any other men come to the house?"

"No, just Uncle Jim and Uncle Peter and the Watkins man. Mummy didn't buy anything. Aunt Maisy came, but she's not a man."

"How many times did the Watkins man come?" He felt like an interrogator for the CIA. Amber began to appear nervous. He'd have to quit with the questioning.

"He came only one time. Mommy says he won't come back if you don't buy from him." Daniel decided Amber's answers still sounded rehearsed but he let the matter be.

He couldn't help but remember how passionate Anna could be. He could understand. But he couldn't forgive. After all, he'd stayed away from other women the whole time he'd been gone.

Thankfully both children, because of their youth, failed to understand the impact of what was happening in their lives. Nonetheless, Daniel ached with grief. He'd probably never see his children again because he knew he would let them go to England with their mother.

Daniel decided he would wait until tomorrow to talk further to the girls. He certainly didn't feel like giving them the gifts he'd accumulated.

The pent-up stress left him craving sleep so he told Anna and the girls he would like to take a nap.

But Amber wouldn't let him leave. She was still too excited about his return. "Daddy, we're going to have a brother or sister. Mommy says it's in her tummy. I hope it's a sister. I don't like boys."

Anna's face was wild with agony and he knew she wanted to stop the conversation.

Daniel's voice filled with authority. "We'll worry about the baby in Mommy's tummy tomorrow. Right now, I'm going to sleep." Amber and Crystal both backed away from him in obvious alarm.

He abruptly turned and went into the bedroom, closed the door, which squeaked a little, and peeled off his clothes. Habit made him fold them neatly and place them on the floor.

Clad only in his underwear, he climbed into the bed and pulled up the covers. Late afternoon light filtered into the room. He felt safe in here. Safe from all of the craziness of his life.

He would let Anna handle the evening chores and the making of supper. He knew he wouldn't be able to eat anything. He would soon be as thin and bereft as Anna.

Despite his mental exhaustion, Daniel didn't sleep. He lay awake, feeling like an inert mass existing in shock.

He needed to think what to do and yet he couldn't face up to his problems. He wanted to stay in this bed for the rest of his life and sleep and sleep and never wake up.

Bedtime finally arrived. It must have been hours, but it felt like only minutes had passed before darkness had fallen. He'd have to once again face his life when the night ended.

Eventually, Anna came to bed. Daniel turned away and feigned sleep. The happy reunion he'd longed for had turned into the worst predicament of his life. Yet he wasn't going to let her know how much she'd hurt him.

He heard her changing into her nightgown, hanging up her clothes in their small closet, fluffing up her pillow, and then gently lying down on her side of the bed. Due to her pregnancy she seemed to take up a great deal of space.

She said nothing but he could hear her smothered sobs. His heart grew icy. What else could she expect?

* * *

The next day, after a near sleepless night, Daniel awoke to a feeling of disbelief. How could this be happening? How could he be so wrong about a person? He felt he couldn't trust any of his instincts.

He somehow summoned the resolve to act normally so he arose before Anna. He wanted to avoid any further encounters with her. He skipped breakfast because he was too upset to eat, and made his way to the barn and other out buildings. He milked the cow and fed the pigs and chickens. The animals treated him like a stranger. Chocolate was his only friend. He felt useless and totally alone.

173

The sun rose in the sky and it promised to be another fine day, weather wise. So he went into the field to stack hay bales.

He had no idea what he would've done if it rained. He felt too upset to further confront Anna, yet he knew he would have to. She had ruined his life. She didn't deserve his compassion.

Despite his sore shoulder, the physical labour helped to ease his emotional pain. It also afforded him time to think. He didn't know if that was good or bad.

He may have to go live with his parents, but he'd still have his land, which he loved almost as much as Anna. He realized with a shock his every thought reminded him of Anna and the present crisis. He attempted to force himself to wipe her from his thoughts. Yet found it impossible. His mind whirred with emotions.

One minute he thought of how much he still loved Anna. And he tried to believe she'd been raped. It was a terrible, evil thing for a man to do to a woman. It brought fear and physical and emotional pain. During those moments he could forgive her for ruining his life because it wouldn't be her fault.

The next moment he would, in his mind, declare her story ridiculous. And he would never pardon her for leaving him mocked and deceived. At those times he hated her almost uncontrollably.

Daniel was tossing a bale up high to the top of the stack when he heard a familiar voice behind him.

"I'm bleeding. Bleeding badly. I think I need a doctor."

For a moment, just a moment, he felt the urge to tell her to go find her lover and let him deal with her problems. However, he would never do such a thing. He'd have to turn around and see if she really was consumed with agony. Maybe she just wanted his sympathy.

He turned and saw Anna's face contorted in what appeared to be agonizing pain. Worse still, fresh blood soaked her dress and ran down her legs. He placed his hand over his hammering heart. *Anna could die.* Panic assailed him.

Nonetheless, he knew he'd have to act quickly and instinct took over. He would carry her. He began to lift her. But she clutched her stomach and shrieked. "No, you'll never make it that far carrying me."

She was probably right. He had no choice but to help her walk. He clasped Anna's small, cold hand and helped her walk through the field.

The fact the crop had been harvested made walking easier. Nonetheless, at one point Anna tripped on the uneven ground and would have fallen if Daniel hadn't managed to keep her upright. Neither of them spoke. *Was she hemorrhaging?* He didn't know how much blood she could lose and still survive. The clasp of Anna's hand grew weaker and weaker.

Finally, he did pick her up. She didn't resist.

At first she seemed light in his arms. However he found himself gasping for breath by the time he entered the yard and saw the blue Chevrolet he'd purchased a couple of years ago.

Yet, despite his burden, Daniel ran the last few yards to the car. He thanked God the keys were in his pocket.

Although he found it difficult, he somehow managed to continue to hold Anna and still open the passenger door. He lifted her onto the seat. She slumped against the window when he closed the door, barely conscious. Despite his peak physical condition, his arms and back ached. The pain in his shoulder was excruciating.

Daniel's hand shook as he inserted the key within the ignition. *Thank God. The car started immediately.*

He left the yard and headed down the gravel road as fast as he could. Both his and Anna's heads bumped on the roof of the car. Daniel feared he would lose control of the vehicle, an easy thing to do on gravel. He feared slowing down even more.

He was relieved when he remembered Amber and Crystal played over at Jim and Maisy's. He certainly didn't have time to go find them now. He'd give his brother a call later.

Sweat poured off his forehead as he prayed silently this ordeal would have a happy ending.

Anna moaned and she slumped further in her seat, as floppy as a dust rag. *Please God. Don't let her lose consciousness. Anna must not die.* He realized how much he still loved her. Even if she wasn't innocent, he loved her. Her voice, her warmth, her gentle mannerisms all contributed to his love.

Loving her now may not be logical or rational. But he still did, and he would forgive her. His love was unconditional. The same kind of love he used to believe she gave him. The kind of love everyone needed.

She'd been left all alone in difficult circumstances. She'd been vulnerable. And maybe she didn't lie. Maybe she'd been raped. If Anna lived, he would believe her story and love her even more. He would never mention the rape again.

Daniel prayed aloud. *"Please God, let Anna live. I'll love her for all eternity."*

He took his eyes off the road long enough to glance at Anna. She still sat slumped against the passenger window. More and more blood accumulated on her dress and pooled on the floorboards. Her face was as pale as a winter morning after a snow storm. She winced every time they hit a bump on the road.

He didn't see any other vehicles and he didn't slow down. A high speed was more important than eliminating Anna's discomfort.

For the first time on this journey, Anna spoke. "I feel like I'm going to faint. Oh Daniel, I'm so afraid." He had to strain to hear her words.

Daniel gripped her arm. "I love you. I won't let anything bad happen. Here's the city now."

Daniel sighed with relief. He could finally drive on pavement. He pressed down harder on the accelerator, ran two red lights and almost hit a car. He didn't encounter any police.

176

They reached the hospital. Daniel parked on the grass because the lawn was situated close to the entrance. He ran inside.

He encountered a nurse or receptionist, a short, stocky brunette, dressed all in white, who looked like nothing would hurry her. She started to say, "We have to process all our patients. Are you..."

Daniel, his face red, shrieked, "Get a doctor. Do it *now*. My pregnant wife is bleeding something terrible. If you don't do something immediately she'll die."

A half dozen people, mostly well dressed, were seated in the nearby, stark waiting room. Their faces registered curiosity and alarm. Daniel failed to notice any of them.

The nurse moved her bulky body at an abnormal speed and walked rapidly through a swinging door. "Dr. Reynolds. There's an emergency. There's a woman with a great deal of blood loss and an overwrought husband. Please come immediately." Despite the fact she used the word "please", it was a command.

A tall, thin man with a mustache immediately answered the summons. He wore a blue shirt and blue striped tie underneath a white lab coat. A relieved Daniel saw the doctor moved rapidly. "What caused the bleeding?" Daniel motioned to the outdoors and both men ran into the parking lot.

"I don't know, but she's pregnant." Daniel found it difficult to breathe, the result of anxiety. Not exertion.

"Has she been getting vitamins and proper prenatal care?"

Daniel knew she probably hadn't, considering the conditions under which she'd been living. He groaned. "I've been away for several months so I haven't been able to properly look after her. But I kind of doubt it. I just got back yesterday."

He'd been going to tell the doctor he hadn't known of the pregnancy. He decided against it. If the child lived, he wanted everyone possible to believe him the father.

* * *

Daniel reached the car before the physician. When Dr. Reynolds arrived, he peeked in at his new patient, "I believe she's lost consciousness. We could get a stretcher, but it might be faster if you carry her."

"Of course," He gently but quickly lifted his wife out of the car. The adrenalin-charged Daniel found her light as eider down.

The doctor closed the car door and followed Daniel and Anna into the hospital.

Within seconds, a stretcher arrived. Two staff members in white lab coats wheeled Anna up to the operating room. Blood continued to pool under Anna.

Please God. Please make Anna live.

Dr. Reynolds and Daniel followed the stretcher down the long hallway. As they walked, the doctor explained, "We're going to do an emergency C-section."

Daniel didn't know what that meant and he felt too frightened to ask for an explanation. However, he was relieved Anna appeared to be in qualified hands.

A nurse appeared; this one tall with dark curly hair and a florid complexion. Daniel would have found her attractive in other circumstances.

She took Daniel by the elbow and guided him to another room. It smelt of antiseptics, "Dr. Weinstein will do the operation. He's an expert on the procedure."

The nurse closed the door behind them yet still spoke softly. "Your wife has excessive bleeding. The placenta has to be removed. It's dangerous. We'll give her blood transfusions. She'll have the baby by Caesarean Section."

She opened the door and motioned for Daniel to follow her. "You'll have to wait in the room with the other expectant fathers."

* * *

Daniel's throat was dry as he entered the waiting area. It was a sunless space with comfortable looking brown furnishings and a green rug over dark linoleum. Magazines littered the wooden coffee table. He spotted several copies of National Geographic.

He found the room occupied by three men. One quietly read a newspaper. He wore a green work shirt and dark blue overalls. He smiled at Daniel. "You look nervous. This must be your first. Edith, my wife, is having our sixth. There's rarely something to worry about. Sit down and relax."

Despite the comfortable looking furniture, Daniel knew he couldn't sit. He was filled with fright. However, he knew he'd have to respond to this man. "This is Anna's third." He found he still couldn't say "our. "And there's plenty to worry about. Anna has lost a lot of blood. She might die."

Daniel felt as if he'd been hit with a hammer. Suddenly, his head felt too weak for his body and he lowered it. He looked as if he examined the floor. Talking about the situation had made it more real.

All three men looked shocked and grave and introduced themselves.

Doug was a handsome blond young man with a terrific grin. Andy was short with sandy brown hair and freckles. Andy said, "We'll be praying for you. So don't you worry." Steve was the man who'd first spoken.

Daniel softly stated his own name. None of the other men spoke further about Daniel's worries but three pairs of eyes conveyed their sympathy. They obviously could think of nothing further to say.

Daniel paced around and around the large room. He couldn't bear to just sit. The movement helped him relax just a little. He smoked cigarette after cigarette until he ran out. He was too agitated to make the trek to the smoke shop so he was forced to do without.

179

As he silently paced, he thought of Anna and her story of rape. Suddenly he felt like a jerk for not initially believing her. And he could understand why she couldn't have an abortion. He would be a father to the child he secretly wished would be a girl. He didn't want a junior Willy around.

Doug finally left his chair and tapped Daniel on the shoulder. "Doctors can do a lot these days. Let's go down to the cafeteria. You need to relax. You look as if you're about to explode."

Daniel tried unsuccessfully to smile. "No thanks, I'm going to stay right here. I don't want to be away when they come to tell me about Anna. And you're right, I'm about to explode."

Daniel knew the men just tried to help. But no one but God could help him. *Please God. Don't desert us.*

* * *

Soon Steve, Doug and Andy had left the waiting room with happy congratulations from the nurses. Other expectant fathers, all of whom conveyed sympathy with words or gestures, soon replaced them.

Hours passed and Daniel still paced. He longed for a cigarette, his familiar antidote to tension. But he knew he wouldn't leave. He hadn't eaten all day but didn't feel hungry.

Finally, at about six o'clock p.m., a short, slight man entered the waiting room and approached Daniel. Like every other doctor he'd seen, he wore a white coat splattered with blood. Anna's blood.

This must be the surgeon, Dr. Weinstein. He looked tired and wan but he spoke with energy. Daniel thought he detected relief in the doctor's eyes. Daniel willed God to let this intuition be right.

Daniel held his breath as the man spoke. His voice sounded deeper than Daniel had expected it to be as Dr. Weinstein was a small man. Daniel had never listened to anyone more attentively. "Your wife, thanks to transfusions, is going to be fine. In a moment, we'll bring you your daughter, who is also just fine." The doctor had small, white teeth and a genuine smile.

Daniel felt the tension leave him with a wonderful sense of relief. Anna would be all right. God had answered his prayers. *Thank you, God. Thank you."* He grabbed the doctor's hand and pumped it so hard Dr. Weinstein winced. "You're a good doctor. No, you're a great doctor. Thank you."

Moments later, a petite red-haired nurse came in carrying a baby wrapped in a pink blanket. The nurse pushed her long hair behind her ear, and smiled. "Would you like to meet your daughter?"

Daniel, still shaking with emotion, took the child, a tiny perfect bundle who appeared awake but not fussing. She had dark hair and a rosebud mouth and a complexion like Anna's when he'd first met her. In fact, everything about her looked a lot like Anna. He could and would love this child.

She didn't look wrinkled and crushed as Amber and Crystal had. Perhaps it had something to do with the C-section birth.

He said to the nurse, "Yes, this is my daughter. I love her."

* * *

Two days later, the hospital staff finally let Daniel see his wife.

After meeting the baby, he'd gone home to look after the girls. They'd enjoyed playing with their cousins.

Playing mother hadn't been easy. They'd survived almost exclusively on peanut butter sandwiches on stale bread. And canned soup, which he managed to burn. Furthermore, the laundry piled up and he'd had no idea how to do it. He realized anew how much he appreciated what Anna did at home. He wondered how he'd ever contemplated living without her.

181

* * *

He wore his navy blue suit and a white shirt and blue-striped tie the day he went to visit Anna. Maisy whistled in appreciation when he came to drop off Amber and Crystal.

Maisy's blue eyes were bright with happiness. "You look great, brother-in-law. I can see everything's working out and I'm glad. I love Anna like a sister. In fact, I love her more than my sister because Louise is too bossy."

Daniel grinned then. His wide, lopsided grin. "I like Anna better than Louise, too. Say, do you happen to know where there's a good place to buy flowers? I want the best for Anna."

Maisy, demure in a red checked housedress covered by a white apron, smiled back. "I would try the hospital's gift shop. They'll have flowers."

Sure enough, Daniel found a dozen red roses, Anna's favorite flower. The florist told him red roses signified passion. Something he felt almost as much as tender love. He carried them through the maze of corridors that constituted the obstetrics portion of the hospital until he found Anna's room. Fortunately, she was the only occupant.

Anna, dressed in a shapeless hospital gown, sat up in bed holding the baby with a wide smile on her face.

The infant was bundled in a pink blanket Daniel surmised must have been supplied by the hospital. He hadn't thought to bring any of Amber's or Crystal's baby clothes but he knew there must be some around the house. Anna never threw out anything useful.

Anna smiled tentatively when she saw Daniel. The smile widened when she saw the flowers.

Someone had combed Anna's hair, and although she appeared pale, she looked rested. She winced with the pain of movement as she reached out her hand so Daniel could hold it. "Thank you for the flowers. They're beautiful."

Daniel put the vase of flowers on the table next to Anna's bed and he noted how much they brightened the sterile room that had been painted a hideous green.

Daniel pulled up a chair and placed it so he could be as close as possible to his wife, "Those flowers have nothing on you, kid."

He clasped Anna's hand between his two large ones. "I've been a first class heel. I believe you were raped. I love you and I'm grateful to God you didn't die. I could never live without you."

Colour returned to Anna's cheeks. She sighed with happiness and smiled. "I love you too. So very much. I'm relieved you believe me. It's true, even if hard to fathom. And Pearl is beautiful and a part of me. I hope you'll get to love her."

Daniel reached out and pulled back the blanket so he could once again take a look at the baby, a miniature Anna. "I love her already. Pearl, is that what we're calling her?"

"Yes, if you like." Suddenly, Anna once again became beautiful. Her cheeks glowed and her eyes appeared warm with happiness. She looked just like she had on their wedding day.

"I like. She looks like a luminous pearl. My daughter is beautiful like her mother. I'll always love you." Tears of happiness filled Daniel's eyes.

The red-haired nurse entered Anna's room. "You'll have to go now. Mrs. Armstrong needs her rest." She spoke with compassion.

The nurse left. Daniel planted a chaste kiss on his wife's cheek. I'll always love you."

PART 4
1957

Chapter 12

May brought spring all new and fresh. Anna had spotted more than one robin, a harbinger of this delightful season, and the grass was green and beautiful.

Anna looked ahead to the coming summer. Besides her vegetable garden, she planned to plant some rose bushes and carnations. Together the two flowers made beautiful bouquets.

The Armstrong family drove to Lethbridge in Daniel's aging blue Chevrolet. Everyone had things they wanted from town. Daniel needed hardware from McLeod's, Anna groceries, and all three girls wanted nail polish.

They even planned to paint their toenails. Anna told them they could each choose a polish. She knew they would all choose red, the colour currently so much in style.

Anna gazed at her reflection in the rear-view mirror and pondered just how good the last five years had been for the entire family.

Certainly their finances had much improved. And Anna bought and grew the best of food. It not only reflected on her face, which had filled out, but also on her figure. Her chest and hips were fuller. And despite the birth of three children, her waist remained small.

The feminine clothes of the 1950's suited her. Like a page out of her mother-in-law's style book, Anna wore black under her new spring coat. The dress featured a fitted bodice, nipped-in waist, and a flared skirt. She wore silk nylons and black pumps. She'd had her hair cut so soft waves framed her face. Daniel loved the hairstyle and said it made her look like Lauren Bacall.

They'd all purchased new clothes for Easter and were glad to once again have an opportunity to wear them.

Anna glanced into the back seat to check on her children. Miraculously, they weren't fighting or giggling. They all seemed to be engrossed in their own thoughts.

Amber, now eleven and looking more like her father daily, appeared radiant in a gold dress and matching sweater.

Crystal was, as always, beautiful. Her long blonde hair almost reached her waist and her blue eyes were fringed with thick, dark lashes. She wore emerald green.

Pearl, in her fifth year, wore a pink coat, white leotards and black shoes. The colour pink suited her. She wasn't as beautiful as her sisters. She was, after all, sired by Willy, not Daniel, but she exuded her own special brand of prettiness.

More importantly, Pearl had a delightful personality. There was no evidence of Willy's nastiness. She reminded Anna of Crystal. Both girls were placid and even tempered. And, compared to their older sister, unambitious.

Pearl loved to sing. She would listen for hours to songs on the radio and then sing them. Anna would've liked to get a piano for Pearl but they lacked space in their home for such a luxury.

Pearl enjoyed a happy existence with few people remembering her conception. She believed Daniel was her father in every sense of the word. Anna hoped she'd never have to learn otherwise.

Even George and Grace now accepted her although it hadn't all been easy. At first, they'd avoided Anna and Daniel and the girls as if they all had smallpox before the vaccine.

Then, about four years ago, this changed. Crystal spotted George and Grace at school. They'd come for a special meeting. She ran up to them. "Granny, Grampa, I miss you."

She'd peered up at them, her face as cherubic as an angel. "You never stop in to see us, you just drive by. And I miss Christmas Day at your house."

A tear had filled her left eye and run down her cheek. "You've never even met Pearl and she's really nice and pretty too with dark eyes. Why don't you come see us anymore?"

That had been enough for Grace and George to issue an invitation for dinner. It didn't hurt that Daniel happened to be the only son who'd produced girls.

Now Anna had no reason to fear her in-laws. They almost ceased to treat her like a heathen. The Armstrong clan was less divided.

Life was good. They'd built onto their house. It now contained three bedrooms and the veranda Anna had always wanted.

They purchased rocking chairs. Anna and Daniel loved sitting out on the veranda on warm summer nights when the mosquitoes weren't too ferocious.

* * *

The short trip to town ended and the Armstrong's were all in the elegant post office building gathering their mail from box 571. Daniel turned his key in the lock and opened the brass door. Numerous bills, advertisements and even letters fell out of his hands and onto the floor.

One particularly interesting looking envelope caught Anna's attention and she bent to pick it up. She saw the return address originated from an apartment in Birmingham, England. Anna immediately recognized her sister, Patsy's handwriting. It was a pleasant surprise because Patsy rarely wrote letters.

Anna tore open the envelope and shrieked with joy. "It's a wedding invitation from Patsy.

"Mum said she went with a fine chap but I didn't know she was getting married. This is very exciting. She doubts we'll be able to come but on the chance we can, she wants

186

me to be her matron of honour. Wouldn't that be great? It's too bad we live so far away."

Anna caught the eye of a large, stout man also gathering his mail. He glared at her and she realized she made way too much noise.

Daniel rubbed his chin. An indication he was mired in concentration.

After a couple of moments elapsed, he smiled happily. "Maybe it's not impossible. The crops have been good for several years now and we've got quite a bit of money in a savings account in the bank. I'm sure Jim will do the chores."

He took the invitation from Anna and glanced at the careful writing, as if to ensure its authenticity. "The wedding isn't until June, after the crops are seeded. So I say we go. That is if you can stand another voyage."

Anna felt herself fill with shock. She had dreamt of this, longed for this and now it would happen. She'd be able to see her parents and Patsy and Robert and England, the land she still thought of as home. She began to smile and it broadened until her cheeks ached.

Daniel continued to plan. "I guess we'll have to be gone for about eight weeks. At least four will be devoted to travelling but that should still give us time for a nice visit." Daniel's eyes were clear and untroubled. Crystal clapped her hands. "We get to meet our other grandparents, and we'll see England. Mother has told us so much about it. I can't wait."

Daniel nervously cleared his throat. "No, I'm sorry but we can't afford to take you kids. And there won't be room for you in Michael's and Margaret's small house. You'll have to stay with Granny and Grampa."

Crystal and Pearl both appeared near tears.

However, Amber became so excited she almost screamed. "I'll save up my allowance. I'll get a paper route. I'll find the money."

Daniel sighed and his voice grew stern with finality. It rose above the sound of footsteps on the floor. "No, it's impossible. Your allowance is too small. You can go when you're older. I'm sorry."

Anna touched Amber's shoulder. "We'll find you girls something nice in England and maybe something special today besides nail polish. What do you say?"

All three children appeared at least partly placated.

Daniel turned and walked rapidly towards the exit. His footsteps thudding on the floor. He held the door open for Anna and the girls. However, Anna saw some of his characteristic unhappiness return to his face. *Thoughts of the war were never far from his mind.*

Despite this, she beamed.

* * *

They travelled by train to Montreal. Anna found, in contrast to her trip out to Canada as a war bride, she now enjoyed the journey. She decided this must be because Daniel was much better company than a gaggle of frightened English women embarking on a wild trip to an unknown land.

The train had a berth, which Anna loved. She enjoyed sleeping in the small, cozy room with what seemed like the whole world passing outside their window. And she loved it when the conductor joked with them as he made up their beds.

The dining car produced excellent meals served with fine linens and silverware.

Anna discovered both she and Daniel had a taste for luxury. They particularly enjoyed having their morning coffee, and bacon and eggs served by friendly, solicitous Canadian Pacific staff.

Nonetheless, the journey seemed never ending and the scenery often bleak and boring. There seemed to be nothing but trees in northern Ontario and they all looked alike.

Daniel told Anna she'd enjoy travelling to Vancouver by train, the journey through the mountains apparently beautiful. She made him promise to take her soon.

They made friends with several other couples and one of these couples reminded them of Reg and Julie, their long-time friends from when Anna and Daniel first dated.

This new, friendly, good-looking couple, Allan and Sylvia, loved to go to the bar car where they happily consumed good scotch whiskey. Not surprisingly, Allan's ancestry traced back to Scotland. Sylvia, a tall blonde from the Yorkshire countryside, had also been a war bride. They'd gotten on the train in Moose Jaw. The two women exchanged addresses and Anna promised to write.

Anna still wrote to Reg and Julie and through the mail they followed each other's triumphs and tragedies. Julie had miscarried twice but had finally produced a daughter, Luella, who looked much like her mother.

Anna had sent pictures of her three daughters. Julie had written back with her thanks and added both she and Reg enjoyed good health. Their farm prospered.

Anna couldn't wait to write to them and describe this trip back to London.

* * *

At Montreal, they boarded a grand new ship, The Empress of England.

Anna felt like a princess as she saw the beautiful, luxurious vessel. They had only booked tourist class cabins, but had access to the delightful Empress Room where they enjoyed entertainment and the best of food and drink. All a flagrant contrast to the crowded Aquitania she had travelled on before when she journeyed to Canada.

She now enjoyed a small yet extremely comfortable state room. There was a complimentary bowl of fruit. Maids cleaned and made their bed. Anna felt extremely pampered.

She had many occasions to wear the black dress she'd purchased for Easter. Each time she wore it Daniel told her how sexy she looked.

Fortunately, Anna managed to escape seasickness because of a calm ocean.

189

As on her previous journey, the food tasted scrumptious. However, unlike on the journey to Canada, Anna had become used to delicious, plentiful food so she took the fine meals more or less for granted.

Anna felt, throughout this whole journey, as if they'd gone on a honeymoon. A honeymoon without the threat of war or absences. She didn't have to cook or care for children. It wasn't she didn't like these activities, and they actually gave her a reason for existing. Nonetheless, it was wonderful to take a break from them.

She had Daniel all to herself and they had time for sleeping in and lovemaking. Daniel remained handsome and sexy and she enjoyed sex completely. It was wonderful to not have to worry about the children listening in from their nearby bedroom.

Just like on the train, they made friends and once more exchanged addresses. There were stimulating activities and just the right amount of time for rest.

Anna and Daniel talked about everything. They found their values still meshed. Daniel was an ideal husband. Even with his continuing struggle with shell shock, she grew to love him more and more each day.

Daniel told Anna his psychologist, Dr. Mathews, had suggested he take a side trip to nearby Normandy while he vacationed in England. Apparently Dr. Mathews thought it might just exorcize his demons. Daniel had found Dr. Mathews at Anna's urging. The two men had established a rapport. Anna prayed for Daniel's recovery, but didn't feel overly optimistic.

* * *

Mid-morning on a sunlit day, the ship docked at Liverpool. Anna and Daniel soon began the process of disembarking. They had changed into their best clothes. Anna wore her black dress and Daniel his only suit. They looked affluent and stylish.

The ship sounded its horn and its resonance momentarily silenced the din of voices.

Then, Anna once again heard Canadian accents and British accents and even some Irish and Scottish. Together they created an excited cacophony of sound.

Anna raced ahead of Daniel who carried the large, heavy suitcase. She became a part of the throngs of people at the docks. She was so excited her heart raced. She told herself to slow down. There was high blood pressure on her father's side of the family.

Eventually, she realized she'd left Daniel behind. There would be no going back. All momentum was forward.

Anna heard a pleasant, familiar, female voice calling out her name. She pushed through the crowd as rapidly as possible. *She must reach the voice.* She felt almost suffocated in the process.

Finally, she saw her mother. She almost failed to recognize Margaret. Her hair had turned white and she'd gained weight. A lot of weight. Her face looked puffy and her eyes and mouth were almost lost within the flab. However, her blue eyes looked the same. Happy and warm as a summer day.

She also spotted her father. Michael didn't have white hair because he had lost it all. He walked with a cane. His warm smile revealed a good fitting pair of false teeth. His eyes had filled with tears of joy.

The obvious aging of her parents reminded Anna of her own mortality. Someday she would be old. Someday she would die. She must live in the present as she'd done during the war years, despite her present happiness.

Both Margaret and Michael held out their arms to Anna and she ran into them. They became a tight threesome. They hugged and cried and laughed. Anna looked around and saw many other people reacting the same way. Lovers kissed and wives and children met husbands and fathers. Mothers wept with happiness.

Anna sensed Daniel by her side. "I'm so sorry, darling. In my excitement, I forgot all about you and that heavy suitcase." She was so excited she was almost breathless.

Daniel smiled. "It's not so bad. It's just difficult to navigate through these hordes of people. Daniel rubbed his damaged shoulder.

Margaret reached out to Daniel, grabbed his right hand and held it between her own. "My goodness, you're handsomer than ever. And a welcome sight. Thank you for bringing her back to us. You're a good man." Tears filled Margaret's pretty blue eyes.

Michael transferred his cane to his left hand and shook Daniel's with his right. "Anna is looking terrific. It's obvious she's happy with you."

Anna reached out and put her arm around Daniel's waist. "And I'm happy with him. I'm sure I couldn't find a better husband." However, she grew concerned. She feared Daniel might have one of his nightmares and awaken her parents. She'd never told them about these evil dreams. This deception by omission only partly due to the fact she didn't want to embarrass her husband.

Daniel reached for a cigarette and expertly lit it. He took a long puff. "I've wanted to make this trip for years. Now it's finally happening."

Michael motioned for his daughter and son-in-law to move away from the centre of the crowds. There was entirely too much confusion. He also feared pick pockets. Anna and Margaret were too excited to guard their purses.

They found comparative privacy on the fringes of the crowds. Michael took control. He glanced at his watch. "We've at least a three hour drive ahead of us. I suggest we stop for tea. I spotted what looked like a good place just a few blocks away. Perhaps we could walk."

Anna eyed her father's cane but didn't say anything, although she feared he would have difficulty trekking any distance. Yet the man obviously wanted to walk, as did she and Daniel. It would be great to get some exercise after their long journey.

Anna clapped her hands in excitement. Her cheeks looked uncharacteristically rosy. "That would be great. It's so good to be here. To see you. I've waited for this moment as long as I've been in Canada and it's here. It's finally here."

Daniel and Michael stashed the luggage in the boot of the car. Anna and her mother hugged each other over and over. They kept repeating how happy they were to see each other.

The four of them began their walk. They moved slowly because of Michael's limp. They talked and talked. However, Anna found herself unable to say anything of consequence. Shyness overtook her. She realized how little letters had done to assuage her loneliness.

Margaret also seemed destined to talk about nothing more significant than the weather. "The sun is shining today and it's a welcome sight. This past week we saw nothing save rain and I'm sick of it."

Anna momentarily lost her inhibition because her mother presented her with an opportunity to tell about Canada. "It hardly ever rains in Lethbridge. The farmers are usually delighted anytime it does. We're on an irrigated farm, yet it's still nice when it rains."

Anna tripped over a crack in the sidewalk, recovered without falling and continued without missing a breath. "Talk of the weather is frequent in Lethbridge and I've often seen the farmers looking up at the sky." This last statement reminded her of the terrible hailstorm.

Anna savoured the beauty of England and the warm companionship of her parents, a dream come true.

However, despite her happiness and the fact the sun shone, she was aware of a dampness that seemed to pervade her. In many ways Canada had the more desirable climate.

* * *

The tearoom proved delightful. It was prettily decorated with blue floral tablecloths over white tables and filmy, pale, blue curtains on the windows. The place appeared quintessentially English, just as Anna wanted.

They seated themselves at a comfortable table and the men lit cigarettes. They ordered a large pot of English breakfast tea. Anna wondered when her parents had stopped drinking Earl Grey. They also ordered scones with apricot jam. Margaret wanted two.

Their tea and scones arrived. Anna's scone tasted so delicious she almost wished she'd ordered two like her mother. Glancing at her mother's increased girth she was glad she hadn't.

Anna asked Margaret if she would like to see the newest pictures of the girls. "We just had this studio picture taken of the three of them and it's quite lovely." Anna fished in her purse without waiting for Margaret's reply.

Margaret put down the teacup. "Oh my, yes, I sure would." Margaret smiled as she intently examined the photograph.

In it, all three girls wore white satin dresses and white stockings and black, patent-leather shoes. The dresses had been purchased on sale at Eaton's and were almost identical. Amber sat in the middle, Crystal to her right, and Pearl to her left. All three looked especially attractive.

Margaret sighed with pleasure. "The girls are beautiful. One of these days we'll come to Canada and meet them. We hope to make it sometime in the next two years. Wouldn't that be grand?" Margaret beamed.

Anna gave a loud whoop of joy. It caused the other patrons of the tea house to turn in her direction. Anna failed to notice. "Mum, that's wonderful. You'll see the girls and Canada. It's greatly different from England though I'm sure you'll like it."

Anna became aware of her complete happiness. The perfect, beautiful present felt wonderful. She had her parents and England to enjoy. Upon her return home, she had her husband and her children. Life didn't get any better than that.

Margaret reluctantly began to return the picture to her daughter.

Anna said, "No, you keep it. It's yours. We had several made."

Margaret radiated happiness. And with a gesture that reminded Anna of why she adored her mother so much, Margaret clutched it to her heart. "Thank you. Thank you so much. I don't know how we'd have survived without Amber's and Crystal's school pictures. But this is the first I've seen of Pearl since her christening picture. I don't see anything of Daniel in her, but she looks just like you did at that age, except she's dark."

Margaret continued to gaze at the picture. "All three of my granddaughters are beautiful."

* * *

Their tea consumed, the four individuals walked back to the car. The light exercise left Anna relaxed and happy.

She enjoyed herself so much she almost felt sorry when they reached the car. It was a gray Austin Michael and Margaret had recently purchased. This was the first time in their lives they'd owned a car. Obviously the hardware business prospered.

Michael said, "It's a small car and we may need a shoe horn to help us all fit. It does well in the damp, and we have a great deal of damp in England."

Daniel laughed. "It looks like a fine, sturdy, little car. Much more suitable for the small English roads than the big Chevrolet we drive in Canada."

Daniel sat up front with Michael and they soon began talking about farming and hardware, topics that interested them both.

Eventually the conversation halted, and Daniel rested his head on the top of the passenger seat. Soon he was asleep. Anna prayed he wouldn't have one of his nightmares.

Anna, too, grew fatigued. However, she was too excited to sleep and she and her mother kept up a constant, if rather boring, conversation.

Suddenly, Anna's reticence left her and she couldn't stop talking to her mother. They talked about their homes, their husbands, and world events. And, of course, the differences between Canada and England.

Suddenly, Margaret said words that struck terror in Anna. "I believe I told you in a letter, Charles Harding has married. He still asks after you, so I've invited him and his wife, Dora, to tea tomorrow."

Anna clapped her hands over her mouth and swallowed to quell the nausea roiling in her gut. Her voice shook, hard and defiant. "Mum, I have no wish to see Charles. Tell him I'm sick. Tell him anything. I won't sit at a table with him. " *Charles was manipulative and narcissistic. She hated him.*

Margaret's brows knitted with alarm. "It's not like you to be so unsociable. You turned Charles down and he's finally gotten over it. He's an asset to the business and a fine man."

Margaret pointed her index finger at Anna. "Not that I don't like Daniel. He's a wonderful person. I just can't help thinking if you'd married Charles you wouldn't be living so far away and I would know my granddaughters."

Anna's tone sharpened. "Trust me, Mum. I made the right decision." She clamped her jaws together and pressed her lips into a hard, thin line.

Margaret was obviously hurt. However, her words suggested a truce. "Yes, I understand. I love you and I know a girl has to follow her heart."

* * *

They arrived in London and Anna's heart swelled at the sight of the Thames River glistening in the sunshine. She was nearly overwhelmed by its beauty. However, London didn't all look as beautiful as the Thames. There were still many bombed-out buildings. And, as London derived its heat from coal, dirt clung to the old buildings and left the air foul. She'd never noticed it when she lived in London.

Flowers bloomed profusely and the city was so green it almost hurt her eyes. The sight of Big Ben, Buckingham

196

Palace and Westminster Abbey created sheer delight. She saw red, double-decker buses and Rolls Royce taxicabs; beautiful things she only remembered in her dreams.

Margaret told Anna she'd have to go the butcher's and the grocer's tomorrow. They apparently had enough baking on hand. Then they could go to the park. *How Anna longed to see the park again!* The waiting would be hard.

Anna remembered supermarkets didn't exist in England. She realized as well she missed Safeway. She liked only having to shop for groceries once a week. Anna wondered if she couldn't be missing Canada as she'd so often missed England.

She saw with relief the rubble was gone from around the movie theatre where she and Daniel had been trapped.

She shivered as they passed, although now it was a new, well-kept building. She remembered the choking dust and claustrophobic surroundings. However, she also remembered the reassuring voice of the man who'd become her husband.

The tour ended and they entered the part of England where Anna had grown up. She sighed with pleasure when she saw all the familiar houses on the street. She felt so filled with nostalgia her eyes grew moist with tears of happiness.

* * *

Finally, Michael parked the Austin in front of the dearest house on the street. The family got out and walked up the front steps, now surrounded by blooming rose bushes. Anna commented on their beauty as they ascended the steps. The house had been painted white with green shutters. Anna liked these colours better than the brown with beige trim the house used to be.

Inside, the home had changed very little. African violets still sat on the windowsill and a Boston fern, lush and green and gorgeous, occupied a low stool. Anna had tried unsuccessfully to grow ferns in Canada. They needed humidity. There was now hardwood flooring in the living

197

room, accented with a soft, green plush area rug. Thank God. The Morrison table had been replaced by a stylish chrome set.

Dad's store must be making money. Anna and Daniel both exclaimed over the beauty of the hardwood floor. Margaret and Michael beamed.

Anna knew they'd soon have a simple, cold meal and a cup of tea, both much looked forward to.

Margaret wouldn't let Anna do anything to help with the preparations so she sat and watched her mother. She remembered her first miserable foray into bread making in Canada.

Now it seemed funny and she recalled it all, complete with Dolly, the cow, chasing her. Soon both women laughed so hard their stomachs hurt. Of course, Margaret had heard this anecdote in letters. But Anna knew it was much funnier hearing it in person.

Anna could hear her father and Daniel growing animated as they discussed the hardware business. Daniel appeared to have some insights into it.

They talked of playing cards after their simple yet delicious supper. But this suggestion failed to be acted upon because all four adults had so much to say.

At about 10 pm, Anna said, "I'm sorry. I'm going to have to go to bed. I can't keep my eyes open a moment longer." Everyone else felt the same way.

Anna hummed softly as she pulled her nightgown over her head. It felt almost illicit somehow to share her childhood bed with Daniel. But in a good way.

She told him so as she snuggled close to her husband. She always appreciated his warmth. Tonight this was especially so. The sheets were cold and damp.

As Daniel held Anna close, she thanked him again and again for making this journey possible. Daniel responded by kissing her shoulders and caressing her breasts. "I love you, Anna."

He put his arms around her waist and drew her close. "I'm pleased the farm is doing so well and I want to be generous and make you happy. I brought along some extra money and I want you to go shopping. There are lots of stores here we don't have at home. I'm sure you'll find something you like. You know more about fashions than I do. I'm just a poor slob of a male."

"That's so kind. So very kind of you."

Her mind started to hum, "I'll shop for the children, of course. They felt so disappointed they couldn't come along. I'll look for new shoes and possibly a new dress for the wedding. And what would you like? We could find you a new suit here?"

"Naw, my old suit is good enough. I would like a new shirt and matching tie, though."

"I shall find you something perfect that brings out the green in your eyes. You're an incredibly handsome man and I love everything about you."

Anna maneuvered so she could kiss her husband on the lips. He responded with warmth.

They hesitated to make love because only a thin wall separated their bedroom from that of her parents.

They lay silent for a moment or two. Daniel spoke again, in a low, quiet voice. "I hope I don't embarrass you with one of my nightmares. After the wedding, when I go to Normandy, I'll find out if Dr. Mathews is right. I sure hope so."

"Daniel, he's a trained psychologist. Of course, he's right."

Secretly, she wasn't so sure. *Please God. Make Daniel well again.*

* * *

The next day, after trips to the butcher's and grocer's shops, Anna and Margaret went to the nearest park. It was just as lush and green and beautiful as she remembered. It even contained a fountain that reminded Anna of a sculpture.

The vegetable gardens of the war years had been restored to flowers. These flowers looked so gorgeous

Anna wished she'd brought her paints. She saw daisies, hydrangeas, mums and roses.

Canada contained beauty in June as well, with the scent of lilacs perfuming the air. Anna realized she missed her very own bush.

* * *

In the afternoon, they took the tube to Harrods, London's most famous department store. Anna was nostalgic as they rode along. They both found seats. *Good. Anna hated standing on the tube.*

She looked at all the people she saw with interest. She saw two young women in tight, low-cut dresses. One blonde with obviously dyed hair. The other a redhead with an equally improbable hair colour. They both wore bright red lipstick. Were they prostitutes?

There was a man dressed in a black tuxedo and top hat. He carried a black cane inlaid with gold. When he saw Anna staring at him he smiled, lifted his hat and bowed from the waist. "Good afternoon, young lady."

Anna returned the greeting with a smile and pleasant, "Hello, it's nice to see you," She reflected on the great variety of people who used the tube in London. Could anywhere on earth be more colourful?

Nonetheless, she realized she felt like a tourist and not someone returning home. She missed Daniel's Chevrolet and the wide, spacious streets of Lethbridge. Driving was very convenient and Daniel was a competent driver. There was no fear of catching a cold or worse from fellow passengers, and she didn't need a ticket. *Was she becoming more Canadian than English?*

They finally reached their stop and climbed up out of the Underground station to enter the throngs on the streets. A large, black haired man in a beige trench coat grabbed Anna by the shoulders and spun her around. "I'm sorry. I'm sorry."

Anna doubted he felt sorry at all. She was convinced he meant to rob her. She clutched her purse tightly to her bosom. "Don't be sorry. I'm fine." *Wasn't it the Canadian way to be polite at all times?*

In fact, despite the melee of crowds, she was afraid. This man might not be just a robber, but instead another Willy Jones. Goose bumps rose on Anna's arms and legs.

Anna forgot the man when she glimpsed Harrods department store. It consisted of five stories of magnificent stone. She couldn't wait to go inside.

Somehow, she felt the need to tell her mother about Lethbridge's post office building. Although much smaller, it, too, looked beautiful. And it existed without the suffocating crowds.

They entered Harrods, and Anna said to her mother, "Let's go look in the French Room. It's a showpiece of high fashion and it's fun to look. Of course, I would never buy anything there. The prices are sky high."

Margaret agreed, although her face appeared red and shiny with sweat.

This worried Anna. "Are you sure you're all right? Maybe we should go find a place to sit outside. I don't have to go to Harrods."

Margaret sighed. "Oh yes, you do. I'll be fine. I'm just a little hot. The doctor keeps telling me to lose weight. I guess he's right. I just love food and it's such a pleasure to eat now the rationing is over."

They found the French Room and Anna almost cried with the beauty of the merchandise. She touched silks and high quality wools, and crisp linens and cottons all fashioned into elegant clothes. This was in direct contrast to the Harrods Anna had known during the war years.

They left the pinnacle of beauty and entered the heart of the store. The crowds almost overwhelmed because of a sale with massive markdowns.

Anna held onto her mother's hand and pulled her through the masses so they could both look at the hats, coats, scarves and gloves. If only there could be this quality of merchandise in stores in Lethbridge. When Anna lived in London, the crowds were a minor nuisance. Now she found them cloying.

They entered the area of the store with drastic markdowns and Anna began to shop in earnest. She once again pushed through the crowds until she found a rack of cashmere sweaters. She swooned with delight when she found a blue sweater in her size marked down several times. The fine, soft, light fabric felt wonderful in her hands. She knew better than to try the sweater on because of the astronomical lineups for fitting rooms.

However, after a fifteen minute wait at the checkout counter, she purchased the sweater. She knew she would remember Harrods and this moment whenever she wore it. She silently blessed Daniel for his generosity.

They made their way to the main level and the slightly less congested cosmetics and perfume department. Chanel No. 5 was on sale. She planned to buy a bottle. It'd been Daniel's first gift to her.

Shopping made the two women hungry so they made their way to the food department and Anna found herself thrilled with its splendor. Anna treated Margaret to fish and chips wrapped in newspaper with dark vinegar. This was an English treat she'd definitely missed.

Margaret ordered two pieces of fish. Anna noticed Margaret often ate at least three scones for breakfast and stifled the urge to say anything. She didn't want to spoil this special outing.

Anna looked for a dress and shoes and gifts for the girls, but found everything too expensive. She planned to do the rest of her shopping at Selfridges.

Of course, the trip to Harrods had to end as both women were exhausted.

They made their way back on the Tube. It was now crowded and very hot. Anna held her breath as the scent of perspiration flooded her senses.

They arrived back at the house. Both women decided they needed a nap. The men had apparently gone to the hardware store. "Daniel and Michael are getting along like father and son. You have brought your father much happiness by marrying Daniel."

Anna smiled and met her mother's eyes, "Thank you for saying that. I appreciate it more than you can imagine."

Anna enjoyed the days she shared with her mother. It felt so good, so right to drink tea in Margaret's immaculate kitchen and talk. They used the old brown betty teapot. It produced the most excellent tea Anna had ever tasted. This closeness reminded Anna of her relationship with Maisy.

Talk eventually led to the subject of their husbands. Margaret sighed. "I love your father and he's a good man. But, there are times when he frustrates me because he can be so controlling. I hope you don't have that problem with Daniel."

Anna truthfully answered. "No, Daniel lets me do whatever I please. I'm lucky." Anna felt a strong need to tell her mother about Daniel's shellshock. Loyalty to him kept her silent. Daniel deserved his privacy.

Anna took a sip of strong, black tea, and placed her half-eaten scone on a plate. "Mom, you don't know how glad I am you and Dad are coming to Canada. You'll see your granddaughters and our dear house with its veranda. You'll love Canada as I love Canada."

Anna realized, as she spoke, that as much as she enjoyed this trip to England; she loved Canada more. It was home. Pride filled her for the beautiful, free, safe country where people immigrated daily.

She would never miss England so strongly again.

* * *

Soon it was the day of the wedding. Her nephew, Robert, acted as usher. He'd grown tall and handsome. Anna longed to reunite with him but realized she must wait until the ceremony was over.

Anna walked down the long, beautiful, red aisle where she'd walked as the bride several years previous. There was abundant sunshine. Margaret said she must have brought the sun from Canada. Anna felt almost as holy as the Virgin Mary as she basked in the light reflected from the stained glass windows.

The wedding guests assembled also luxuriated in the warm glow. Anna heard excited whispers from those attending. The church was beautifully turned out with pots of blue, mauve and white hydrangeas.

Anna, as Matron of Honour, wore a blue, high necked sheath accented with faux pearls and her comfortable black pumps. She carried a bouquet of pink roses and white carnations. The scent was magnificent.

The organist, dressed all in black, played "Here Comes the Bride." She was a talented musician and Anna suppressed a strong need to sing along. Anna couldn't help comparing this wedding to her own. Much was the same. She'd married a man she loved. Now Patsy did the same.

Somethings had changed though. Bounty replaced war-time restrictions. Safety replaced danger. Now, Michael and Margaret were happy; then they'd been saddened.

Anna reached the altar, and a hush fell over the sixty guests. She turned enough to see Patsy and her father walk down the aisle. Michael wore a new charcoal suit. He'd shed his cane and Patsy helped to keep him in balance.

Patsy had always been good looking; now she looked beautiful enough to inspire poetry. Her dress, a long, white, loose-fitting silk garment with matching veil looked simple and elegant. Under her veil, Patsy's blonde hair cascaded around her shoulders. Although her father clung to her, she walked with her head high.

Anna cried with happiness when she'd been reunited with Patsy. She realized she hadn't been aware of how much she'd missed her sister. Time just fell away as they'd hugged and kissed and recalled childhood memories.

Despite the crowding in Margaret's and Michael's small house when Patsy and Roger arrived from Birmingham, the six adults all managed to enjoy themselves. Anna and Patsy shared their childhood room. Daniel and Roger stayed at a bed and breakfast, The English Rose, only a few blocks away. They all got together in the evenings to play Hearts. Daniel usually won.

The first evening Patsy had arrived at the house, Anna and Patsy stayed up all night talking as if they'd never been parted. At one point Patsy said, "I may not be virginal but I'm going to look virginal on my wedding day. I've given up on tits and ass."

Patsy sighed with contentment. "Roger, of course, knows about my past and he's fine with it. And he keeps me happy. I'm so lucky I found him."

Patsy fluffed up her pillow and propped it onto the headboard. "To make him even more perfect, he makes a good living in a high-class bank. The exact same bank where I work as a secretary. It's in one of the finest buildings in Birmingham."

Anna instantly liked tall, thin Roger, who possessed wispy blond hair and was only two months younger than Patsy. Somehow he missed being good looking but Anna couldn't discern the diminishing feature. He dressed, even in casual clothes, like one would expect of a high-class banker. But, unlike the typical banker, he possessed a great sense of humour.

Daniel declared his new brother-in-law a "jolly good bloke," and everyone laughed at Daniel's attempt at talking like an Englishman.

When Anna had shown Patsy a recent photograph of her daughters, Patsy had studied it for a long time. "Your girls are all beautiful. You must be so proud. I would like to have a child with Roger. But I'm too old. Fortunately, Roger and my darling Robert get along.

Anna was lost in these thoughts as Patsy and Roger said their vows. She found their voices warm and loving and somewhat hypnotic. When it came time for her to hand over Patsy's wedding band, she managed to successfully complete her small part in the ceremony.

The groom kissed the bride and they all signed the register, both Anna and Patsy with shaking hands. Everyone went outside to enjoy the clear skies. Anna reflected upon how much she loved the sun on her shoulders and the pleasant scents of mingled perfumes, when she spotted Charles Harding. The blood drained from her face and goose bumps formed on her arms. To her relief, he shuffled by without speaking or meeting her eyes.

Anna exhaled. She didn't realize she'd been holding her breath.

As usual, Daniel charmed friends and neighbours. Anna heard a couple of women she'd gone to school with say what a handsome, thoroughly nice man Anna had married. Anna couldn't concur more.

It surprised Anna when several people commented on her Canadian accent. Everyone in Canada thought she still sounded English. She was now a true Canadian. Canada was her home. It didn't bother her she had become something of an outsider in England.

Anna shook the hand of Glen Clarke a friendly neighbor who kept his garden immaculate; when she noticed a tall, blond, well-built young man glancing in her direction. She smiled and he strode towards her. "Aunty Anna."

They hugged. His body felt strong and very male in her arms and reminded her of Daniel. The scent of Old Spice clung to him.

It's so very, very good to see you. I'm so sorry I missed much of your growing up. You've turned into a fine young man." Her eyes were damp with happiness. She opened her arms wide and they embraced once again. Anna still loved Robert as much as if he was her own son, and not Patsy's.

Robert began to tell Anna about his studies at the University and she said she felt "proud to be his Aunty." He studied political science and hoped to eventually get into law. Anna was pleased with the small part she'd played in his upbringing. He may have grown up a bastard but he'd soon be a member of the elite.

Robert had brought a friend. Pretty, auburn-haired Ginny. She wore a green shirtwaist dress and wide-brimmed hat. The outfit suited her colouring and dainty figure. "Ginny, this is Aunty Anna. She's the woman who took such good care of me when I was growing up."

Anna and Ginny shook hands. Ginny said, "It's a pleasure to meet you. I've heard nothing but good things about you." Anna beamed. She hoped this young woman would become part of the family.

Ginny studied to become a teacher. Anna assured her she would do the job perfectly. "I can just tell. I can see you teaching young children in grades one or two. They'll love you. I can tell you'll be patient and kind."

Ginny blushed with gratitude.

They held the reception in the basement of the church. The room was filled with pink and white carnations. Anna found their scents so delightful they were almost intoxicating.

The room grew crowded with the sounds of laughter and pleasant observations. She heard one young man comment, "Patsy sure is a looker."

Anna, always a lover of food, decided to have a look at the offerings for the sixty or so guests. The buffet style meal looked delicious with turkey, mashed potatoes, peas, carrots, devilled eggs, pickles and even olives. There was a separate table for desserts, which included pies, cakes and squares. The entire meal had been catered.

Roger and Patsy obviously did well at their jobs to be able to afford such splendor.

* * *

Daniel led Anna over to a table populated by a number of her old neighbours where there were four empty chairs. They invited Anna and Daniel to join them. They sat near the open door. A fresh breeze would keep her cool and comfortable.

Anna and Daniel had just settled into their seats when Dora Harding, Charles' wife, rushed up to claim one of the unoccupied chairs. Anna knew from her mother's letters Charles had married a school teacher eleven years his senior. Dora was a massive, full-faced woman. Her bulk was encased in a dark green suit and matching hat that sat precariously atop her large head. Anna wondered if she reminded Daniel of the tank he'd commanded.

Please God. Don't let Charles follow his wife.

207

Thankfully, Margaret had been true to her word and cancelled tea with Charles and Dora earlier. Anna hoped Dora wouldn't ask about her assumed bout with the flu.

Dora said, "Charles come sit beside Anna and me. Anna won't bite. You sit beside me and I'll sit beside Anna." She barked the orders like an army officer. *Damn the woman.* Anna moved as far away as she could without seeming rude.

Reluctantly, Charles shuffled over and slowly settled into a chair. He looked very much alive, despite the sinister letter he'd sent her on her wedding day.

Anna silently thanked God she hadn't married him out of pity, or guilt, and she'd kept his secret, just as he'd requested.

Charles had put on weight, so his hips appeared even wider than they'd been when she'd last seen him. His cropped hair had gone completely gray. She noticed his hand shook as he brought the teacup to his lips.

Anna decided to speak to Dora and ignore Charles. "Dora, I would like you to meet my husband, Daniel."

Anna heard none of the chatter and laughter that filled the crowded room. Daniel gave a curt, unfriendly nod. Charles' shoulders slumped as he sank deeper into his chair. Anna remembered how Daniel had chivalrously defended her from Charles' unwanted attentions. It was obvious the two men still hated each other.

Dora snapped back, louder than necessary even in this noisy room, "We met in the reception line."

She turned all of her attention back to Anna. "So, you're Anna. I've heard all about you. However, it's not all been accurate, though." Dora leaned in closer. "You're much prettier than I expected and you're definitely not too thin. Your husband is a handsome man. Not a brutish chap at all." Dora paid no attention to anyone else at their table.

"Yes, he's handsome. I'm a lucky woman." Anna smiled at her husband and reached for his large, warm hand. Her own were cold as snow.

She turned once again to Dora. "As you mentioned, I have gained weight since moving to Canada. In England, during the war, I suffered like everyone else with rationing."

She tried to swallow the lump in her throat. "In Canada, there's no end of food. I have a huge vegetable garden and strawberry and raspberry bushes. I do all my own canning in the fall."

Anna feared she might be prattling, yet she couldn't help herself. The woman appeared almost formidable. Anna babbled on. Now mostly about the weather.

Dora, apparently bored, ignored Anna. She turned and addressed her husband. "Now Charles, remember not to talk with your mouth full. Sometimes your table manners are appalling."

Charles blushed and his eyes focused on the table top. Anna almost felt sorry for him.

Abruptly, Dora turned back to Anna. "You may like the fair skies in your beloved Canada, but all the sunshine can be bad for the complexion. One can't be too careful." She stared at Anna's face. Anna clenched her jaw under the scrutiny.

She took note of Dora's complexion. Dull and sallow. *Damn. She was too polite to criticize.*

Muriel Fletcher, a kindly, gray haired neighbor dressed in regal purple, turned her soft blue eyes on Dora. "So Dora, are you still teaching?"

Dora sniffed. "I'll be teaching until I die. The hardware store doesn't make enough for us to live on. Charles should have taken up a profession like medicine or law. Her voice carried across the room.

"I do enjoy teaching. There's none of this silly kindness from me. I keep my classroom silent, the only atmosphere in which my grade five students can learn."

Dora adjusted her hat. "When I need to discipline my students, and I have to frequently, I have them stand with their arms outstretched and pile books on them. They receive the strap if they drop them too soon."

Anna wondered what Robert's darling young girlfriend would think about such methods.

Anna volunteered to accompany Daniel to Normandy but he refused. He needed to follow his psychologist's orders by himself. He'd felt terrifyingly alone on D-Day, even though he'd been with thousands of other soldiers. It needed to be the same now. Something he wanted to face alone.

Daniel was almost rigid with fear at the sight of the large, brightly-painted double decker ferry that would take him to the coast of Normandy.

The waters were calm and the sun shone, all in contrast to D-Day. He compared it to the rough, choppy crossing, which in itself had resulted not only in seasickness but also in numerous drowning deaths.

Daniel stood behind the other passengers and vehicles, outwardly calm but vibrating with acute anxiety.

He had no luggage, coat, nor sunglasses. He was aware of the chatter of the people behind him, but couldn't discern what was said even though they stood close by.

Daniel trembled as he had on D-Day. The ship neared capacity and people crowded each other in their eagerness to get on board. *Please God. Let there be no room for me. Then I'll have an excuse not to board.*

The scene reminded him of when his ship from Canada arrived in Liverpool; except, of course, then he'd been with Anna and very happy.

The excitement and pleasure of his fellow passengers as they greeted one another, some in English and some in French surrounded him with laughter and conversation under a pall of cigarette smoke. Most of these people appeared affluent. Their obvious happiness failed to alleviate his anxiety and made him more conscious of his feelings of isolation.

Despite the day's warmth, Daniel's hands were chilled as he paid for his return ticket. He couldn't answer the friendly clerk when this round-faced, ruddy cheeked man asked in cockney English why he travelled. The man appeared surprised when Daniel turned away without speaking. Daniel paid for the voyage in English pounds and had to be reminded to pick up his change.

The kindly clerk shook his head and muttered "I've never seen the likes of him."

Daniel wordlessly handed his Canadian passport to the government agent. The stern-looking French man quickly stamped it and motioned for Daniel to proceed.

Daniel was the last passenger to walk up the ramp onto the boat. He moved slowly, with his head down, like an old man. Bile rose in his throat and his stomach churned.

Twice, he almost turned around. But a member of the crew, a tall, well-built blond man, walked close behind him. Suddenly he wished he had Anna with him.

A cold wind blew as the ferry pulled out into the open water. Many of his fellow passengers struggled into their coats. A couple of men lost their hats. Daniel remained unmindful of the change in temperature.

He knew better than to go through the small door into the part of the ship where they sold coffee and soft drinks and cigarettes to the throngs of happy passengers. He couldn't stomach anything and he had enough cigarettes.

Daniel wanted to stay away from other people. He stayed on deck and smoked. The crew member who'd followed him on board watched him carefully, but made no attempt to speak to Daniel.

Daniel looked over the horizon. Images of the D-Day invasion were superimposed over the beautiful sunshine and shining water. The ships tossed on the seas, the planes overhead, tanks, and, the swarms of infantry. The beach crowded beyond capacity and the noise overwhelming. Fear was a tangible thing, hanging in a miasma over the scene, sharp in his nostrils and on his tongue. He lit a cigarette with trembling hands but it did little to calm him. Nearby a group of students lounged in the sunlight laughing and joking.

He'd fought for these young people and was glad he'd done so.

Suddenly, he was in the Firefly with the blood and entrails and fragments of brain all around him. It was like his nightmares. Only worse. He vomited over the railing. The pain of retching was satisfying in a strange way. A purging. Daniel heated with embarrassment from the surreptitious glances of the other passengers. The sickness gripped him again and the other passengers moved indoors.

He raised his head and wished he hadn't. Buried in the mud of the shore was a Firefly Sherman. The pounding of his heart sent dizzying waves sweeping over him, his vision blurred and he gripped the rail to stay upright. *I wonder how its commander died?* The errant thought flashed his mind. *Would the war never end for him? Was he destined to be stuck on the beach forever?* The landing came closer which set his heart racing faster. He was safe here on the water; when the ferry made land he'd have to disembark and make his way to Juno Beach.

The ferry shuddered as it came to rest against the docks. Daniel let the crush of passengers carry him off the ferry onto the docks. There was a town nearby which he had no desire to visit. The narrow cobblestone streets between towering buildings, though peaceful now under the French sun, would ring with gunfire and screams in his mind. The world swam before him and he fought to force breath into his lungs. His chest constricted painfully.

* * *

In order to avoid going directly to the beach, Daniel decided he would wander the Normandy countryside.

The other foot passengers had been picked up by friends or relatives and most everyone else had driven their car or bicycle away from the harbour. The ferry wouldn't be returning to England for hours so few people waited.

Daniel forced himself to put one foot in front of the other and follow the near-deserted pathway.

He came to a beautiful, secluded spot surrounded by maple trees and poppies. His senses rebelled when he realized he'd entered a vast, well-maintained cemetery. The restful sounds of the wind in the trees and the chirping of song birds seemed a mockery of the mangled bodies hidden under the green grass.

Simple yet elegant white crosses were arranged in rows, neat and tidy, hundreds of them. They seemed to go on forever.

Daniel staggered through them. So many lives. Why wasn't he one of them, why had he survived?

Daniel shivered in a sudden cold breeze and wrapped his arms around his chest. White transparent figures dart past him. *Ghosts? Yes. Would they harm him? Yes.*

He'd never laugh when he heard a house was haunted again.

Daniel thought of looking for the graves of the men from his tank. Didn't he owe them that much?

He fought the urge to bolt from the beautiful, haunting place. His legs refused to obey him. Away. He must get away. Daniel sank to his knees between the silent crosses, convulsed in tears. "I'm sorry. I'm sorry," he choked on the words. There was no one except the ghosts and birds to hear him.

Damn Dr. Mathews. He was a sadist.

Eventually, the sobs reduced to hiccups and shuddering breaths. As he calmed, the realization came to him along with a wave of peace. The ghosts flitted around him, brushing his clothes as though in benediction and forgiveness. "I'm a good father and a good husband. What happened wasn't my fault. I owe it to all the young men who died to live my life with integrity and honour, to live the best I can in their memory," he whispered. Anna's words came back to him, everything she tried to tell him was true; he saw that now. How lucky he was to have a woman like her as his wife and partner.

Daniel got to his feet, wiping his wet cheeks and left the cemetery. He wandered aimlessly for a bit and suddenly realized his surroundings were very similar to home. It comforted him. The Normandy coast was beautiful in the sunlight with cattle grazing and green fields. The shining blue skies contained only a few fluffy, white clouds. Apple

213

blossoms covered the trees, their heady scent perfuming the air.

A couple of girls passed on bicycles. Their shining dark hair glistened in the sunshine. They laughed and called something in French. There was peace here, a peace he'd helped bring about. Daniel came to a junction. He turned to follow a little-used road. Birds sang and wildflowers bloomed.

To his surprise, a car approached, the noise and smell turned his stomach. Daniel quickly retreated to the side of the road.

The driver, a dark haired man with a neat mustache and a jaunty cap, called out something in French. Even from a distance, Daniel could see the man's very white teeth.

Daniel exhausted his French. *"Parlez-vous Anglais?"* *Please. Let him speak English.*

The man shook his head. *"Non."* He gestured for Daniel to get into the gleaming green Peugeot automobile.

Through motions, Daniel did his best to politely decline although he assumed the man's intentions were genuine. He needed to be alone.

Daniel didn't know the French words to thank the man for his offer. The Frenchman seemed to understand. He gave a small wave and drove slowly past. The Peugeot's tires looked new. After the driver had gone several yards, he sped up leaving a plume of exhaust in his wake.

Daniel walked on, the activity relaxed him. His anxiety slowly dissipated. He enjoyed the warmth of the sun. It seeped through his trousers and long-sleeved shirt.

For the first time since he'd boarded the ferry, Daniel wished he'd brought a hat.

Normandy seemed a walker's paradise, and he found the exercise cathartic, exhilarating and relaxing all at the same time.

He didn't check the time and paid little attention to directions. He was confident he could find the ferry again whenever he might be ready to leave.

In the distance, fishing boats and a small, secluded sandy beach came into view. There couldn't have been a more tranquil scene. There were even fields of wheat. In a few months, the wheat would be golden and incredibly beautiful. Just like it was at home.

He looked in the other direction, and saw what might have once been a castle or at least a fortified house. It was obviously very old. Tall grass grew up around the sides of the ruined structure, and wind had eroded much of the stone. Nature had overtaken it.

What it would have been like to live in such an edifice? While it appeared elegant, it probably would have been cold and drafty, even with a fire blazing. Perhaps the peasants had it better in their cottages.

The ancient structure reminded Daniel there had been wars and a need for protection long before his war, World War II. He believed his had been the most terrible because it affected him personally. The war was over, he reminded himself. Now, there was no need for protection. Normandy was as safe as Canada.

The wind blew, soft and silent. Nothing like Lethbridge's roaring gales. It caressed his face. *Daniel was happy. Actually happy.* He would tell Anna he hadn't the courage to lift the hatch on his Firefly. She would understand. She loved him unconditionally as he loved her.

He filled with an immense sense of peace. Joy filled him and overflowed into the bright afternoon. He was free from his bondage at last.

The End

I have lived in Calgary all my adult life. I love Calgary, even on days like this when it's late March and still snowing. I have been happily married to Bruce Bohnet for the past 45 years. We have travelled extensively. We both enjoy experiencing new places and meeting new people